And from thence he went against the inhabitants of Debir: and the name of Debir before was Kirjathsepher: And Caleb said, He that smiteth Kirjathsepher, and taketh it, to him will I give Achsah my daughter to wife. And Othniel the son of Kenaz, Caleb's younger brother, took it: and he gave him Achsah his daughter to wife. And it came to pass, when she came to him, that she moved him to ask of her father a field: and she lighted from off her ass; and Caleb said unto her, What wilt thou? And she said unto him, Give me a blessing: for thou hast given me a south land; give me also springs of water. And Caleb gave her the upper springs and the nether springs.

—JUDGES 1:11–15 (KJV)

Now the people of Judah approached Joshua at Gilgal, and Caleb son of Jephunneh the Kenizzite said to him, "You know what the LORD said to Moses the man of God at Kadesh Barnea about you and me. I was forty years old when Moses the servant of the LORD sent me from Kadesh Barnea to explore the land. And I brought him back a report according to my convictions, but my fellow Israelites who went up with me made the hearts of the people melt in fear. I, however, followed the LORD my God wholeheartedly. So on that day Moses swore to me, 'The land on which your feet have walked will be your inheritance and that of your children forever, because you have followed the LORD my God wholeheartedly.' Now then, just as the LORD promised, he has kept me alive for forty-five years since the time he said this to Moses, while Israel moved about in the wilderness. So here I am today, eighty-five years old! I am still as strong today as the day Moses sent me out; I'm just as vigorous to go out to battle now as I was then. Now give me this hill country that the LORD promised me that day. You yourself heard then that the Anakites were there and their cities were large and fortified, but, the LORD helping me, I will drive them out just as He said."

—JOSHUA 14:6–12 (NIV)

MYSTERIES & WONDERS *of the* BIBLE

Unveiled: Tamar's Story
A Life Renewed: Shoshan's Story
Garden of Secrets: Adah's Story
Among the Giants: Achsah's Story

MYSTERIES & WONDERS *of the* BIBLE

AMONG THE GIANTS
ACHSAH'S STORY

Jenelle Hovde

A Gift from Guideposts

Thank you for your purchase! We want to express our gratitude for your support with a special gift just for you.

Dive into *Spirit Lifters*, a complimentary e-book that will fortify your faith, offering solace during challenging moments. Its 31 carefully selected scripture verses will soothe and uplift your soul.

Please use the QR code or go to **guideposts.org/ spiritlifters** to download.

Mysteries & Wonders of the Bible is a trademark of Guideposts.

Published by Guideposts
100 Reserve Road, Suite E200, Danbury, CT 06810
Guideposts.org

Cover and interior design by Müllerhaus
Cover illustration by Brian Call represented by Illustration Online LLC.
Typeset by Aptara, Inc.

ISBN 978-1-961251-55-7 (hardcover)
ISBN 978-1-961251-56-4 (softcover)
ISBN 978-1-961251-57-1 (epub)

Printed and bound in the United States of America

AMONG THE GIANTS

ACHSAH'S STORY

Dedicated to my father and father-in-law, who shared Christ's love with so many and provided for those in need.

CAST OF CHARACTERS

Biblical Characters

Achsah • the daughter of Caleb

Caleb • one of Joshua's generals, and one of the twelve spies who believed the Promised Land could be taken

Elah • son to Caleb, Achsah's brother

Iru • Eldest son to Caleb

Joshua • Moses's general and, later, leader of Israel

Moses • deliverer and leader of the Israelites escaping from Egypt

Naam • son of Caleb, Achsah's brother

Othniel • a close friend to Caleb

Sons of Anak • Ahiman, Sheshai, Talmai, the giants who lived in Hebron and various cities, also known as the Rephaite

Fictional Characters

Ari • a guard employed by Caleb

Avraim • Caleb's son and Achsah's older brother

Bel • a rescued woman from Hebron who serves Caleb's family

Dov • a friend of Haim and childhood friend of Rebekah

Eli • a weaponsmith interested in Achsah

Haim • one of the descendants of the twelve spies who refused to enter the Promised Land

Hur • Caleb's son and Achsah's older brother

Marduk • the king and descendant of the Sons of Anak

Rachel • younger sister to Othniel

Rebekah • daughter of Iru, niece to Achsah and best friend, same age

GLOSSARY OF TERMS

abba • father

Anakim • descendants of the Nephilim, the name is derived from the Hebrew word "Anak," which means "long-necked" or "necklace"

Asherah • female Canaanite goddess of fertility

Baal • Canaanite god, Prince of the Air, god of storms

cubit • seventeen to twenty-two inches, an ancient linear measurement

El • Canaanite god, sometimes used to replace Yahweh in Israelite worship

imma • mother

kiddushin • the Hebrew betrothal, a contract between a man and woman to promise to marry

mezuzah • a container placed near the door to remind and declare that the Israelites of that particular house serve God. Deuteronomy 6:9

Nephilim • giants, the fallen ones, described as the offspring of the daughters of men and the sons of God

parasang (parasa) • a Hebrew unit of measurement, equal to roughly four miles

pithoi • a large clay jar for storage, often used for water, wine, or grains. A few pithoi from bronze age Israel have carvings indicating Yahweh and Asherah together.

Sheol • the underworld, the grave, the abode of the dead

Yahweh • God

CHAPTER ONE

Outside of Hebron

The taunts of foolish boys followed twelve-year-old Achsah as she marched toward the well. Clouds of powdery dirt swirled beneath her new sandals and belted tunic, coating her toes with dust. In her urgency, her long braid danced behind her, slapping her back as she rushed up the hill. Beside her, Rebekah, her niece and closest friend the same age, struggled to keep pace.

"Wait!" Rebekah called out, her high voice breathy from the long walk. "I am not as fast as you. It is only Haim. He means no harm."

Achsah slowed for but a moment, but her skin crawled as she clutched her water jar to her chest. Haim always meant harm, but arguing would ultimately prove useless. Of course, she would never retreat to the safety of her courtyard. Not with *Abba* as one of the greatest generals in all of Israel. But despite her bravado, a tremor had rippled through her when she passed a gathering crowd of six young men at the edge of Hebron, including the lean but ever-growing Haim who now towered over her.

"I am not afraid of Haim. I am merely tired of his squawking," she retorted as she kept her gaze trained on the stone well, despite the urge to see if the boys had followed her. The well waited, quiet at this early-morning hour. Which meant she had only Rebekah to count on, should trouble arise. Next time, she would take her older servant. Bel would know what to do.

Brash laughter rippled in the breeze, sending a smattering of prickles across Achsah's skin. The weather felt hot and dry, thanks to the changing season, while the sun shone bright in a cloudless sky. All around her, the densely overgrown hills, covered with thick pine, oak, and mighty terebinth trees, provided plenty of hiding places for the mischievous youths. The land, too rocky for sheep, had been burned to clear the brush, layered into undulating terraces of grain and barley, lentils and millet.

Surely the boys ought to be in those very fields, working side by side with their fathers instead of loitering at the well, spying on girls.

"Achsah!" one youth, as tall as her abba, cupped a hand by his mouth to shout. She darted a quick look at him before catching herself. She refused to stare at him and give him the satisfaction of knowing that he had, indeed, rattled her. Taking a deep breath to steady her nerves, she set her clay jar on the dusty ground. Oh yes, she recognized the owner of that deepening timbre.

"I think he wants your attention," Rebekah whispered loudly as she glanced over her shoulder.

Haim, at sixteen years of age, was proving to be a thorn in Achsah's side.

"Let him try," she said through her gritted teeth as she snatched the rope that dipped into the watery depths. "I am too busy today to bother with the lot of them."

After several yanks, the water bucket appeared, sloshing precious liquid over the sides. As carefully as she could, she set the

2

bucket on the thick stone lip. She had just reached for her jar when Rebekah gasped and a long muscular arm reached out to slap the water bucket back into the well.

The wooden bucket clunked against the walls, the sound hollow and taunting until, at last, a splash reverberated deep below. Achsah whirled to see Haim's grinning face flashing a mouthful of crooked teeth. Somehow he had crept up behind her with nary a sound. Why hadn't Rebekah warned her?

"You really ought to offer me water." He crossed his arms across his chest. "After all, you are a girl, and I am a man. A very thirsty man."

Brown curls, greasy and far too long, clung to his perspiring forehead. And the breeze brought a hint of stale odor that made her nose wrinkle.

She leaned forward, furious that, despite her recent growth spurt, she barely reached his chin. That pesky fact didn't stop the roil of rage from kindling inside of her. "No."

"Oh, leave her be, Haim," another boy called out. Lanky and thin, with a shock of auburn hair, he trailed after Haim just about everywhere. "She is the daughter of Caleb, and you do not want to make her abba mad. Trust me."

"Be quiet, Dov," Haim growled. The young men had predictably followed Haim's example, as they had done a year ago. She understood some of it, after growing up in a military home—the way they pressed in to follow the strongest leader, like a pack of wolves in need of an alpha. The boys stood, almost as if indecisive, unsure whether to stay and see what might happen next or hurry to the fields before someone spotted them.

She squared her shoulders and kept her face impassive. But all her resolve to appear as fierce as her father only brought laughter.

Haim jabbed her shoulder, his finger sure to leave a bruise. "You need not put on such airs around me. I do not care what the other villagers say about your abba. He is old. An old, useless dog who does what he is told. One day, no one will listen to him or Joshua."

Her father's name, Caleb, truly meant faithful servant or dog. But she had never viewed the name as a slur. Instead, for years men had whispered about his battle exploits with awe. Battler of giants, they said. The right hand of Joshua and Yahweh. The man with a sword in his hand and never a plow.

Hearing Haim's derision proved too painful to bear. Worse, his family remained an enemy of hers, ever since the twelve spies sent by Moses returned with nothing but tales of woe regarding the Promised Land.

Scorn dripped from her voice like vinegar. "And your grandfather is a coward. He spread lies about the enemies, leaving Joshua and my abba alone to bear Yahweh's command. Why don't you scurry back to the wilderness since you think it is safer?"

To prove she didn't find Haim a threat, she yanked on the rope and hauled up the bucket with a mighty heave, despite her age. Laughter, much louder, tainted with barbs aimed at Haim, filled the morning air.

Rebekah stood by, her eyes wide and her mouth rounded. But no help came from Achsah's niece and closest friend.

As soon as Achsah placed the bucket on the lip of the well, Haim leaned over and knocked it into the shadowy depths again, where a sound echoed. *Thunk. Thunk. Thunk.*

Like the beating of her heart about to leap out of her chest.

Silence ensued. She felt the weight of the young men's stares and the weight of expectation regarding what a young daughter of a famed military leader might do. If they expected her to cry big salty tears, they would be sorely mistaken. Instead, fire crept into her cheeks when she saw Haim's smug grin as he folded his arms across his chest.

Before anyone could stop her, she rushed him, planted the flat of her palms against his chest, and shoved with all her might. He stumbled backward, flailing, and might have landed in the well if he hadn't caught the stone edge just in time.

The chuckling turned to shrieks of laughter as Haim jumped to his feet, his cheeks a mottled color.

"How dare you!" He clenched his fists at his sides, as if to strike her. "You think you are so special because of your abba and Joshua? We have had enough of your airs, with your nose pointed to the sky. When Joshua dies, we will finally be free of Caleb."

She braced herself, shifting on the balls of her feet while the youths pressed closer, ready to duck as her abba had once taught her. Rebekah released a timid shriek.

"Stop!" a harsh voice cried out. The crowd parted, revealing a glowering young man. With black hair and the beginning of a beard darkening a square jaw and lean cheeks, he swung his molten gaze at Haim.

With a shiver of relief, she recognized Othniel, a family friend who spent most of his days at her home. Now seventeen years of age, he had spent countless evenings with her brothers and abba rather than with his family. She had grown used to his silent company.

In fact, she had heard him utter hardly any words at all in the years she had known him. Today proved to be quite astonishing. Othniel shouldered through the young men until, at last, he faced

Haim. Wearing a rough-spun tunic and a bow replete with arrows slung over one shoulder, he appeared ready to face any threat as he worked the fields.

"Haven't you children work to do? The men have already begun harvesting," he demanded, jabbing his thumb toward the terraced hills. "Why are you pestering the young girls?"

Othniel's chiding had the intended effect as the now sheepish boys turned away from the well, leaving only Haim. After a strained pause, Haim blew out a harsh breath and brushed past her, his face drawn in sullen lines, leaving her, Othniel, and Rebekah behind.

Othniel glanced at Achsah, his expression unreadable for one long moment. Without another word, he followed Haim down the hill, toward the wealth of barley crops waving in the distance.

Exhaling, she watched him descend as clouds of dirt swirled beneath his sandals. She had expected him to chide her, just like her brothers enjoyed doing, but once again, Othniel returned to silence.

"Achsah, why must you provoke Haim so?" Rebekah protested as she tucked a stray lock of brown hair behind her ear. Her gaze wandered to the youth fleeing toward the rippling fields.

Achsah pulled on the rope, her hands shaking so badly that she could hardly pour the water into the jar. Somehow she managed, even though cool water sloshed onto her wrists and her olive-hued tunic.

"I am not provoking him. I do not even look at him most days. He brought me the fight, and I finished it for him."

Rebekah bit her bottom lip while she waited for her turn. "Thank goodness for Othniel's arrival. At least cooler heads prevailed. Did you see Dov with Haim? How tall he has grown this past summer."

Dov, the pasty-faced youth who loomed like a pole? He barely said much of value either, offering only the limpest of challenges to Haim's terrible behavior. Did Rebekah truly like someone as weak as Dov?

Achsah shot a glance at her niece, who was carefully pouring the water into her jar. Othniel's timing proved impeccable. He stayed close to her family, though she couldn't quite determine why—except for Othniel's great regard for her abba. A pity Haim didn't carry the same respect. Instead, he seemed eager to battle with her at every chance. But then, Haim's abba and grandfather had fought against her abba's desire to claim the Promised Land. Old family resentments ran deep, especially because Abba had been allotted some of the choicest property in the area surrounding Hebron.

"Haim cannot be trusted. He hates our family and makes it clear with each passing day. All because my abba shamed those spies for their cowardly refusal to enter the Promised Land and still continues to shame them," she said, although it was doubtful Rebekah would listen.

Rebekah hoisted the jar to her chest. "Perhaps. But my abba says Haim's family is not completely to blame. After all, we have had nothing but war these past years. War with the tribes of the giants and the Canaanites and the Jebusites and the Philistines and the Ammonites. Anyone whose name ends with 'ite.' We have been at war with everyone!"

Achsah hoisted her water jar and pressed her lips tightly together. By now the sun shone brightly, chasing away the faint pink dawn. In the distance, women came in small groups to draw water before the heat of the day. Rebekah's opinions shouldn't surprise her. Her niece was just echoing what her abba and Achsah's oldest brother, Iru, complained about to everyone who would listen. So many Israelites protested further war these days.

"We have done our share," Iru often grumbled when visiting Abba's home. "Let the others fight if need be."

No wonder Rebekah hadn't come to Achsah's defense. Only the silent Othniel provided help. A sigh escaped Achsah as she began descending the powdery slope. When she glanced over her shoulder, to her surprise, Othniel stood in the distance, his gaze in her direction.

She shifted the water jar to her left arm and raised her right hand to wave at him, but he was too far away for her to catch his expression. Regardless, after a pause, he raised his hand. Almost reluctantly, to her way of thinking.

"Othniel remains a favorite of Grandfather, and he is not even family." Rebekah tugged on Achsah's sleeve. "My abba says Othniel wishes he could be adopted into the family. I hope Grandfather will do no such thing. We cannot afford to divide our land any further."

As her friend led her away, Achsah frowned. Did Othniel linger at the family table because he had designs on Abba's vast holdings? It wouldn't be the first time someone fawned all over the mighty general, hoping to secure some sort of favor.

"I also heard that Othniel is poor, with an abba who died in the wars. So, whatever you do, Achsah, do not look at him and give him any foolish ideas."

"I am not giving anyone ideas," Achsah retorted, clutching her water jar close to her chest. Still, at the bend of the road, she turned her head ever so slightly to let her gaze wander to the fields where the men were headed, but Othniel was gone.

CHAPTER TWO

N ot too much spice," Bel, one of the older servants, warned as Achsah sprinkled dried powders into the bubbling stew. Evening fell as they cooked outside in the courtyard. She bit the inside of her cheek as her gaze drifted toward the open door where the sound of men arguing floated in on the cooling breeze.

After drawing water, Achsah had raced home to tell Abba about the unfortunate encounter with Haim, only to find her brothers clamoring in a meeting. By the sound of the voices rising from within the great room, things were turning heated.

She spied her abba sitting cross-legged on a mat with her brothers, and the temptation to eavesdrop was far greater than attending to the meal preparation.

"Achsah, watch the stew!" Bel said with an exasperated smile as she brushed back the auburn strands sticking to her face. Although she was in her midthirties, vestiges of beauty clung to the older woman, along with a hint of mystery. "Trust me, any more leeks and salt, and your brothers will run home with their tongues on fire."

Would that be such a terrible result? Achsah tamped down that rebellious thought before it flew out of her mouth and invited further trouble.

"Abba likes his food with plenty of flavor," she reminded Bel, who hovered over the steaming pot like a bird of prey, ready to peck at every one of Achsah's flaws. Indeed, Achsah could hardly fry the honey cakes well enough or cut the vegetables small enough to suit the woman who had been her nursemaid.

Without Achsah's dear *imma* to teach Achsah such skills, Bel had taken it upon herself to turn her into a proper daughter. But Bel was nothing like Imma, who had passed away from a fever the previous year. Even now, the memory brought a sheen of hot tears to Achsah's eyes. She blinked them away, focusing on the chunky stew and the faint conversation just beyond her reach.

"Age will do that to a man, stealing his taste," Bel grunted as Achsah stirred the contents with a large wooden ladle. "Your poor abba is not as young as he once was."

The lamb meat mingled with far too many leeks and an array of mushy vegetables—thanks to Achsah's straining to hear her abba's concerns. She ignored the heat emanating from the pot, the steam stinging her fingers and wrist as her concentration strayed to the hushed conversation. Someone hit the mat with his fist. Trouble indeed.

Abba had called for an emergency meeting, demanding his sons abandon the harvest to talk with him. Although they usually resisted such an interruption, on this occasion they ran to him, their faces strained. Whispers of border trouble brought anxiety. Amid the threat of renewed conflict, word came from a young servant boy that Joshua had collapsed, perhaps dying of old age. Israel's future was at stake.

Haim's declaration that his family would never follow Abba's lead haunted Achsah. She dumped in another handful of coarsely chopped leeks, only to groan within when she belatedly realized her mistake. Thankfully, Bel had turned her attention to slicing the pale melons into juicy wedges.

Would Abba leave her alone yet again? Every skirmish brought a sense of fear mingled with steep pride at how much the tribe of Judah needed her father.

"The stew, dear child! The stew!" Bel snatched the spoon from Achsah's hand, shooing her away.

At least Achsah had bowls of roasted grains and flatbreads to serve, along with platters of grapes. She couldn't ruin grapes, could she? More than anything, she wished she could sit cross-legged with her brothers and listen, leaving the cooking to Bel. Especially today, of all days.

As Achsah ladled the stew into wooden bowls, a familiar lean form rushed through the courtyard. Othniel glanced at her, his gaze brief and cool. Without a word, he slipped into the grand house where the men clamored to greet him, leaving her trying to keep the clay bowls from tipping over.

An exasperated huff escaped Achsah's lips. Perhaps Rebekah was right. Perhaps Othniel would edge into the family and supplant everyone since Abba loved the young man so much. As grateful as she was for Othniel's intervention this morning, it hardly seemed fair that he received such elevated treatment, while she, the last of Abba's children and the daughter of his beloved and final wife, stayed on the outskirts. But that was the way things were done.

Muttering under her breath and ignoring Bel's eye rolls, Achsah loaded the last of the steaming bowls onto a wooden tray.

"I will take it, my little mistress," Bel protested as she reached for the tray. "I can see that you are far too distracted this day, and we do not want hot stew landing on your brothers." Her sleeve fell back, revealing strange markings that carved a raised path along her arm. The secret of their origin remained locked inside Bel no matter how much Achsah had pried as a young child. This moment proved no exception when the older woman calmly yanked the linen over her arm, hiding the scars while ignoring Achsah's curious stare.

"We will carry the trays together," Achsah replied firmly. She rose, carefully balancing the four bowls. At least serving would allow her to eavesdrop much more efficiently. Before Bel could utter another protest, Achsah ducked into the house, with the tray wobbling in her grip.

The spacious hall declared Abba's rise to prominence. Whitewashed walls and woven mats offered luxurious comfort to the guests. Earlier in the day, she had plumped the feather-stuffed crimson pillows for Abba, who needed his mattress to cushion his bones. Not that he would ever admit such weakness, but she had seen him cut back on his sword maneuvers these past months, his gait much slower. Old war injuries, Bel had explained. Certain to haunt a man later in life, no matter how strong he might have been in his youth. The way Bel spoke about Abba always carried a hint of awe, as if he were one of the greatest men ever to walk the earth, second only to Moses and Joshua.

When Achsah approached her brothers, her abba's fierce gaze softened. With his white hair long and wild, and his face wrinkled from age and sun, he remained a powerful figure. But she had never feared him. He motioned her forward, his lips curving ever so slightly. Of course, she served him first and then the eldest of her brothers. Yet she couldn't help but notice that Othniel sat to Abba's right, instead of her brother Iru.

Iru ignored her, as he usually did. Now in his late fifties, with streaks of gray at his temples, and as the son of Abba's first wife, he treated her like a child. Not that he treated his daughter, Rebekah, Achsah's niece, any better.

Iru leaned forward, his beard bristling with unconcealed fury. "I am not taking my men for another spy excursion. I have heard of no significant trouble at the border."

"With all due respect, I have heard of raiders," Othniel spoke up, drawing attention since he rarely offered advice. "Now that Joshua lies on his deathbed, some of the giants have ventured from the safety of their walls. They took a girl only the other day."

"A girl?" Iru's eyebrows nearly shot to his forehead. "We are planning a mission because of a missing girl? How do you know she did not run away? When will this madness of yours end, Abba?"

Abba bristled, his gaze hardening. "I will not stop until all the cities in the Promised Land belong to Yahweh. He commanded Moses and Joshua to take them. Now my dearest friend may be dying, and the need to secure our land remains unfulfilled, as demonstrated by this missing child!"

Iru sat straight up instead of lounging on the luxurious cushions. "I see no reason to fight for all of Israel, let alone one child. Joshua made you give up Hebron after we worked so hard to capture it. What will I get in return for risking my life again?"

"You have enough farmland," Abba said mildly as he dipped his bread into the stew. But he did not bring the bread to his mouth. "How much more land do you need?"

Hur, another brother, with an equally bushy beard, reddened as he wiggled on the mat, nearly jostling the bowl in front of him. "The

Israelites promised us cities, Abba. Cities! Why did Joshua go back on his word and take back what he promised us? Iru is right. I have no desire to rescue a runaway, let alone start another war."

Achsah bit the inside of her cheek. Hard. How could her brothers be so callous as to ignore the suffering of a helpless girl?

"Get those Levites in the sanctuary cities to actually lift a sword for once," another brother, Elah, insisted. "Let them fight the giants instead of us. Let them retrieve this child. Do not the Levites owe you, Abba, after all you have done for them?"

Achsah crept behind her brother Hur, making herself as small as possible so she could listen in on the conversation. No one noticed her except perhaps Othniel, who, to her great surprise, flashed her a small smile, not unlike her abba's amusement when he caught her doing something she shouldn't.

She tore her gaze from Othniel and focused on Iru instead. Iru usually convinced his brothers to follow his lead. He pursed his lips as if tasting something sour.

Abba dropped his bread into the bowl. "No one owes us anything. Yahweh wishes for our nation to establish six cities of refuge, spread throughout Israel. If someone dies in an accident, the accused will find a safe place to wait until justice is determined. We need such centers throughout Israel if Joshua passes away, and he will die, as will I one day. The priests will ensure that the surrounding tribes continue to follow Yahweh's commandment."

"I do not want to lose any more men or my sons to yet another battle," Iru protested as he cracked his knuckles. "Your priests could not even bribe me with the loot of a city."

"Do you not see that Joshua's illness has encouraged the Canaanites to test our strength and our resolve? We remain surrounded by enemies. The Hittites. The Canaanites. The Jebusites. Yahweh gave Joshua and Moses the command to clear the Promised Land for our people to live in *safety*," Abba answered quietly. "A stolen child matters."

Achsah crouched lower behind Hur's broad back. She shuddered at the idea of being ripped from family and home. With her six brothers, she had plenty of protection and security. She couldn't imagine the terror the girl might be feeling.

Iru looked unconvinced. "I want to live in peace with the nearby cities. They are our neighbors, true enough, and perhaps it is time we chose different methods. A truce might bring more favor, yes? I have talked with other Israelites in the valley. Most of them want to farm. To grow their vineyards and enjoy their wives. I am not about to throw out all that progress we worked so hard to achieve. Our glory days of fighting are over."

All of her brothers spoke at once, their voices sharp and strident, demanding to be heard. Some agreeing with Iru, and others protesting that Abba might be right. Only Othniel remained silent, just as she did.

She sucked in a sharp breath between her teeth. Surely Abba wouldn't let such an insolent remark from Iru go unanswered.

Abba, however, remained unruffled. He raised a scarred palm, stilling his sons. "How can you say that, when we must reclaim the land Abraham had purchased so many years ago from Ephron, the Hittite? Because of my obedience, Yahweh rewarded me with hill country and a family. But we cannot rest. We must rout out the last of the giants before it is too late. We did it at Hebron, and we can do it again with Kiriath-sepher."

Wrapping her arms around her middle, Achsah pictured these men who were rumored to be over six cubits tall, taller than her mighty abba. An impossible feat, it seemed. Yet they remained a blight, hovering on the horizon, their presence a continual threat despite an uneasy period of peace. Worse, the settlement of giants lived within the mysterious Kiriath-sepher, its name meaning "the city of books," which boasted an immense library filled with clay cuneiform tablets. They dominated the nearby trade routes, forcing many Israelites to take different roads.

"Abba, why not concentrate on leading the cities instead of starting another war?" Elah, protested thickly. His mouth had been full of food, so he swallowed and wiped his bearded chin. "You could do more good that way. If Joshua dies this week, we will need to get all the tribes together and assure them that you will lead. We do not need more fighting. Give them a leader. A king. That will silence our neighbors, and they will slink back in fear when all the tribes unite. Imagine the most powerful general rising to the throne!"

Abba shook his head, the spark in his eyes dimming. "No, Yahweh must guide us and be our king. He led us into the wilderness with a pillar of cloud during the day and a pillar of fire during the night. If only you could have seen the miracles I witnessed. You would not doubt His decree to fully possess our land or His strength to enable us to do mighty things. I am old…too old to replace Joshua or fulfill what God called me to do. But you are in your prime. Take out the sons of Anak. They have killed many of our people, but you, my sons, seem content to leave them be. Remember, we are warriors, not rulers."

A sullen silence fell across the gathering. Achsah held her breath, her ears nearly ringing from the effort. Even Bel seemed fixed at the threshold, her puckered mouth rounding with shock as she clutched a wine pitcher to her chest. The older servant's horrified gaze slid to Achsah's. She jerked her head toward the doorway. A silent warning, perhaps, to Achsah to leave before anyone noticed her presence.

Achsah shook her head. She had no intention of leaving. She wanted to know if her brothers would actually honor their abba. *Her* abba. Didn't they understand the risk of letting the enemy lie at Israel's door? Had they forgotten the stories of the Rephaim, the enormous men inhabited by the spirits of the dead who were rumored to be residents of Sheol? Some Israelites whispered that the giants were the "divine ones," the sons of "gods," although whenever she brought that idea up, Abba told her in no uncertain terms to be quiet.

The brothers eyed each other while Abba dipped his hand into a bowl of roasted grains.

Avraim, another brother, spoke up, almost hesitant. "We are farmers, Abba. Please, let us enjoy the fruits of crops and the—"

Her abba clenched his massive fists until the knuckles gleamed with skin stretched taut. "They will attack. They will wait until you are asleep in your bed, glutted by your feasts and your vineyards, and they will strike when you least expect it. Why must you choose to be so complacent? So—"

"So cowardly!" The hot words burst from Achsah before she could slap a hand over her mouth to stop. Her cheeks heated even more when every head swiveled, sixteen pairs of eyes staring at her.

"You, little sister," Iru spoke slowly, his voice like gravel, "should be in the kitchen as is appropriate."

"And you, my elder brother, should honor your abba, my abba, as is appropriate!" she retorted. Yahweh help her, but she had come this far. Why back down now?

Abba sighed. Suddenly, he appeared drawn and tired, the lines more prominent on his forehead and crinkling about his eyes. But his voice, unlike Hur's, remained as kind as she remembered. "Go, child. Such talk is not for you."

She struggled to rise, her foot now half asleep and full of shooting prickles. With as much dignity as she could muster, she bowed slightly to Abba and tried not to limp out of the room. But not before she heard Hur's comment. "Should you not arrange for a marriage for her? Although, perhaps, with that big mouth—"

Laughter filtered through, changing the mood, at her expense, unfortunately. Her eyes burned again with unshed tears. Not for the first time, she longed for her mother, Nahib, to whisper some kind of wisdom on how to manage such an unruly gathering of men. Imma had always known how to soothe tempers while changing hearts and minds with a gentle word of advice.

Achsah knew only anger these days. She joined Bel, loading the next array of plates with dates and gleaming grapes.

"I will take the fruit," Bel whispered, her tone kind for once. Achsah nodded, yet her gaze strayed again to the men sitting on cushions, the voices now hushed. She glimpsed Othniel sitting next to her abba, his expression transfixed on Abba. What could the younger man be thinking?

"I heard Marduk, one the sons of Anak, has a bed nearly nine cubits long and four cubits wide, nearly like King Og's iron bed," one brother noted. "They are fearsome men, brutal and cruel. Perhaps we should take them out."

Iru folded his arms across his chest, appearing unconvinced. "Most of our enemies have been subdued. The sons of Anak have remained quiet for several years. Maybe they are more frightened of us than we are of them."

"You should be frightened," Abba's voice echoed. He sounded irritated and tired. "If we do not follow what Yahweh asks us to do, calamity will arrive when we least expect it. If none of you will remove the threat to our villages, then I will do so myself."

Achsah couldn't take any more listening. Her appetite fled. She hurried farther into the courtyard where the shadows collected with the approaching evening. Beneath a swaying palm, she tried to slow her rapid breathing. One day, Iru would lead her family. Already, he seemed determined to push against Moses's decrees. If Iru refused to fight, her brothers would follow suit, leaving Abba to deal with the threat alone. Her abba, although formidable, could no longer match the younger men when they sparred in the courtyard.

She pressed a fist against her mouth, quelling the frustrated sound rising from her throat. Must she lose another beloved parent? Only Abba loved her, as had Imma. Her brothers tolerated her, viewing her value in terms of whom she could marry and what alliance she could bring to the family.

Why hadn't she been born a boy? Her gaze fell to the small armory where the grindstone for sharpening blades waited for the next battle. The sound of rasping swords had followed her throughout her childhood. A familiar sound. Not entirely unpleasant to her ears—a comment that had made Abba laugh when she dared to tell him. If only she could help him in his quest.

She pushed open the door to the armory, greeted by the scent of metal and leather. In the gathering gloom, the swords and shields hanging on the whitewashed walls called to her. She reached out a finger to touch the nearest sword hilt, the metal cold. Then, before she could second-guess herself, she pulled it free from the rack. It felt heavy. So heavy her arm sagged from the weight of it.

Regardless of the weight, she carried it outside to the courtyard. Oil lamps flared from the open windows, bathing the beaten pavement of the courtyard in rectangles of golden light. Her brothers remained inside. Bel, too, had disappeared, likely cleaning the remaining bowls.

She would not have another moment alone like this. Unhindered. Unseen. With all her strength, she swung the sword, just as she had seen Abba do countless times as he practiced in the courtyard. In the privacy of her bedchamber, she had practiced the same battle moves as the men, lunging on one leg with a wooden stick repeatedly until her muscles ached the next day. The sword felt much more unwieldy than a mere stick.

"A good effort," a voice came to the right of her. "Just like your abba too. You even hold the sword the same."

She whirled to see Othniel standing close to the palm tree, his arms crossed over his chest. Intent on mastering the move, she hadn't even heard his approach. If she expected to find derision in his expression, she could find none. He uncrossed his arms. "But that sword is not the right balance for you."

Before she could say anything, he ducked into the armory, returning a moment later with a smaller blade curved like a sickle. He handed it to her, motioning for the larger weapon in her hand.

She handed it over and took the smaller blade, wrapping her fingers around the leather-covered hilt. Already it felt better.

"Try again," he encouraged as he extended his blade, showing her the stance. Legs partly crouched. "Keep your back leg for exploding forward and your front leg for balance and stability."

He lunged, his leap far eclipsing any attempt she might try. The sword sang in the air, whistling as he swept it in an arc.

She tried the same, just as her brothers poured out of the house, their servants carrying torches to aid in the darkness. Yet, ignoring the surprised shouts, she mimicked Othniel.

"What do we have here?" one of her brothers cried. "Is that you, Achsah?"

"Why is she holding a sword? Do not encourage her, Othniel. Next, she will be running off to do battle herself."

Achsah swung the blade again. "I would help Abba, unlike the lot of you."

"That will do, little sister. Who can stand against the sharpness of your tongue? Perhaps that is how we defeat our enemies. We will send you to *talk* them to death." Iru smirked as if tolerating a troublesome child and then motioned for his retinue of servants to follow him.

Laughter filled the courtyard while her throat tightened. At least the cover of evening hid her embarrassment and mounting ire at being dismissed so readily.

Her abba came readily to her defense as he stood in the doorway. "Leave Achsah be. She has twice the courage of most men." He glanced at her, his brows lowered as if angry, but she heard the tenderness of his tone. The protectiveness. "You all would do well to learn from her example."

Her chastised brothers hurried to exit the courtyard. Iru first, his mouth pinched tight as he shoved open the gate. Her other brothers filed past with their servants, everyone armed for the trek home. Only Othniel remained by her side.

"Will no one stand with Abba tomorrow?" Her voice sounded so small in her ears, so weak, yet fear rumbled inside her. Fear that she might never again see the one she loved most if no one helped him. "Will no one watch over him when he fights the giants?"

Othniel hesitated beside her. Then he placed his hand over his chest, the action solemn and comforting all at once. "I will do it, Achsah. I will make sure no harm comes to him. I swear it with my life."

Something like a sob rattled in her throat just as he leaned in closer to her, his voice low in her ear. "Keep practicing with the blade. Your spirit brings hope to your abba, especially when he stands to lose his closest friend, Joshua." At that moment, the moon broke free from the clouds, illuminating the young man beside her.

He handed her the heavy sword with that slight smile again. And as she replaced the weapons inside the armory, she overheard him talking with her abba in a low tone. When she ducked out of the armory, she spied Othniel exit the courtyard before she could thank him. She couldn't remember another time when he had spoken so much to her.

Her abba waited for her, extending his arm when she reached his side. "My little girl with the heart of a lion, a warrior fit for the tribe of Judah."

"If only I had been born a son, Abba. I would do as you ask. I would clear out any border threats and ensure the safety of our lands."

"I know you would," he said thickly, patting her hand which rested in the crook of his arm. "But I like you just as you are. My one daughter. I would not trade you for ten sons."

"Will you seek a betrothal for me soon?" she asked, unable to resist considering Hur's comment. "Rebekah speaks of nothing else these days. I find her conversation so wearying."

Her abba's grip tightened—not painfully but reassuring in its strength. "I will not give you to just anyone, Achsah. He will need to be worthy. And kind. Most of all, he will need to serve Yahweh with all his heart. When I find such a man, I will let you know. May He bring you a husband and Israel a new leader."

She exhaled with relief as they entered the house. *Her home.* Her place would always be beside her abba. She had no desire to marry. Not at all. Instead, she would take care of her father and his every need. Yet as she mulled over his last statement, a ripple of unease occurred in her. Did Abba truly despair of finding a man worthy to lead after Joshua? Surely one man would prove wise and strong enough to unite all of Israel.

"I heard you say you will not take Joshua's place. Why?"

Abba smiled at her. "The Israelites have not asked me, other than your brothers, who dream of power and wealth, not service. More importantly, Yahweh has not selected me for such a task.

Someone else must rise to the occasion. One day, Yahweh will choose that very man to guide our people."

"Will you go fight, even now? Will you rescue the girl?"

"Tomorrow." He clasped her shoulder, the weight of his hand comforting despite the unsettling nature of his answer. "I cannot imagine a poor child left all alone to fend for herself."

"Will my brothers go with you?"

Her abba pulled at his beard, his steps slowing. "Othniel promised to come with me. Do not worry about the trouble at Kiriath-sepher, my treasure. No harm will come to you. I will ensure it."

Later, as she lay on her pallet stuffed with sheep wool and scented with fragrant herbs, she drew the heavy covers up to her chin and shivered in the darkness, watching the moonlight slide through the slats of her shuttered window. She rolled over onto her side, her breath coming quickly, stoked by an emotion she hated most of all. Fear. She squeezed her eyes tightly and tried not to think of swords clashing and men bleeding, regardless of what she had seen these past years.

Abba called her his treasure, for her name meant "bangle." Something fine to adorn a beautiful woman. Her imma told her that Abba had chosen the name when he first laid eyes upon her. No one loved her as much as Abba did.

Surely Yahweh would protect her from losing the one person she loved best.

Surely He would hear her cry.

CHAPTER THREE

Dawn crept over the horizon, the color a faint blush warming the barley crops that rippled in the gentle breeze. A beautiful, peaceful scene, but Othniel had no time to enjoy it as he raced over the fields toward Caleb's villa, his sword slapping against his side.

Earlier this morning, Othniel had left his imma and siblings at the farm nearby, warning them to stay close to the men who worked the fields.

"Another child taken?" his imma had whispered late the previous evening, when his sister Rachel lay fast asleep on the rooftop beneath a canopy of stars. "How did you learn of such news?"

He had kissed his imma's forehead and wrapped an arm around her thin shoulders, refusing to admit that he'd been spying on behalf of Caleb. But as he monitored the area of Kiriath-sepher, which defiantly remained within Judah's territory, he had run across a troubled family who had begged his help to find their missing daughter.

"You are going, are you not? So like your abba, in every way," his imma said with a hint of pride, though tears filled her eyes. "Whenever Joshua or Caleb called, your abba came, laying down even his life."

Yes, Abba had proven himself to be one of the truest soldiers in service to the general. Caleb had never forgotten the sacrifices made by Othniel's family.

Othniel placed both palms on either side of her cheeks. "Imma, that missing girl is the same age as our Rachel. How can I do nothing when someone has taken a child to Kiriath-sepher? Would you not want someone to search for Rachel?"

Of course, Imma agreed, even as her face paled. "I do not know what I will do about our crops. It is too much for Rachel and me to maintain alone."

"Caleb promised us barley and servants whenever we need it. But truthfully, I would go to Kiriath-sepher regardless of what Caleb gives us. Our crops will do us no good if the enemy comes to set fire to everything." He dared not tell her of the enemy spies sent out from the sons of Anak, hunting for weak spots among the villages and hamlets. She would never sleep again.

Now, as Othniel pushed open the heavy wooden door, he found Caleb waiting inside the courtyard with his sons Elah and Naam and a host of fifty men. Caleb was the leader of the tribe of Judah, appointed by Moses, and surely more men ought to follow the old warrior. Caleb's sons Hur and Iru remained conspicuously absent.

Caleb greeted Othniel with a smile, and Othniel noted in the early-morning light that his mentor's eyes were undimmed with age even though his hair, now pulled back in a series of braids, glowed white in the sunlight.

"Today, we will fulfill what God commanded. I am still as strong today as the day Moses sent me out; I am just as vigorous about going out to battle now as I was then. Follow me this day and see Yahweh's deliverance."

Last night, after they had enjoyed bowls of hearty stew, Othniel had heard the low murmuring of Caleb's sons as they traded stories of the giants remaining in the last outpost, a well-fortified city with thick walls. Even if Hur and Iru refused to believe the warning signs, Othniel couldn't. He had grown up listening to his imma's hushed stories of men who worshiped strange gods and offered stranger blood sacrifices. Nor was he immune to the fear that someone might kidnap his beloved sister. Nor could he imagine the terror the missing girl must be feeling at this hour—alone and taken from the safety of her home to become someone else's property.

No, Iru erred in his desire for peace.

The men clustered around Caleb and cheered the rousing speech. As Othniel joined in, he glanced toward the house and spied a slight form pause at one of the open windows. Achsah watched for a moment and then disappeared into the shadows of the room.

He felt a pang for Caleb's young daughter, who tried so hard to be brave, even after losing her beloved imma. It was the same pang he felt for his younger sister, who had hugged him tight this morning with tears in her eyes, begging him not to go.

I will watch out for your abba, he silently promised Achsah, his hand touching his chest again. Whether she saw the action, he did not know, but compassion filled him all the same. His young sister had wept many bitter tears when they lost their abba in battle four years ago.

The resounding blast of the shofar, blown by Elah, stirred his blood as the men roared, raising their fists or swords as one. Othniel pictured the famed ruined city of Hormah—the images so vividly described by his abba. The place that Caleb and Joshua had conquered as one, leaving a mound of bones and earning them the sobriquet "the Fathers of Destruction."

Victory seemed so close.

With another harsh battle cry, Caleb led the men out into the cool morning air with Othniel by his side. One glimpse of that fierce, older visage, with the white hair tied back and his teeth bared like a lion's, sent prickles skittering across Othniel's skin. Perhaps it would be Othniel or the younger men who needed the protection after all.

"We must hurry," one warrior hissed at Othniel later that evening. Arrows pierced the ground, narrowly missing Othniel despite the cover of darkness. He gasped when something sharp grazed his skin, leaving a trail of fire in its wake.

Thankful for the thick covering of clouds obscuring the full moon, he touched his arm and felt wetness on his fingertips. That arrow had flown far too close. In the distance, the city of giants loomed. For too long, Kiriath-sepher lay untouched, surrounded by the tribe of Judah. One stubborn city refusing to budge. With the Philistines and Canaanites to the west of Hebron, near the cities of Gaza and Ashkelon, controlling access to the Great Sea, the tribe of Judah lay in the middle, flanked by the Salt Sea to the east, and beyond, the tribe of Reuben. The city of giants bothered the Israelites like a festering wound that refused to heal. During some seasons, they lay low, almost to the point of being friendly. At other times, they had carved a path of terror when it was least expected.

Othniel knew fighting the giants would prove a trying task. With Caleb's desire to strike quickly and fiercely, taking the enemy by surprise, the plan had promised to work. But not this day. Why had Yahweh withheld His blessing? Was it because the men of Israel no longer wanted to listen to His voice? Was it because they had forgotten Yahweh's mighty deliverance from the slavery of Egypt?

He couldn't ask such questions, not with arrows whistling through the air, landing with soft thuds all around him. Their attempts to free the servant girl had ended in futility. Had the sons of Anak known that Caleb would come for them? Instead of surprising the city, Othniel and his fellow warriors found themselves under a vicious assault with the soldiers popping up from the fortified walls to strike without relenting.

"We cannot take them," Caleb's son Elah muttered as he crouched beside Othniel, ducking low just as one round stone flew past his head. The stone bounced, leaving an imprint in the soil. "The giants have the high ground."

Othniel peered over the large boulder, one of many strewn across the landscape. The walled city glowed in the light of the flickering torches the enemy giants held up along the fortified walls. Just as Elah said, any attack seemed more and more impossible with each passing moment. A row of archers and men with slingshots provided a near-constant assault.

Would they ever rescue the girl? Rumor had it that she remained hidden behind those thick stone walls, sold by a slave trader. Othniel groaned under his breath, his heart pounding like a drum as he thought of his little sister being trapped behind those impenetrable stone walls.

"Where is the mighty dog, Caleb? I hear only the yipping of a wounded pup!" an unnaturally deep voice yelled from the top section to the west of the wall. "Tell the old man that Marduk will hunt him down and slit his throat!"

Othniel ground his teeth together. This giant, newly arrived, towered over the others, his shoulders massive as cedar trunks. His features, though too far to see clearly, appeared gruesomely distorted by the wavering torches until he resembled something altogether unnatural.

"The man shouting is one of the *Nephilim*," a man beside Othniel moaned. "We cannot beat such demons."

"With Yahweh, we can—" Othniel insisted, but his desperate plea all but died when another man cried out with terror.

"Caleb! Caleb has been hit!" a man yelled during the panicked rush to escape from the onslaught of slingshots.

"Hush!" Othniel warned them, lest the enemy hear. He rose while maintaining a crouching position and scurried past several boulders, heading toward the shout.

There on the ground lay the white-haired warrior, the father of destruction, clutching his leg where an arrow jutted from the flesh below his knee. And at that moment, the moon broke free of her constraints, flooding the rocky plain with a cold, clear light, illuminating the frightened men of Israel. A mighty scream—like the braying of jackals—rose from the city walls. Skin prickling, Othniel scrambled to the side of the man who had been like an abba to him.

As Caleb lay on the ground, the arrow's presence was impossible to ignore. The shaft protruded menacingly from his calf, a cruel reminder of the battle's chaos. The decision couldn't be clearer—the arrow had to be removed before Othniel could even consider moving Caleb to safety.

Yahweh, help.

Othniel took a deep breath. With a swift and measured motion, he unsheathed his knife and assessed the situation. The fletching lay crumpled on the ground, no longer providing the stabilizing balance it once did.

Recognizing that a quick extraction would prove impossible, Othniel carefully cut the arrow shaft close to the wound. He gauged Caleb's reaction.

"This will hurt," he told the older man. "I cannot dig out the arrowhead. Not now with the enemy approaching."

With a low moan, Caleb dug his fingers into Othniel's arm.

"I will need to carry you. We cannot linger here," Othniel said, glancing at the city walls. How long did they have to make their escape?

Blood oozed from the wound. Othniel wasted no time cutting and using part of Caleb's tunic to staunch the bleeding.

"No, you must rally the men and try once more," Caleb hissed, each syllable laced with pain. "You must do it!"

But the screams from the wall only grew in strength, and, with the exception of Elah, Caleb's younger son, the men who had come with Othniel and Caleb now darted away, using the strewn boulders for cover.

"Not tonight," Othniel said as he looped Caleb's arms around his waist and rolled them both until Othniel was on his stomach and the older man lay on top of him, and then with a grunt, Othniel rose onto his knees, holding Caleb's dead weight. Long ago, Hur had shown him how to remove an immobile man from the battlefield, using the wounded's weight as leverage. Yet, even with Caleb's arms wrapped around Othniel's neck for support, Othniel staggered under the older man's weight.

"Leave me be!" cried Caleb from behind Othniel's ear. The old man clung to him all the same, his grip like a vise over Othniel's neck and chest.

"Never."

"We need to get to the horses," Elah said, sounding strained, as he came to a halt to the left of Othniel. Moonlight reflected off his sickle blade. He pointed it toward the hills, now obscured against the night sky. "And we need to ride through the night and lose any trackers in the hills."

A horrible thought considering Caleb's wound.

Even more disturbing, the howls of the enemy drew closer and closer, echoing across the plain while the moon shone in full glory, illuminating the fleeing Israelites who scattered in every direction, leaving their comrades behind in their desperate attempt to escape the giants.

The gates of Kiriath-sepher opened with a clash, and more torches flooded through the gaping opening, like the mouth of a monster threatening to swallow Othniel and his countrymen whole.

Elah eyed Othniel with a look of disbelief. "What have we done? We have stirred the depths of Sheol tonight, and the Nephilim will take us captive."

Caleb, however, didn't answer, his head slumping against Othniel's shoulder. How much blood had the general lost? He needed to get Caleb to safety and bind that wound as soon as possible.

A failed mission. Was such a thing even possible with the greatest warrior from the tribe of Judah? With a muttered prayer for the girl trapped in the city of giants, Othniel glanced at his friend and said only one word.

"*Run.*"

Two days of running and evading the enemy, two days trying to lose the giants in the labyrinth of terraced hills and terebinth trees while Caleb protested.

"Enough, Abba!" cried Elah, who, as a younger son, usually deferred to Caleb's commands. "You would see each of us slaughtered by the sons of Anak? We cannot risk such an action, and you cannot walk, not with that arrow lodged in your leg."

"It is but an arrow," growled Caleb, though whenever he tried to take a step, he buckled to the ground. Only grudgingly did he accept Elah's offer of a horse.

Night swathed the land again by the time the weary trio returned to Caleb's abode. The rest of the Israelite warriors had fled, each to his home. Caleb's household lay swathed in darkness but for one light flickering near a window.

As carefully as he could, Othniel helped the older man off the horse, bracing himself yet again for the dead weight. With Naam's help, they carried the general into the house. Instead of complaining, Caleb only grunted, pressing his lips together to keep any further sounds of pain from escaping. Othniel and Naam carried Caleb between them like a rolled-up rug.

"You feel hot. I fear infection might be starting in the wound," Othniel admitted to the general as he maneuvered sideways, his arms beneath Caleb's arms while Naam held his father's feet. A most undignified position for a mighty man of war.

"It is nothing a priest cannot handle. Heat a blade to cauterize the wound and be done with it," Caleb hissed as he struggled to free himself from Othniel's and Naam's grip.

Any attempts to remove the arrowhead had failed during the rushed trip, since the Canaanite giants had sent their best warriors to track down the Israelites, leaving no opportunity for treatment.

"Bring him to his chambers," Elah commanded, as he motioned for Othniel to follow. "I will rouse the servants, and we will find someone to tend to him. I could send word for one of the Levite priests, but we will be forced to wait for the nearest priest to return from Hebron."

Othniel and Naam carried Caleb through a series of corridors until, at last, they reached the largest chamber, where a mattress, stuffed with straw and sheep wool, waited. The patter of bare feet running distracted Othniel, but the approaching light of yet another clay oil lamp allowed him to see better as he and Naam lay Caleb on the mattress.

"Abba!"

The light drew nearer, revealing the owner of that voice. Achsah, her hair unbound, held the clay lamp high just as Othniel removed Caleb's sandals.

"I am sorry," he said to Achsah, his throat tightening when he spied her look of horror. "Your abba took an arrow in the leg just outside of Kiriath-sepher. We escaped with our lives."

Her eyes, a luminous brown, widened, and for once, he saw her lips tremble.

"What do you need me to do?" she whispered as she reached out to touch Caleb's sleeve.

"This is no place for a child. Leave me be, Daughter," Caleb said through gritted teeth, yet, despite all of his growling, his skin had paled to an unnatural hue.

She straightened her small shoulders. "I shall do no such thing, Abba. I know I can help."

"We need fresh water, just as the priests decree, to cleanse his wound," Othniel told her as he unhooked his sword from his belt and set it aside on the rug. "The freshest water you have. Not something that sits in an open bowl, used by others. We need clean cloths to bandage his leg. Your brother plans to find a priest to help, but in the meantime, we must do what we can. Also…find me a stick with no splinters."

She placed a hand against her abba's forehead, her voice even, then turned to Othniel. "I will get what you need."

No tears or sobbing, to Othniel's surprise. No helpless wringing of the hands. He found himself vaguely impressed with her resolve as she rushed from the room, raising her voice to call the nearest servants. Her orders flew quickly, and even her older brother, Naam, deferred as he left to join her.

Good. With her out of the room, at least he could inspect the wound better without injuring her pride. Despite her bold show of strength, even the strongest soldier could retch at the sight of a gaping flesh wound. With the aid of the flickering lamp, he saw more than enough when he moved aside the foul robes to further inspect Caleb's leg. No other weapon ensured death quite like the arrow. Thankfully, it hadn't struck bone, but it had caused enough bleeding to make a man faint.

"You must get the cursed arrowhead out," Caleb whispered. His eyelids flickered, as he wavered in and out of consciousness.

Let him sleep, Yahweh, Othniel prayed as he watched the older man take deep breaths.

Naam returned with a heated blade, glowing hot from being immersed in the coals, and Achsah brought a pitcher of water, a basket of linens, with a stick lying on top. The servant woman, Bel, followed close behind with extra linens, a jar of salve, and a bowl.

Othniel poured the water over his hands, allowing the water to splash into Bel's bowl. Then he cleaned Caleb's leg as best he could. After a pause, he asked for the stick. Achsah flinched when he instructed Caleb to open his mouth and bite down hard on the stick.

"You may not want to stay," Othniel muttered under his breath, slanting her a look.

"I agree," Bel added quickly.

"I am not leaving my abba," Achsah answered, narrowing her eyes at Othniel, her challenge clear. Blowing out a harsh breath, he turned from her and focused on the task at hand, especially when Naam handed him the blazing knife.

He lost all sense of time as he prodded for the arrowhead embedded in the torn flesh and removed it as best he could. After he finished, Bel cleansed Caleb's leg with a solution of vinegar and hyssop. But before he could dress the seeping wound, Achsah showed him an open alabaster jar of strong-smelling salve.

"It is a healing ointment. My abba keeps a pot for use following his skirmishes."

The powerful aroma of cedarwood and other spices filled his nostrils when she edged past him to tend to the wound in the calf muscle.

She bit her lip as she smoothed the oily paste across the torn flesh. When she glanced at Othniel, he thought he saw a flash of fear.

He straightened, suddenly lightheaded. Spots swam in his vision as he braced himself with a hand, lest he crumple to the floor.

"Have either of you eaten anything?" Achsah asked him and her brothers. Othniel shook his head.

"Go, eat, Othniel, before we need to take care of you too," Naam said wearily as he hunkered down beside Caleb. He shoved a hand through his thick hair, perhaps as despondent as Othniel felt. Bel stayed as well, the lines on her face deepening as she fussed over the sleeping general. He wondered at her manner, so tender for a servant. In fact, he might have sworn that her whispers were prayers. Her right sleeve fell back as she tucked a damp strand of hair behind her ear, revealing the mark of a temple prostitute branded for service.

But before he could dwell further on such thoughts, Achsah tugged on his sleeve to lead him to the main room, where he had sat on finely woven mats with Caleb's sons, discussing Joshua's collapse and the threat of giants over bowls of roasted grains and a fragrant stew. How long ago it seemed...yet only mere days had passed.

Shame at failure filled him as the taunts of the sons of Anak reverberated through his mind. Would Marduk seek his revenge and strike Caleb or Caleb's family? The thought terrified him.

Why did You not intervene, Yahweh? Why did You allow me to taste failure? No answer came from Yahweh, leaving Othniel to ruminate.

Setting the lamp on a low table, Achsah motioned for him to come closer, and the servant woman bowed and hurried from the room to prepare some food. How quickly Achsah had grown into her role as mistress of the house, taking over the household responsibilities.

She pointed to his left arm. "You also were struck with an arrow."

"Grazed," he corrected, covering the spot with his hand. A mere scratch didn't compare to what Caleb had endured, and, amid the danger of fleeing, he had forgotten about it until now.

"I will treat it all the same. Sit down, and I will retrieve the salve." She didn't wait for him to answer. But as soon as he sank onto the nearest woven mat, exhaustion hit him and he saw lights dancing in his vision.

When Achsah returned, she came with the pot and a pitcher, and an assortment of cloths draped over her arm. He kept silent as she worked. Silence somehow felt easier. Far more comfortable. Usually his imma or sister filled the quiet with their pleasant chatter, teasing him about his silence.

Should he say something now? Offer comfort? He had no skill with pretty speeches. All words fled, however, when Achsah looked into his eyes and asked bluntly, "Will my abba walk again?"

He swallowed hard, his mouth dry at such a question—one he had fretted over during the past hours. Finally, he forced himself to move his lips. "I do not know." Something—an expression he couldn't quite decipher—flickered in her eyes at his curt answer. Mentally, he chided himself for not protecting Caleb better. Shame heated his skin. Shame and fear, for he couldn't imagine a world without the wisdom of either Caleb or Joshua. Might both men pass away during the night? And if so, what would happen to all of Israel and the tribes?

"I am sorry," he said thickly, trying his best not to move and disrupt her ministrations. "I wish I could have protected your abba better."

Achsah blinked suddenly and ducked her head. Her face was hidden by her long hair as she cleaned his arm and rubbed the cedarwood salve before binding the wound with strips of linen.

A ragged sigh escaped him as he thought of the young Israelite girl—so similar to Achsah and his sister Rachel—trapped in the city of giants. Caleb was right. Peace would elude them as long as evil men lived within the boundaries of Judah.

All thoughts were cut short when a pounding at the door arrested his attention. The visitor didn't wait to be invited in. Instead, the door flew open just as Othniel's hand reached the dagger hanging at his side.

The man's eyes bulged as he bent over, gasping for air, as if he had run at full speed across the winding barley fields.

"Forgive me," he panted. "But I am to bring word to Caleb that—"

Achsah cast a look at Othniel. He stood slowly, dread threading through him, the knot in his stomach growing with certainty.

"Joshua is dead."

In that moment, Achsah straightened her shoulders, and Othniel found himself a bit in awe of her, for one so young to be so resolute... so fearless. And so unlike his beloved little sister. "I will tell my abba the news. Come and rest with Othniel."

The young man shook his head, sweat dripping down the side of his cheeks as he bent over, hands placed on his knees while he struggled to regain his breath. "No, mistress. I must run to Hebron and warn the priests before more trouble breaks out."

"We will send one of our servants." Achsah paused in the great room that led to Caleb's chamber. "Someone who is not winded."

Ah, that sharp tongue of hers. Othniel might have chuckled in different circumstances if he didn't feel the immediate swell of panic at the realization that Israel had lost one so formidable as Joshua.

Yahweh, help us.

The young man reached out a hand to stabilize himself against the door while Othniel inhaled a sharp breath. Othniel wasn't exactly fresh either, after rushing from the giants while experiencing a humiliating defeat.

But the priests at Hebron would listen to him. And they knew he hung onto every word of Caleb's. As for Caleb's sons…

He dared not entrust the message to the eldest, Iru. Time was of the essence if they were to rally the cities before the surrounding Canaanites learned of Joshua's death.

"I will go. If we need an army ready, then I will send word." Othniel turned to the young man. "When you are ready, go to the next villages. We will send a warning to every corner of the land of Judah and far beyond."

The young man nodded, still gulping great lungfuls of air. His voice quavered with fear. "Who will lead us now?"

Who indeed, Yahweh?

CHAPTER FOUR

Nine Years Later

Y ou do not look happy for me." Achsah's niece, Rebekah, pouted as she sat cross-legged across from her on a newly woven mat.

Achsah sighed, threading a crimson string through her loom. Dressed in a new tunic of luscious saffron and smelling of sweet perfume, Rebekah had arrived early in the morning to share the news of the wedding date. She tugged at a dangling silver earring while waiting for Achsah's reply.

"Nothing would please me more than to see you married," Achsah finally answered as she pulled the string tight, the action mirroring the tension coiling inside her. Before her, rows of vibrant colors, each carefully organized, taunted her with their near perfection, unlike the state of her current life. "What woman does not want to have a home of her own and children? It is just—"

Her chest fluttered. How ironic that right this very hour, Abba would be speaking with someone about *her* hand and…

Somehow she couldn't quite poke the crimson string through the myriad of tightly woven threads that waited as a testament to hours of careful artistry. She let the stubborn string fall and glanced at Rebekah, who stared at her with her full lips pinched tightly together. "It is *Dov*."

Rebekah folded her arms across her chest, her cheeks blooming like twin flowers. "You say his name like it is a slur. I know you have never liked him. The moment you heard about the betrothal a year ago, you actually snorted at me and gave me all the reasons not to accept."

Achsah resisted the urge to defend herself. It was true. Dov ben Raphu had never earned her respect. He spent far too many days in the Canaanite cities, bragging about his trade routes and deals with the enemy. He had never left Haim's side—whose very family had proven to be an enemy of Abba's, despite the ties to the tribe of Judah. Was it wrong to want so much more for a dear friend and family member? Born the same year, they were more like sisters than anything else. Couldn't Rebekah see the danger?

Sometimes, Achsah wondered if Dov found the Canaanites far more palatable than the tribe of Judah and the strict priests who oversaw Hebron. He certainly wasn't Eli, who had spent the last several evenings with her brothers, sitting at her table and sending flirtatious grins or winks her way whenever she glanced at him.

"Dov seems very determined to move you far from family. Do you think it is wise to live so close to the Canaanites and the Philistines?" Achsah asked, running a finger across the tapestry in front of her to keep her expression from revealing too much. A tsk from Rebekah drew Achsah's attention away from the loom.

Rebekah tossed her brown curls over her shoulder, her tone similar to the chiding one might give a small child. "We have been mostly at peace, Achsah, for the past nine years. We would do well to pursue better relationships with our neighbors rather than eye them with suspicion. Maybe if we were not so inclined to war, no matter the tiny provocation, they might lay down their swords as well. Besides, have you seen the goods the Canaanites and Philistines sell at their markets? Purple cloth from Tarshish and the most beautiful beads of amber and gold I have ever seen. And the perfumes! You will smell so wonderful, no man will be able to resist you."

Achsah blew out a long breath, her fingers already tensing. She picked up the shuttle to pass the horizontal thread through the shed, the space created by lifting the vertical threads. An intricate pattern took shape, slowly but surely. The soothing act of weaving, however, did little to curb her mounting irritation. "You know we cannot trust the Canaanites. They have been raiding borders again."

"Dov thinks he can negotiate a peace treaty and placate the leaders of the Canaanite and Philistine cities, including Kiriath-sepher. Especially after Grandfather's failed campaign all those years ago. If anyone can bring peace, it is Dov."

The way Rebekah spoke of Dov, with hushed tones of reverence and eyes wide with wonder, made Achsah want to throw up her hands in disgust.

Shifting on her mat, she strove to keep her tone even. "Purchasing a few trinkets from the nearby cities is one thing, but the worship of Baal or his goddess, Asherah, is an entirely different matter."

Rebekah batted aside the suggestion as if it were but a bothersome fly. "Of course, we will not abandon Yahweh. I am rather insulted that you would assume so poorly of me, Achsah. Have we not known each other since we were children?"

Achsah leaned over, placed her hand on Rebekah's arm, and squeezed gently. "Forgive me if I offended you. It is just that Abba often says how difficult it is to keep Yahweh's commandments when our hearts remain divided. We have seen too many Israelites forsake our way of life and the commandments handed to us by Moses."

"How can I ever forget those lessons of your abba, those very long-winded lessons? No, I will not abandon Yahweh. I would not dare, or I shall never hear the end of it," Rebekah said as a giggle burst free from her.

Achsah removed her hand, her smile dying on her lips. Her brother Iru held the same flippant attitudes as his daughter. He refused to clear out the land of the giants, as commanded by Yahweh and Moses. As a result, her other brothers copied his example with complaints whenever Abba reminded them of their duty to the tribe of Judah.

"We must plant our crops."

"We have grandchildren and vineyards to enjoy. Have we not earned this right?"

"I am building a new threshing floor. I could not possibly help during such a busy season. How will I feed my family?"

For nine years, she had watched her family slide into growing complacency, content to let others fight instead. Meanwhile, her abba's urgency to fulfill Yahweh's commandment fell on increasingly deaf ears.

"I can see that you are busy. I just wanted you to hear the good news. How we will celebrate at the wedding feast!" Rebekah cast Achsah a sly glance. "And perhaps, one day, I will be the first to hear of your betrothal?"

The loom now a helpless project in light of current distractions, Achsah rose when her niece did. And though she embraced Rebekah, the action brief, it at least gave her a moment to compose her features.

Truly, she wanted marriage for her niece. Together, they had watched their friends marry and discover the joy of motherhood. But while Iru controlled Rebekah's every choice, Abba offered Achsah the freedom to choose.

"You will have to accept an offer instead of rejecting it, yes? Although…it has been years since someone has asked you," Rebekah prodded, her eyes twinkling despite the cutting remark. "We are not getting any younger."

"When I find a man who follows Yahweh, I will consider marriage."

Rebekah laughed, the sound tinkling like the silver earrings dancing from her earlobes. "You will refuse him as you have the last six men. Do not deny it. My abba says you are determined to rule this household. But what happens when Grandfather passes? My abba says you must marry and he will choose for you. And who will have you when you are far older than all the other available maidens, far past your childbearing years?"

"Then at least I shall be content on my own, as I have always been," Achsah said with a rueful smile. She had endured such chiding before, evenly brushing aside such remarks. So why then did she ache today? Was she too old to be considered for marriage?

Was she truly destined to refuse everyone? Because, in all honestly, very few men lived up to her bold abba who loved her so faithfully.

Then again, why should she become any man's property and leave that circle of protection? Her abba never tried to silence her or make her feel less than his other children. Would Eli prove as honorable and kind if he offered to marry her?

Such thoughts regarding suitable men brought to mind the troublesome subject of Dov and his friendship with Haim. Dov had no sense within him to see evil. A shiver rippled through her shoulders as she led Rebekah out into the sunny courtyard.

"Achsah, do be reasonable. Perhaps Dov can help you find someone. He is connected with so many others, thanks to his trade routes—"

"There is a man," Achsah blurted before she could stop herself. Inwardly cringing at her impetuous admission, she plunged ahead, regardless of the consequences. Anything to silence Rebekah and return to the loom in peace. "He is well respected by my abba."

Rebekah paused in the courtyard, her eyes shiny as she reached for Achsah's arm. "Why have you not said anything? What is his name?"

Of course, Rebekah would want a name, and it would spread throughout the tribe of Judah in a fortnight. Why had Achsah thought to open her mouth at all, except for the newly acquired shame of reaching the ripe old age of twenty-one, when most women had a household full of children?

Rebekah, with her silver bangles tinkling, shook Achsah's arm. "The name!"

"Eli." The weak admission left her in one gush. In fact, if she dared admit it, she rather hoped her abba had gone to speak with Eli this morning and perhaps encouraged the man to pursue more than just a few admiring glances whenever she saw him in Hebron. But that bit of information lodged in her throat, thankfully, just at the last moment.

Rebekah let go, her expression full of delight as she crowed her triumph. "I should have known you would be drawn to such a handsome man, and I believe Eli trained with your abba this past year. It is clear why you have refused all the others."

"I have refused every other man because none of them who have wandered through my door worship Yahweh as Moses decreed. For far too long, the young men of our tribe have crept into the nearby Canaanite towns to do as they wish, including your betrothed Dov, sampling nothing but trouble, yet always returning. I fear he will only lead you astray with his restless longings for a different life."

Rebekah drew back, her dark brows lowered as if to do battle. For a moment, Achsah feared her niece might stomp a foot or yell, but instead, tears flooded Rebekah's eyes. She sniffed loudly.

"Dov is right. Your tongue stings like an asp. Who would want to endure your poisoned fangs?" In a whirlwind of fabric and billowing veils, Rebekah rushed out of the courtyard, leaving a trail of sickly sweet musk behind. Within moments, the courtyard door slammed, the echoing sound a jolt.

CHAPTER FIVE

Chiding herself, Achsah rubbed the back of her neck. Had she said too much yet again? But if she didn't warn Rebekah about Dov's shameful behavior, often whispered about within the courtyard by the servants, how could she live with herself?

Why didn't her brother Iru see through Dov's pretense? Then again, Iru saw nothing beyond the wealth of his granaries and ever-enlarging vineyards. He had kept Rebekah from marrying, seeking only an arrangement that would suit him financially. Would he profit from Dov's trading routes? She knew her brother would take full advantage of Dov's connections.

A snort escaped her just as the courtyard door opened again. However, instead of a tiny figure swathed in an embroidered saffron gown and delicate veils, her white-haired abba limped into the courtyard, his meaty hand clasping a rough-hewn cane.

Beside him, another man followed close behind, his tall frame, though not as broad, matching her abba's in height. A man whose presence felt as familiar as family over the years.

Shielding her eyes against the harsh sun, she smiled in welcome. "Abba, how was your walk?" Part of her wanted to demand to know how his conversation with Eli went, yet with Othniel now shutting the courtyard door, she stifled her mounting impatience.

Her abba snorted, much like her, but all the same, the fierceness of his features softened as he limped toward her. "I have been to the edge of our land, and I ran across Othniel in the fields. He's come back from scouting near Juttah and Jattir."

Othniel raised his head and met her gaze, his eyes dark and unreadable. Black hair, far too long, curled about his neck and fell over his brows. His nose took a crooked path, thanks to a punch. Even from where she stood, she could smell him—the hours spent beneath a scorching sun, baking on the rocky landscape with only some brush for shade, were evident. His tunic was coated in pale dust, as were his hairy legs and arms. Wherever he came from, since she was certain he had seen more than just Juttah near the Sea of Salt, he clearly hadn't bathed in days.

She offered him an absent smile, one reserved for her brothers, who visited occasionally when they had a free moment between harvests. While she encouraged her abba's excursions, she couldn't quite shake herself free of the dread that something awful might occur to him. "Abba, I thought you had plans to visit our neighbors," she said quietly, slowing her steps to accommodate his uneven pace. He hated being treated like an invalid, especially after the old wound.

He leaned on his cane, his face pinched—either because of her request or the ache in his leg. "I would have, but more important matters arose when I met Othniel. The sons of Anak raided another border town, Jattir, snatching men or women caught using the trade routes."

She flinched, pressing a hand against her chest to stop the fluttering inside. The news, though hardly unexpected, brought more than a sliver of unease. "And you wish to rally the tribe again?"

"We must."

She lowered her voice to a near whisper, although she felt, somehow, Othniel could hear the rustle of a mouse across the courtyard. "Abba, no one listens to those warnings anymore. They are deep into the harvest, preparing to glean the barley. They dare not let the crops wait without risk to the kernels."

"One day, it will not be just a child or a woman taken here and there. We will lose an entire town, and what then, when invaders sweep across our land intending to destroy us? What will we do? Hide in our caves and thresh our grain in secrecy?"

She silently groaned even as she outwardly shook her head. Arguing with Abba proved an impossible feat. Truthfully, she agreed with him about the increasing danger prowling the borders. Regardless, she ached inside for his crushed expression. These days, it seemed only she listened to the rumblings of an old man. Well, she and perhaps Othniel.

"Achsah, Moses told us to take the land. A commandment from Yahweh. How can we live in such blatant rebellion, absorbing all the Canaanites do? I have heard rumors of new worship poles erected in the name of the goddess Asherah, along with groves reserved for their wicked rites. By our own people, no less!" Her abba actually blushed when he said this, but she was no naive maiden, ignorant of what went on in those so-called sacred fertility groves.

Would Eli and the others head off to defend the border? A throat cleared beside her, and she glanced at Othniel.

"You will stay for supper." Her statement came out more clipped than she intended, but ire somehow bubbled up inside of her. If only Abba hadn't run into Othniel. If only Abba had fulfilled his promise to her and sought Eli to see if he might be interested in marrying her.

Othniel nodded slowly. She glanced at his hands, noticing the long scratches marring the skin. A faint trickle of blood dripped down his forearm.

"I will not feed you until you wash those hands." She pointed to the edge of the courtyard where a pithoi of rainwater waited. "There is fresh water in the jars and a ladle beside the pithoi on the bench."

He blew out a long breath and nodded again. The man's silence grated on her because all she wanted was to sit with Abba and privately discuss what would happen next with Eli.

"Do I even want to know what happened to your hands out in the bush?" she asked, motioning to Othniel's arm.

He appeared not to hear as he moved toward the pithoi, running a hand through his hair to shake the dust out of it.

"Stop, Achsah. Othniel goes routinely to see about the people taken from the villages. Those he can rescue, he does. It is in the city of giants, however, where he finds only failure." Her abba sounded peeved. Peeved at her, of all people.

"Why does he keep going back, alone?" she insisted under her breath. "Why does he insist on endangering himself?"

"He searches for a young woman, the same age as his sister. Your age, too, I believe. Someone took her all those years ago when you were only twelve years old. Whenever he hears rumors of Israelite slaves, he searches for her and the others taken. He always remembers the lost and wishes to bring them home."

For once, she was speechless, her heart pounding at the idea of a helpless girl—now a woman—trapped behind the thick walls of the city of giants with no one to remember her except for one farmer who dreamed of being a warrior like her abba.

She treated all the men in her house the same. Othniel proved no exception. The older she got, the sharper her tongue—just as Rebekah had accused earlier. Tears of frustration burned in Achsah's eyes as she marched into the house to grab linens and her precious jar of cedarwood salve. When she returned with her hands full, she heard her abba's voice, low and fierce. "If no one else will lead the men, then I will do so again."

Othniel kept his tone respectful. "Caleb, I have returned from the priests and the other tribal leaders. Our only hope is to travel to the other tribes and ask for help. Neither you nor I can take the city alone."

"We should not wait. We cannot afford another raid."

As she removed the clay lid of the pithoi and dipped the ladle into the water, she motioned for Othniel to come forward. "Abba, listen to Othniel for once. Clearly, he gives you good advice."

When Othniel moved closer, she poured water over his scratches until his skin appeared clean, water droplets clinging to the dark hair of his arms. Faint white scars lay crisscrossed over his forearms, disappearing beneath the sleeve of his filthy tunic.

Just like Abba's arms—a record of each battle and skirmish fought during the wilderness and far beyond.

And at that moment, her gaze met Othniel's. His mouth parted as if he wanted to say something to her.

She arched an eyebrow, waiting for him to speak.

"Thank you," he finally said in a low tone. "I cannot convince your abba without your help."

If Abba did not listen to her or Othniel...

Anxiety bubbling within as she set the ladle on the bench pushed against the plastered wall, she inhaled deeply to compose herself. Better to focus on the task at hand. She opened the alabaster jar, the fragrance of the balm's oils so strong that her nose and eyes watered. In the meantime, Othniel described some of what he had seen near Juttah, Jittir, and Eshtemoa.

"I ran into some Philistine merchants who thought I was one of them. They hinted that the sons of Anak might plan another uprising soon. The giants have hunkered down in the city of Kiriath-sepher for years, and no one can make them budge. In the meantime, they hold the roads leading past the city, taking slaves as they wish. No one dares travel past Kiriath-sepher without endangering his or her life."

"Is it true that the Anakim are indeed the Nephilim?" Achsah interjected quickly. "Like the mighty men of old from Noah's age before the Great Flood?"

The Nephilim, rumored to be from the union of the sons of God and the daughters of men, had long cast fear among the Israelites. Some people claimed the Anakim were just as wicked and powerful as Nephilim had been. Some whispered that evil spirits dwelled in these giants, giving them unusual powers. A jolt rippled across Achsah's shoulders at the idea.

Othniel must have noted her reaction. His amber gaze softened. "They are big men, it is true, but in the end, they are just men like your abba or me." He raised his scratched arm. "Even giants bleed."

She dipped her fingers into the oily paste and pulled his arm down so she could smear her medicinal ointment. "But perhaps you and Abba might bleed more in the end. You must be careful. Did you find her? The girl captured so many years ago?"

He winced at her question, but he did not pull away from her grip. "No," he answered hoarsely.

She didn't have the heart to probe further, her mind whirling with images far too troublesome and heartbreaking to linger overlong. Why must Rebekah move to the borders? Surely Dov could find trade routes elsewhere or settle in Hebron if need be. Hebron needed merchants.

But she knew the answer as soon as the question flitted through her mind. Dov would have to face the priests daily. At least, near the Canaanite cities, he could live as he pleased without ever hearing another word of condemnation. Just like his awful friend, Haim, who had only worsened with the passage of each year.

A sigh escaped her as she placed the last dab of ointment on Othniel's knuckles, rubbing it as gently as she could. His hands, though large, were not nearly the size of her abba's.

"Do you remember doing this task nine years ago, after I brought your abba back from battle?" Othniel asked after a pause, breaking into her tumultuous thoughts.

She replaced the lid on the alabaster jar with a decided clink, shaking her head. No, she had completely forgotten, truth be told. Indeed, all she could remember of that fateful evening was her abba lying in pain and sorrow, his private tears at being abandoned by his eldest son even more bitter to bear.

"I am sorry for what happened that night," Othniel said, much to her surprise. He leaned in closer. "I never wanted to see your abba hurt."

Her nose wrinkled as she stepped backward, but regardless, she appreciated his sincerity and the grief shining in his eyes. "It is not your fault. And I count myself blessed to see my abba's face each morning, and that is because of you bringing him home alive and in one piece. If only I had been born a man, I would have gone out with him. I would have done all that he asked and more." She sounded brighter and more confident than she felt.

"I remember a twelve-year-old girl saying as much," Othniel replied with a rare sparkle in his eyes. Eyes with flecks of gold, she noticed, being this close to him.

She huffed a laugh as she stepped away, but any humor stilled as soon as it left her lips. Again, the image of a woman trapped behind the gates of an enemy city brought a wave of nausea cresting within her. "I spoke harshly to you earlier. You have done a good thing, Othniel, son of Kenaz, searching for the lost and the forgotten. My abba is right to trust you in such matters. I do hope you will join us for the evening meal, as always. Just…wash behind your ears, please."

He swallowed, suddenly silent again.

Had she embarrassed him? She hoped not. She ribbed Elah mercilessly, despite him being years older than her. Never had she encountered someone so silent…so awkward, and it set her on edge some days. Carrying on a conversation with Othniel reminded her of untangling a massive knot snagged in her loom. It took so much effort and care not to break the fragile threads.

She left him and Abba in the courtyard to continue their hushed conversation and found Bel arranging the pillows in the house. "We have a guest tonight. Do we have any grapes left?"

Bel smiled as she plumped one last crimson pillow. She nodded toward a table pressed against the wall. "Iru made certain his servants sent over a basketful of his produce earlier this morning."

The grapes lay clustered in a basket set on a table, each globe gleaming like a precious jewel. Achsah could almost taste the crispness and imagine the juicy flavor exploding with each bite. She took extra care to prepare the meal of roasted lamb, soft cheeses, and round breads. A side of dates and roasted grains were sure to please.

As she and Bel carried out the food, her abba waved for her to take a seat beside him. Othniel's hair appeared wet, as if he had at least dunked his head in a bucket. A stray water droplet traced a path down one lean cheek, and the clean brown tunic on him also appeared new. Perhaps borrowed from her abba.

After serving the men, she took a bowl of the herb-infused lamb for herself. Talk moved to more pleasant topics, including Iru's new vineyards, Hur's ever-multiplying herds, and the birth of Naam's latest son.

"Your sons are indeed blessed," Othniel told Abba as he dipped his hand into the bowl of roasted grains. At least he ate her food, consuming it as quickly as she brought out more platters and bowls loaded with figs and sliced melons.

"Blessed by Yahweh's mercy, but for how long? We fought for our peace, and now most of my sons refuse to wield anything other than a plow." Abba sounded bitter as he picked at his food. "When Yahweh removes His blessings because of the disobedience of Judah and the other tribes, will they then cry out for a deliverer? I remember how often they turned from Him during the wilderness trek. No matter how many miracles they witnessed with their own eyes, they still rebelled. At least, in severe hardship, they cried out for their need for Yahweh's intervention. Now Iru, Elah, Hur, Avraim, and Naam trust their own wisdom. I would far rather have hardship and feel the closeness of the Most High than live in luxury and wander far from His presence."

Achsah reached out and placed a hand on her abba's sinewed arm, yet he trembled beneath her grip.

"Enough of such talk, Abba. The hour grows late, and Othniel perhaps needs a place to stay for the night. Give him one of the spare rooms."

"Are your imma and sister waiting for you?" Abba asked as he retrieved the last piece of bread from the bowl, toying with the piece between his tanned fingers.

Othniel shrugged as he lounged against the cushions, one hand resting on his stomach. He stretched out to his full length. "My imma, perhaps. But she stays with my sister's household these days and finds herself quite content with all of her grandchildren. Content and distracted."

Abba chuckled as he pushed aside his now-empty bowl. "Good for both of them. And what of you, Othniel? A man needs someone to come home to. A family to fight for. Are there no women in all of Judah to hold your interest?"

Othniel's mouth tilted with a crooked smile. He fell silent again, as if lost in thought, as he toyed with the frayed edge of his sash. Curious, Achsah could only wonder at his unwillingness to answer. Othniel, like her, had aged over the years. Why had he never married? Perhaps if she wasn't so busy running her abba's property, she would see if the women at the well could help him find a good wife.

"I am certain there are young maidens who would be happy to accept your offer," she spoke boldly, determined to help an old family friend who deserved some happiness to call his own. "Shall I ask Miriam, Naam's wife, and see what can be done? Surely we can see you married by the end of the harvest."

A soft, strangled sound escaped Othniel as he straightened in the plump cushions. Suddenly, he would no longer meet her steady gaze.

"And what of you, my daughter?" Abba sounded amused. He stroked his beard as he studied her. "Such a bold offer on your part."

She leaned forward, her voice hushed. "Indeed, Abba, there is a pressing situation I would like to discuss privately with you after you have finished your meal."

He frowned, as if bewildered by her request. Had he forgotten about Eli so quickly? With a silent groan, she cleared the empty bowls, nodding at Bel to bring in one last platter of glistening honey pastries to the men. As she drifted back to the kitchen, she pictured Eli with his wiry build and constant smiles. His eyes, a vibrant green like the cypress trees, and the way he laughed, drawing the attention of everyone in the room. Her pulse quickened a notch at the memory of him flashing a white grin, and her pulse hardly ever raced.

No one could look away from Eli. She had never seen a man so handsome or so effortless at drawing conversation back to himself. He never lacked for words. She didn't have to do all the talking, and he didn't seem to mind her chatter either. He actually appeared charmed by her. Nor had she imagined the way his fingers had brushed against hers the last time she served him a meal.

No, Eli would prove the perfect match. As the son of Hezim, an old warrior friend of Abba, Eli had trained hours in this very courtyard, proving himself a master at the sword. Some believed that he might even one day become as valuable a fighter and leader as Joshua. Nor did he farm like most of the other men she knew. Instead, he spent his days making bronze and bronze blades for battle. He had even begun to experiment with iron ore to match the blades of the Philistines. Surely Abba would approve of such an occupation!

Returning to the main room of the house, she breathed a sigh of relief when she spied her abba alone, without Othniel's constant presence. At least Othniel had taken her suggestion to find a room and rest for the night, giving her a moment of privacy.

Now was her chance.

"Abba, I have been waiting all day to hear if you spoke to Eli and Hezim. Will Eli not offer marriage? You promised me you would say something on my behalf, and I am more than ready. Rebekah came this morning to tell me of her forthcoming marriage to Dov. I do not need to tell you that I am not the young woman I used to—"

Abba held up a hand, stilling her passionate speech. "Be at peace, Daughter. I will speak with Eli if that is what you wish. But are you truly certain he is the one? What makes him different from all the others you have rejected? Has he shown any interest? It is the man who must approach and arrange the betrothal, paying the bride price. Not the other way around."

True enough. And that stubborn truth brought a stinging humiliation that wouldn't go away. Yet, in the past several years, all offers had dried up, thanks to the reputation of her unbridled tongue.

"Well, I"—she sputtered, for once feeling off-kilter—"yes, without going into every detail, yes, I believe Eli might be interested. He always has a sweet smile for me. He has been by your side, unlike so many others. He is—"

A rustle at the doorway, left open to the cool air, made the hair on the back of her neck stand on end. There, in the golden light of evening, stood Othniel with his back to her. He shifted, rubbing an old injury on his arm as he stared out into the courtyard, into the deepening horizon where the sun set in a haze of fire.

Had he heard what she just said? He seemed oblivious to the conversation in the house. Her cheeks heated further with embarrassment when her abba answered loudly as he reclined on his cushions.

"Eli smiles for everyone, Daughter. *Everyone.* But I will ask Hezim and get his council once this affair with our border eases."

"Abba! The borders will always have trouble!" she hissed. "Do not tell me you are planning to go out again, not after what happened when I was a child!"

With the help of his cane, he rose to his feet, his expression fiercer than she could ever remember. "I will deal with the border. If no one else will, then I must. I cannot let Othniel work alone. At least my presence might draw other men to the cause. I cannot lie on my couch while others suffer."

Once, years ago, Abba's presence drew men, inspiring them to acts of greatness. His fighting had proven legendary, earning him the respect of all of Israel. But not these days. The world her abba remembered no longer existed, and the men who had fought countless battles were now either too feeble or gone from this world. Othniel didn't have her Abba's way of rousing the men to action. He could hardly even get a handful of words out of his mouth.

Then again, not even Abba could spur most of his sons to defend Israel's borders.

She bit the inside of her cheek hard, the pain a welcome distraction against the mounting frustration threatening to spill over in yet another torrent of angry words. Yet any protest died within her when she again pictured the lost young woman and all the others sold into slavery, trapped behind enemy walls, silently pleading with Yahweh for deliverance. Who would deliver them? Who would deliver Israel, especially with no leader? Why didn't Yahweh do something? Anything to ease the burden of his people?

"I do not want to see you get hurt again," she whispered softly so that no one but her abba would hear.

"I am not afraid. I have lived a good life." He patted her arm. "You know I must rally the men once more. They have drifted from Yahweh since Joshua's death. I had hoped our people would make Yahweh their king. As it stands, they want no leaders. They want to do what is right in their own eyes. If I am to have one last battle, then let me go out in such a blaze of glory that the younger men will stir from their apathy."

"But you are all I have in this world. If you go…and I am left all alone…" Her voice trailed. Her chest tightened until she could barely speak her greatest fear of being an old woman, relegated to the back rooms of her brother's home. A nuisance. No longer needed or wanted.

Oh, Yahweh. I can hardly admit to such weakness.

Such raw admissions would hardly prove speech befitting a daughter of the man who had led Israel's armies into battle.

She closed her eyes tightly before her tears would betray her.

"Do not be afraid, Achsah. Not for me, or for Israel. Or for yourself. Yahweh will prove Himself, as He always has. I have seen Him part the Red Sea. I have watched the men who rebelled against Moses, Korah's men, be swallowed by the earth opening its gaping mouth. I have seen so many things far too wonderful and strange to imagine. You must trust Him."

She put her hand over Abba's and offered her bravest smile to the one man she loved most. Abba had reached the age of ninety-three. Somehow, for so long, he had always seemed invincible to her—even with his limp. But what would Israel do when their lion passed away? What would she do?

CHAPTER SIX

In the days that followed, Abba left with Othniel to speak with the high priest at Shiloh. Achsah worked in her gardens and finished the rug on her loom—a gift intended for Rebekah's coming wedding. The routine of chores did little to ease her anxiety. And, of course, Bel stayed close, offering unwanted advice on how to best bake the round loaves that Abba loved.

When Achsah headed to the marketplace with Bel and a trusted guard named Ari, she heard further whispers about the giants while shopping for goods before the coming Sabbath.

"They make us look like locusts in comparison. Their homes are not like ours, with doors nearly *fifteen* cubits tall. It would be best if we left them alone," one woman with missing teeth said. An exaggeration of the giants' height, Achsah mused to herself as she studied a table of woven textiles from as far as Egypt, the linen translucent enough to see one's fingers through the weave. Somehow the Anakim grew in stature with the gossip.

"Six cubits. Otherwise, we truly would be grasshoppers in their presence. They are nothing more than men, no different than the rest of us," Achsah corrected as she paid for her purchase of a fabric in a deep indigo hue nearly as dark as the evening sky. She couldn't help but remember Othniel reminding her that the giants bled too.

Were they simply big men? Big men intent on using brute force, and not the descendants of the fallen gods?

Mystery swirled around the sons of Anak, much of it blended with exaggeration. Just as Bel handed her a pair of silver earrings with sparkle that would provide the perfect contrast to the indigo fabric, Achsah's ears perked to hear further gossip filtering through from two women deep in conversation at the next stall.

A hand touched her arm, and one of the older women who frequented the well stared at Achsah. "I heard your abba left to rally the armies. Are the rumors true?"

"He left days ago. When he will return, I do not know," Achsah answered. Her abba couldn't enter Hebron without being the subject of loose tongues.

The woman scowled, immediately setting Achsah on edge. "It is madness, what Caleb proposes. The tribe of Manasseh allowed the Canaanites to live at Beth-shan and Megiddo as slaves. The tribe of Ephraim lets the Canaanites live in Gezer."

Achsah recognized the other woman, one with long white hair, as Simi. She joined in the conversation, her basket full of melons purchased from the market. "Zebulun's tribe also made alliances with the Canaanites. So did Asher. Even the men of Naphtali have taken brides from Beth-shemesh and brought them into the tribes. Why should your abba force us to do otherwise?"

"I do not care if all of Israel makes a practice of such things," Achsah said evenly. "You know as well as I do what Moses decreed— straight from Yahweh's mouth. If we had not battled for the right to live in this land, none of you would be here, in this city, safe enough to sample the wares at the market. You would be slaves—just like the men and women snatched from our borders. Why adopt the practices of people who live in defiance of the Most High God?"

She spun on her heel with the bolt of linen pinned beneath her arm, leaving the women speechless, their mouths gaping at her acidic answers.

"You are a fool like your abba, Achsah. The enemy has iron chariots to chase us! Our men have only their sandals to escape!" Simi yelled after Achsah, right in the middle of the market. Heads turned to watch Achsah as she marched through the crowd, past the tables of perfume bottles, melons, dates, and painted pottery, while doing her best to ignore the curious stares. Bel and Ari tried to keep up, Achsah's own noisy puffs soon drowned out by the cacophony of the marketplace.

How was it possible that so many Israelites were complacent in their prosperity, refusing to take a stand while the enemy grew bolder and bolder?

She glanced at the bright blue sky as if an answer waited there, but Yahweh didn't write answers in the clouds for her. And He didn't speak directly to her.

Her abba's voice came back to encourage her. *"If only you had seen what I have seen. The miracles. The wonder of deliverance."*

She stopped in the middle of the beaten road, waiting for Bel and Ari to catch up. Abba had also witnessed great suffering in the wilderness because of the Israelites' lack of faith.

Help me have faith, like Abba.

When Bel finally caught up to her, Achsah reached for her servant's basket.

"No, mistress, I will take it." Bel carried a wealth of goods stacked precariously high in her thin arms. Bronze bangles, more fabric, and even a pot of perfume, as Rebekah had so slyly suggested during the last visit. Plus, additional food to prepare for the Sabbath meal. The two of them looked forward to the day of rest to focus on Yahweh.

Achsah reached for the basket with a smile. "You know I do not mind carrying a load for you."

Bel released a sigh of relief as she relinquished it to Achsah. "I did not get as many melons with your abba and Othniel gone. Nor do I suspect your brothers will come for the Sabbath."

"Should we visit them instead? If one of my brothers hosts it, I would not mind the change for once."

Bel's gaze dropped to her dusty sandals. "I do not believe they have any plans. All their work will be directed to the barley harvest in the coming days. Besides, your older brother says he must prepare for a wedding feast. He has no hour to spare for the Sabbath."

The basket began to slide from Achsah's grip and he fumbled for it, and she would have tipped out the precious contents that would be used in preparing for Rebekah's wedding if Ari hadn't caught it. Would her brothers really be so stubborn to abandon all that their abba had taught them? Did they resent the Levite priests so much for taking Hebron from the family that they would now turn their back on the Most High?

"I did not know that my brothers had abandoned the Sabbath," she said. She gripped the basket closer to her chest as she maneuvered past a farmer and his donkey also planted in the middle of the road. The man jerked on the donkey's rope, earning a loud bray of protest.

"No, mistress, they fear your rebuke too much to let you know," Bel said with faint amusement as she eyed the farmer and the donkey. But then her expression sobered as she met Achsah's gaze. "But perhaps they should fear what your abba will think when he returns."

Days later, from the viewpoint of the window, Achsah watched her abba return to the grand house that his sons had built him. When he passed over the threshold, he paused at the doorway where a carved hollow containing a clay vessel served as a reminder. Tentatively, he splayed his fingers against the wall, not even daring to touch the *mezuzah*, which safeguarded the words of Moses written by a priest. But his lips moved all the same, as if repeating the sacred script tucked inside the vessel.

She knew the parchment by heart.

Hear, O Israel: The Lord our God is one. Love the Lord your God with all your heart and with all your soul, and with all your strength. These commandments that I give you today are to be on your hearts. Impress them on your children. Talk about them when you sit at home and when you walk along the road, when you lie down and when you get up. Tie them as symbols on your hands and bind them on your foreheads. Write them on the doorframes of your houses and your gates. When the Lord your God brings you into the land, He swore to your fathers, to Abraham, Isaac, and Jacob, to give you—a land with large, flourishing cities you did not build, houses filled with all kinds of good things you did not provide, wells

*you did not dig, and vineyards and olive groves you did
not plant—then when you eat and are satisfied, be careful
that you do not forget the Lord, who brought you out of Egypt,
out of the land of slavery.*

He withdrew his hand from the doorpost and leaned on his staff
as he hobbled into the main hall. This afternoon, he allowed her a
moment to fuss over him. No sign of Othniel, which left her freedom to grill her abba in privacy.

"You made it back for Rebekah's wedding. I trust your trip
proved successful?" She stepped back to assess his expression. Dark
circles stained the skin beneath his eyes, and the lines and crags of
his weathered face appeared to have deepened. Indeed, his skin
appeared to be like dried papyrus, fragile and brittle.

"I do not know," he finally answered. "We shall see in the coming days. Truthfully, Othniel did most of the talking when we met
with the other leaders of Judah."

"Othniel?" She raised her eyebrows, shocked at such news.
"Does he truly speak, Abba? He always seems rather tongue-tied
around us. Or with me, at least."

"Never discount a man who listens to a woman. They are rare
enough to find. He needs to learn to speak more, and so I let him
share the latest news surrounding Kiriath-sepher. Yet with our com-
bined efforts, I do not know how many will rally to our cause. Will
it take more tragedy before the men are moved to action? I fear so."

She entwined her fingers together, studying him for the longest
moment until, at last, he blinked.

"What is it, Achsah?"

"Bel told me that your sons are too busy to attend the Sabbath, especially with the harvest. They will come when they can, but who knows when that will be?"

He faltered, his grip sliding on the cane, his face a mask of agony before it settled back into the firm lines. She regretted sharing such discouraging news, especially after encountering the spiteful women at the market who heaped scorn upon her and Abba.

Another matter pressed all the more urgently on her. Part of her debated the wisdom of bringing it up, yet she dared not wait and let the opportunity slip past.

Her words gushed out of her, like a flooded ravine after the rain. "Will you speak with Eli, Abba? Now that you are finally home? One day, if I do not marry, I will be sent to Iru's home or that of another of my brothers and I will have no place other than to tend their wives and children. I do not mind tending to women and babies, but I want a home where Yahweh comes first. I want a man who will honor you."

Her abba sucked in a breath through his teeth before leaning on his cane. "Would that you were born a son, Achsah. Why did Yahweh give me one child who loves Him so completely, in the form of a daughter and the last of my children? My eldest son, who will inherit so much of what I have fought for, does not care like you do."

Her heart broke for Abba. If only there was something she could do to spur her eldest brother to serve Yahweh.

CHAPTER SEVEN

Several Days Later

The sounds of music and laughter filtered through the assembly as Achsah slipped through the packed guests mingling in the Ben Raphu courtyard. Rebekah's wedding proved to be the celebration of the year, with families from near and far gathering to witness the nuptials. Countless enormous pithoi were lined up against the courtyard wall, filled with the finest wines. Roasted meat, turned on several spits, filled the air with a sweet, spicy scent as snatches of conversation filtered Achsah's way, the sound mostly muted, with rumors about the border. Once, she thought she heard her abba's name spoken, but when she eyed the man who uttered it, he grimaced.

Even in the gathering of celebration and marriage, one could not fully escape the reality of existing side by side with the Canaanites. Or the weight of Abba's actions.

She gathered a fistful of her new tunic, the indigo linen a pleasing choice along with the delicate earrings dancing from her earlobes. Although she rarely put so much effort into her appearance, not when she was occupied with running Abba's household, she couldn't help feeling a tinge of gladness when Bel had stepped back earlier with a smile of approval. She might be older than the other young women fluttering around Rebekah, but at least Achsah had kept the blush of her youth.

Iru stood at the edge of the massive courtyard, his arms folded across his chest, his expression smug as he scanned the excited guests. By his side, their abba also watched the celebrations, his mouth pinched into a thin line. Did Abba feel the same way as she did? Disapproving of Dov? Dov's abba, Eleazar ben Raphu, was far richer than Iru, as evidenced by the enormous olive grove rustling outside the grand house. How had he obtained such immense wealth?

When the shofar blew the clear, high note demanding that the bride gather her belongings and head to the bridegroom's house, Achsah had joined the fellow handmaidens to escort Rebekah. Achsah had held her oil lamp high with the other maidens, her light illuminating the rocky path in the evening gloom. Even under the cover of darkness, Eleazar's house appeared as an impenetrable fortress surrounded by mighty walls.

A prison for Rebekah.

Now, the clay lamp long since abandoned, Achsah threaded her way toward the women gathered at the edge of the celebrations, the place where she felt least safe, as opposed to standing by her abba's side. Farther ahead she saw Rebekah, fully veiled in costly attire, approach Dov's side. With a curve to his lips, he fingered the edge of Rebekah's veil, finally lifting it to reveal his bride's features. When he reached for the wedding cup to signify their union with a sip, Achsah averted her gaze, her throat tightening.

A year ago, Achsah had witnessed Rebekah drink from the betrothal cup, sealing a covenant with the *Kiddushin* ritual, promising to be set apart for her husband.

Gritting her teeth, Achsah scanned the crowd for her abba's reaction, but he was tucked away behind several men. If only Dov had kept himself apart, refusing to slip into the Canaanite villages to visit pagan women. But Rebekah had been bought with a price, and nothing could break her vow. And now, as the couple shared the next ritual cup, Achsah couldn't help but notice the irony. Dov would likely never follow his vows—not the way Moses decreed.

A shorter but powerfully built man twisted sideways through the group. Her pulse quickened when she recognized Eli, the armorer, who crafted the most exquisite bronze blades, reserving the very best wares for Abba. His brown hair and trim beard, along with his ready smile, made him one of the most attractive men at the wedding. And before she even realized her actions, she had already smoothed her tunic and readjusted her sash.

Her mouth increasingly dry and her heart pounding like a drum, she slipped away from the women before she lost any residual courage and maneuvered closer to where the men had gathered. Pleasant laughter filled the night air, along with the sound of insects buzzing overhead, glimmering in the flickering torches as they drew too close to the heat and light. So intent on keeping her gaze latched on Eli, she didn't see the foot she had crushed as she marched forward to achieve her mission.

A man exclaimed, and she pivoted to see Othniel just as he hopped backward with a wince.

"I must apologize. I did not see you standing there," she said. His pinched expression tightened even more at her statement, but before she could apologize further for her clumsiness, Eli spotted her and waved.

He cried out, his grin infectious enough to lift her spirits. "I thought I spied Caleb's daughter among the revelers. I had hoped that you would come this evening."

As the flutes and stringed instruments struck up yet another song, Eli edged forward, and Achsah's breath caught when she saw him standing directly in front of her. Nearly the same height as her, he reminded her of an ox. Powerfully built with thick shoulders, just like Abba. Othniel hovered close, making no move to join Caleb or any of the other men. Instead of acknowledging Othniel, Eli kept his appreciative gaze trained on Achsah.

"How lovely you look," Eli said, his voice low and warm. "Will you join the others dancing?"

She stuttered out an answer, while Othniel muttered something unintelligible under his breath. When she shot him an inquiring look, he only raised his heavy eyebrows, as if to challenge her.

Confusing man.

Eli proved so much easier to read.

"I have not danced in so long," she admitted to Eli, sounding even to her ears as wistful as a young girl.

He laughed and joined her as the music swelled and the dancing began. Young women brought out cymbals, and Achsah found herself dragged into the swirling crowd of women, shouting their joy for the newlywed couple. Even if she didn't feel like celebrating this union, she couldn't resist clapping her hands and singing with everyone. Not once but twice, Eli danced his way near her, singing just as loudly and as off-key as she did. He kept to the men dancing in a separate group, shooting her mischievous looks whenever she glanced his way.

Her cheeks hurt from so much smiling as she whirled in a circle, her earrings hitting her neck and her wealth of bangles clinking like the cymbals of the women. If only Abba would look at her and see her joy with Eli. Surely they would make a match this very week.

Danger and despair seemed impossible on such a wonderful evening. While the full moon shone bright in the sky and torches placed around the courtyard provided a warm glow, Achsah forgot all her worry regarding the Canaanites.

Yet her gaze landed on Abba, who now stood with Othniel. Othniel, who apparently didn't care to dance. Their somber expressions and bent heads brought a halt to her dancing feet.

Oh, Abba. You cannot ever rest, can you?

And again, the image of the lost girl came into her mind, pulling her to a full stop as guilt suffused her. How could she rejoice when others suffered so? Her mood dampened, she ducked out of the flailing arms amid the boisterous shouts as some teasingly tried to prevent her from fleeing. Eli continued to dance with abandon, his hands raised high as if to touch the sky. Rebekah and Dov whirled, laughing, while the women clapped to the beat of the cymbals.

But that fleeting moment of joy leached from Achsah as she considered her abba, deep in conversation. Did he ever slumber or sleep when concerned with Israel's safety? What was he planning now?

As she moved toward him, escaping the merrymakers intent on twirling to the flutes, she overheard a man speak her name. She slowed her steps, catching part of a conversation and immediately regretting it.

"Will your sister marry this year?"

And then, to her shock, Iru's rough voice answered, "Who would want such a shrew?"

She glanced over her shoulder, immediately regretting her action. There stood a stranger with Iru...Haim! Haim, who had grown into a lean figure, was nearly as tall as Iru. He laughed the loudest, holding the cup in his hand and spilling wine over his fingers. Why would Iru even associate with a man as awful as Haim—one who hated their family?

Laughter chased her as she hurried again, her humiliation complete with Iru's mockery. Why must he antagonize her so? Why did he resent her? His behavior reminded her that she could never live in his house and find peace.

She could only hope Eli wouldn't hear such awful things spoken about her. At least Abba greeted her with a wan smile as she joined him at the safety of the wall, away from the merrymakers. Without thinking, she slipped her icy fingers into his warm, rough hand, seeking comfort. He squeezed her fingers ever so gently.

"I saw you dancing," he said with a teasing lilt. "And it did my heart much good to see you out there, enjoying yourself. You remind me of your imma in the best of ways." Then he leaned close, whispering. "I saw Eli too. You will be happy to know that I have spoken with his abba. As for Eli, let us see what happens next, yes? We will trust Yahweh to lead, as always."

Should she be satisfied with such a vague answer? Not entirely a firm, enthusiastic yes. But not a no either.

"Is it true that Rebekah will leave with Dov for the borderlands, not even staying with his abba?" Abba asked her.

She stiffened at the question, bracing for Abba's dismay. "I understand Dov wishes to enlarge his trade routes with the Canaanites, the Jebusites, and even the Philistines. He has ambitious plans to increase his wealth, and through our enemies, no less. I would box his ears if I thought it would do any good. I might tell him what I think before the night ends."

A throaty chuckle came from the other side of Caleb. She spied Othniel's toothy grin, flashing so quickly she thought she might have imagined it. Yet his laughter didn't grate on her the way Haim's did.

"You will do no such thing, Daughter," her abba said sharply. He rapped his stick on the ground just as another muffled sound escaped from Othniel. One decidedly of stifled mirth.

"If you say so," she answered sweetly before daring to wink at both men.

Abba didn't respond with humor, instead stroking his white beard while his gaze darkened with the ferocity of a much younger man. "Why did Iru allow this marriage?"

"I am certain it has more to do with finding a groom who can bring further wealth than anything else. Iru is a grown man, Abba, and fully responsible for his own choices," she reminded him primly, softening her answer with a hint of a smile.

A ragged sigh escaped her abba. "True. Very true." He leaned a hand on her shoulder, the weight impressive after so many years. "I must see that you will not be alone, Daughter. That day will come soon enough. I dare not let Iru plan a wedding for you."

The smile on her lips remained constant, though inwardly she cringed. The idea of losing Abba brought more pain than she could deal with in front of so many. "No more sorrowful talk."

Anything to blot out the sound of Haim and Iru's mocking laughter echoing in her mind.

She held out her hand in challenge to Abba and to Othniel, who took a step forward, his lopsided grin appearing again.

"Surely you two old warriors will not cling to the safety of the wall all evening? Why not join the others?"

Othniel readily abandoned the wall, reaching for her just as the shofar blew in the distance, the sound echoing across the plains and over the wedding guests. The flutes shrieked in a strident note and the stringed instruments halted, along with a stuttering clash of cymbals. The shofar echoed again, the sound closer. Louder.

Abba gripped his stick as if it were a sword. The doors to the courtyard flung open, rattling against the mud-brick walls, and two men ran into the gathering, their faces pale with terror.

"Giants! The giants have invaded Juttah and Jittir!"

Achsah stood frozen. Abba rose like a mighty lion as confusion and panic and wailing descended on the guests, affecting men and women and children alike.

"Men of Judah, will you do nothing?" he shouted, reminding everyone of the great military leader who had fought by Joshua's side and earned a place in the Promised Land.

Immediately, several of the men ran in search of a horse, or a weapon—if he had it—while the small children cried in terror.

She grasped her abba's arm. "Please, do not go. Let the other men take your place."

He tore his gaze from the crowd, his eyes bright and hard with a battle zeal that still sent a shiver down her spine even as she felt fiercely proud of him. Desperation to protect him drove her to speak. "Abba, you cannot lead the men into battle with that injured leg. You are ninety-four years of age. This is absurd!"

"I am still needed, Achsah. Can you not see that none of the men will go on their own if I do not help them? Let me die in the battle, if I must." Abba broke free of her grip before her protests had died on her lips. Othniel witnessed the exchange, and she shot him a frantic look to beg him to at least address her fears.

"Help me convince him otherwise," she pleaded with Othniel "Abba can barely ride a horse, with his injured leg."

Without a word, Othniel stalked through the crowd to Abba's side. He stopped Abba, and together they spoke in low tones, leaving her once again outside of the conversation. Would Othniel agree with her, or would he let her abba lead one more campaign?

When Abba placed his arm around Othniel, her heart sank. She bit the inside of her cheek hard to quell the rising anger within her. Of course, Othniel would do as he was asked. Had he no spine to stop her abba?

If only Abba would release his need for control to let the younger men advance. Such traitorous thoughts, but they swirled through her mind regardless, tearing her inside. Yes, she felt a stab of pride when men clustered around Abba and Othniel, everyone speaking at once.

But fear wormed its way into her heart too.

And though she wanted to caution Abba, to remind him to be careful considering his age and old injuries, she kept silent. She would never shame him in front of so many.

Othniel continued to stand beside her abba, his sinewed hand already on the hilt of the sword at his side. Her skin prickled with awe as Eli thrust through the revelers to join Abba's side almost immediately. But it was Othniel whose steady gaze met hers across the courtyard while she stood forgotten by the wall. His brow furrowed as he placed a hand on his chest. The memory of him doing so when she was just a girl, promising to watch over her abba, flooded her anew. Despite her resolve to show no weakness, she trembled when most of the men left with Abba. Several already carried swords wherever they went, but a few others refused to leave the wedding celebration.

Yahweh, keep them safe. The prayer, an old one, worn as much as a threadbare washcloth, brought no comfort this evening. She found Rebekah beneath a canopy and reached for her niece's chilled fingers, holding them tightly with her own. Dov, however, made no move to leave his bride's side. Would he let the other men fight for him?

He sniffed loudly. "A shame to think of all this food that will go to waste. I had planned a feast for several days. Now who will eat it?"

"No one," another man sneered as he approached the canopy. "What fresh madness will Caleb drag us into now?"

Haim. He glared at Dov and then aimed a look of sheer hatred at Achsah before striding toward the rest of the group. The crowd thinned. Beneath the torchlight, silver threads gleamed from the embroidered edge of Haim's expensive tunic, surprising for a man with the smallest allotment of land. He raised a slender hand, an enormous ring winking beneath the torchlight.

"My brothers," he started, then paused, for those left over were mostly female, of varying ages, with their mouths agape as they stared at him. However, a few men elbowed their way to where Haim stood, his hand still upraised for effect.

Haim cleared his throat, his posture pompous as he slowly turned, pointing to everyone in his path. "We cannot be certain that the right response, the first response, must limit itself to war. Perhaps if we spoke with our neighboring cities, we might come to a friendlier agreement and prevent the needless loss of life. Do you want to see your sons and husbands and abbas buried before the next harvest because of Kiriath-sepher? Do we really wish for more fighting over what might be nothing more than a simple misunderstanding?"

"I doubt the sons of Anak wish to break bread with you," Achsah cried out as she let go of Rebekah's hand. "Will you truly do nothing while the rest of the tribe of Judah suffers?"

Haim pivoted in her direction. "It will be the entire tribe of Judah suffering if your abba has his way. And not just our tribe, but all the other eleven! You will bring the wrath of the Philistines and every other nation surrounding us. This will not be a mere skirmish but a war with no end."

"Oh, hush, Achsah. Please," Rebekah pleaded, her eyes watering. "This is my wedding feast. Why must everyone ruin it? And all because of the trouble in one border town?"

But Achsah's blood boiled too hot to let Rebekah's warning slow her down. Achsah jabbed a finger in Haim's direction. "You are just like your grandfather, who quaked before the giants of the land. How dare you speak ill of my abba! It is because of him and Joshua that most of the giants have been driven out. Do you not remember that King Og would have executed all the Israelites when they proposed to pay for safe passage to the Promised Land? Have you forgotten how the five Canaanite kings conspired against us to make us their slaves? Have you all forgotten the cruelty of King Adoni-Bezek, who cut off the thumbs and the toes of his enemies, forcing them to eat under his table like brute animals?"

She ran out of breath, her chest heaving as her neighbors and friends stared at her.

"Despite being crippled, my abba would give his life to protect the women and children of Hebron. He willingly gifted the city to the priests as a refuge to ensure a haven for those seeking justice. Both he and Othniel have taken it upon themselves to rescue the children and women snatched from the fields when no one else cares. He has done nothing out of selfish ambition or greed, unlike some that I know who stand before us, wearing beautiful tunics and enormous rings." She glanced from face to face of those who had turned to listen to her. "We should not trade with the Canaanites. We should not buy their idols, or have we all forgotten the laws handed to us by Moses and Yahweh? Have we forgotten our promises to Joshua that we would serve only Yahweh?"

"Be quiet, Achsah," Dov said, his teeth gritted. He grabbed the wrist of his bride and yanked her away from Achsah. "Not everyone thinks like Caleb. If you were not Rebekah's kin, I would backhand you myself."

Rebekah shrank back, a cry escaping her, but Dov dragged her out into the crowd, his grip unrelenting. Rebekah glanced over her shoulder, her gaze frightened as her eyes met Achsah's.

Dismay filled Achsah as she watched her niece disappear. Would Rebekah pay for Achsah's boldness?

A murmur rippled through the assembly as the guests whispered among each other, echoing either what she had said...or what

Haim had said. For the sake of the tribe, she dearly hoped she had convinced at least the women to agree with her.

Her words must have flown straight as arrows, piercing the women's hearts, because their voices rose as one. Haim listened only for a moment, before marching toward Achsah, his mouth pulled into a grimace.

She refused to budge at his advance, but when he grabbed her arm, his fingers pinching tight, she couldn't escape his hot breath fanning her ear nor his accusation that made her heart falter.

"How many people will die because of your abba's desire to fight?"

CHAPTER EIGHT

Two Days Later

Fires dotted the black landscape, consuming the dry barley crops like a ravenous beast. Too many fires to count created a ring of glowing destruction just outside the village of Juttah. Would the giants destroy all the surrounding crops by early dawn?

Perhaps more disturbing, Juttah lay only two days' journey from Othniel's home, and he had no way to warn his sister or his imma of the impending danger. He had rushed to Caleb's armory to gather additional weapons and supplies as fast as he could and then rejoined the other men to hear Caleb's plan of attack.

In years past, he traveled to the border to push the Hittites and the Canaanites back into their cities and farmland, but tonight... tonight...the enemy cunningly attacked during one of the largest wedding feasts held near Hebron. Likely, everyone in the surrounding area knew of Iru's daughter being given away in marriage. Caleb's granddaughter, no less. The family had achieved a level of fame across the entire length of Judah and far beyond.

The smell of acrid smoke stung Othniel's nostrils, and despite his best efforts, he feared what he might find smoldering among the ruins of crumbled mud-brick homes. Hours earlier, a donkey, half mad with fear, had bolted across the plains, veering wildly away from Othniel's group, until at last, it collapsed, exhausted, on the ground. More animals followed, fleeing for their lives, lost and confused by the sounds of battle.

When he spied the fires on the black horizon, he understood the message of the enemy. This was no mere raid but an act of war. If so, who else had the sons of Anak rallied to the enemy's cause?

"We cannot overtake any chariots," Othniel reminded Caleb as they rode together on two of Caleb's finest horses. Othniel's beast, a gift from Caleb, named Qulal, or "fleet of foot," pawed at the ground with an aggressive snort, as if to challenge Othniel's observation.

Two to three Canaanites, protected by an iron chariot and pulled by fast horses, proved a formidable foe. The men could fling spears or shoot arrows at little risk while darting across the plains.

"Then we must use the element of surprise," Caleb answered. "They expect weakness from us. We will head east, under the cover of darkness, and find their camp and let them think they have achieved success. When they rest at night, glutted by their spoils of treasure, we will attack."

Caleb had insisted on riding into battle, even in his nineties, snapping at any counsel to do otherwise. All the while, Othniel's promise to protect Caleb warred with saving Caleb's dignity in front of his men.

Othniel gripped his reins tightly. He needed Caleb's advice and steady resolve during a battle. No one else knew how to command an army quite like the general. But to ride into battle at this age? To swing a sword?

"My general." Othniel kept his voice soft so that none of the other men would overhear. "I need you to guide the soldiers from the rear. Let me ride at the front and take the risk. You have trained me for such a purpose. If I fall, at least the Israelites will have a man of experience to guide them, for I am nothing but a simple farmer. You have always been their leader."

He heard the creak of leather armor as Caleb shifted on his mount, but the cover of night, despite the full moon, kept the old man's expression veiled. "You are not nothing, Othniel. Your purpose will yet be revealed, so do not say such frivolous things before Yahweh who made you. But I will do as you suggest. I was in my forties when I led my first battle. You will do the same tonight."

Othniel smiled in the dark as he nudged his horse forward to the front of the soldiers. Caleb's reassurance had always comforted him. Like Caleb, he too, carried a mix of foreign blood, thanks to his grandfather and father who fled Egypt to join with the Israelites. But he had always felt more kinship with the tribe of Judah, fully embraced by their God. This, Caleb understood, calling Othniel a brother. And truthfully, an adopted son.

"Then hide behind a rock, Abba," Iru said as he drew his horse up beside Caleb. "I see plenty of them to keep you safe."

Othniel gritted his teeth together to keep from publicly rebuking Iru. They needed no more distractions caused by Iru's rudeness. At least the eldest son had come to fight, and during his daughter's wedding feast, no less.

Eli, who also had one of the few horses, maneuvered himself close to Iru and Caleb. The bronze blades strapped to his back gleamed beneath the moonlight, a fearsome sight. But would they be enough against the iron weapons of the enemy?

The weaponsmith offered no reassurances. "We should wait for a more opportune time to attack. How do we know the sons of Anak have not brought in men from the surrounding Philistine cities to their aid?"

"What would you have us do? Wait for dawn, when we will be as visible as white sheep munching on grass?" Othniel was unable to keep the incredulity from his voice at Eli's reluctance. "If our numbers are less than the enemy and our blades are not as strong as the iron weapons of the Canaanites, we need the element of surprise, just as Caleb has suggested. Stealth will work to our advantage."

Eli cleared his throat. "How do we know they will not be expecting us?"

A good question. One that had bothered Othniel as he flung himself onto one of Caleb's horses and raced across the plains with his sword strapped to his back.

Why did the sons of Anak always seem one step ahead?

A celebration echoed through the night, its raucous sounds twisting Othniel's gut as he compared the sight below him with the celebration he had just enjoyed with Caleb and Achsah. Just as Caleb predicted, the enemy had made camp outside the fallen village, settling into a low area surrounded by sloping hills.

Red embers floated on the breeze, and the men taunted their prisoners, claiming many vile victories while a woman sobbed.

Crawling on his belly, Othniel slid across the raised rocky ground jutting over the gentle valley, with Iru, Eli, and six other men scrambling for a closer look at the raiders sitting in a circle before a fire. Othniel had ordered his companions to fan out, creeping like snakes with heads low to the ground, while a second contingent of men waited with Caleb and Iru near another rocky outcropping. One blast of the ram's horn and Othniel and his men would leap to their feet and scream while attacking, hopefully causing enough chaos to kill before the raiders could strike back. Iru would approach from the opposite side, leading his men to cut off any raiders who would escape.

At last, Othniel reached the edge of the sloping hill, giving him an intimate bird's-eye view of the camp. Women sobbed as they squatted, tied back to back, heads dropping onto chests, unveiled with hair hanging down. One raider shouted, swiveling from his seat near the fire to silence the women with a glare. The sobbing halted, and from behind, Othniel heard the stealthy rustling of the men creeping up from behind and their grunts as they joined him.

He turned his attention back to the fire, counting the women. Eight. No…ten. And children. Four helpless children under the age of ten, perhaps. Three girls and one young boy. His gut roiled as he thought of the missing men and women he had searched for these past nine years since that failed mission.

"Yahweh," he whispered, "give me Your courage. Save the innocent and set them free. Strengthen my arms to do battle for You. I cannot do this alone."

"Well?" Eli said, as he crawled, using his elbows to shimmy forward, his voice far too loud for Othniel's liking. Othniel rolled onto his side and clapped a hand over Eli's mouth, startling the man.

Shaking his head, Othniel loosened his grip against Eli's face. What Achsah saw in the weaponsmith was beyond him. A low fire settled in Othniel's chest as he batted away the thought of her dancing near Eli. He couldn't afford such distracting images, yet the anger lingered, bringing a tension to his fingers. He itched for his sword.

Beside him, on the left, Elah riffled in his tunic, pulling free a ram's horn—a shofar—held by a leather string, and placed it to his lips. Nodding, Othniel raised a single digit as his other hand reached for the sword. The resulting blast of the shofar bellowed a galvanizing blast that sent chills rippling through Othniel. A call to worship... or a call to war.

He sprang to his feet, not even recognizing the roar ripping from his mouth. The bronze blade in his hand felt like an extension of his arm as he immediately swiped for the nearest raider. The rest...

The rest became a blur of movement, his arm a streak of lightning that bolted from enemy to enemy with terrifying speed and precision. When the last of the battle ended and he stood over the only surviving Canaanite with the tip of the blade pressed into the man's throat Othniel found he could speak again.

"Have you taken any other Israelites?"

The writhing man, who lay on his back, his weapons scattered on the ground, had the audacity to spit at Othniel. "Israelite scum, the sons of Anak will avenge my brothers. They will run through every village in Judah, and not even your old dog, Caleb, will be able to defend you."

Othniel pressed his sandal onto the man's chest, pinning him as the blade edged closer until blood welled beneath the tip of the sword point. "Would you like to share your bold threats with the Father of Destruction? He is here."

The man's eyes rounded gratifyingly, but Othniel immediately regretted his heated, careless words when Caleb approached the camp with Iru and the other men. What if other raiders returned to the camp and struck Caleb's men from behind?

"What other towns will be attacked next?" Othniel rasped, dreading the answer.

The man gasped as the blade further nicked his skin. "I do not know. They have paid me. Handsomely by the city of Kiriath-sepher and its ruler, Marduk."

"Do you know of an Israelite slave there—a woman now, brought from the time she was twelve?" Othniel demanded.

"There are many slaves," the man gurgled as Othniel pressed his sandal harder. "Why care about one mere woman? You will all be slaves or dead before the harvest ends."

Red swam in Othniel's vision, and for a moment he couldn't quite get enough air into his lungs. But before he could act, men shouted. He glanced at Eli, motioning for the weaponsmith to watch the prisoner, who rolled over onto his side, coughing.

As he swung his sword, the tension of battle rippling through every muscle yet again, he rushed forward only to see Caleb, supported by Iru, slowly sink to the ground.

CHAPTER NINE

"Mistress, please. Wake up!"

Rough hands shook Achsah, pulling her from a strange dream. She stood in front of Hebron's locked gates, with a man by her side, his features indiscernible to her. Silent as ever, like a pillar of stone. All around her, a dust storm gathered strength, rolling and swallowing everything in its path as it headed for Hebron from all directions.

She sprang up from her mat with a gasp, clutching her blanket to her chest. As she struggled to gain her bearings, she realized she was in her bedchamber, and not Hebron. Bel knelt beside the mat, her loose curls streaming past her shoulders. The servant woman wore a simple shift, not even bothering to throw a robe over the undergarment.

Bel reached out a shaking hand and touched Achsah's cheek. "You must rise, mistress. The men have brought your abba home."

Abba? Terror sliced through Achsah as the memories of her wounded abba reverberated in her mind. Had Yahweh abandoned him again in the heat of the skirmish? Her abba, who did as Yahweh commanded, defending the tribe of Judah? Why did Yahweh seem so distant when she prayed to Him? What more did He want from her or her abba?

A shuddering breath escaped Achsah as she threw back the cover and rose on unsteady legs. Sweat trickled down her neck, the nightmare all too fresh, her fear transferring from nightmares to waking. Perhaps the vision had been a warning of things to come? She scarcely knew what any of it meant.

"What happened?"

Bel flung open a cedar chest and removed a fresh tunic for Achsah. "I must warn you. It is not good. Othniel and Elah brought him back unconscious. No arrows this time. Othniel said it might have something to do with your abba's heart."

His heart? Years ago, her abba told her that men could fall dead from fear on the battleground. She never thought such a thing could be possible for the stalwart man who had raised her.

Achsah changed swiftly, yanking the linen over her head and barely letting it settle to her feet as she moved toward the door. "I will tend to him."

She rushed down the hallway toward the flickering light escaping an open door. The door leading to Abba's chambers. The low hum of men's voices from the room filled her with fresh fear, and her heart beat an unsteady rhythm when she pushed past those lingering in the doorway to see Othniel and Elah hovering over the family patriarch.

Her abba glanced about the room, his eyes distant and unseeing.

"Abba, where do you hurt?" Achsah cried as she reached his side, enmeshing her fingers through his. How cold he felt. He didn't squeeze her hand in response. Instead, he opened his mouth as if to speak, but only a garbled sound came out. Helpless, he blinked at her and tried again, his lips moving with unintelligible words.

"He has no visible injuries," one man spoke from the corner of the room.

"Quiet!" She raised a hand to still the room and leaned close to her abba's mouth to hear him better. "Calm yourself, Abba. Breathe."

He obeyed her, his great chest rising and falling with gasps of air.

"Take...me...back," her abba finally whispered, his speech slurred, and then he closed his eyes as if exhausted by the effort. He licked his lips, his neck straining with effort. "I will raise my hands like Moses...over the fighters, and we will take the city. Please, Yahweh, forgive me...for failing."

He sounded delirious, muttering under his breath with one side of his face slack. She glanced at Othniel, so many questions rattling through her.

"Let him sleep," Othniel said as he held out his hand for her to take, the hint to leave the room evident. She ignored the scarred palm and ordered everyone out of the room while she tended her abba. But the basket of herbal remedies and clean linen bandages kept beside the mattress were of no use tonight. Nor did her prayers seem to reach the heavens.

Abba rested, but she could not leave his side until she was certain there was nothing more she could do.

When Bel came to offer Achsah a respite and watch over Abba, Achsah finally rose, clutching the basket to see if any of the other men needed help. There, in the great room, on her way to the kitchen, sat Othniel, speaking with one servant and a few of the other soldiers. Her brother Elah was nowhere to be seen, perhaps having already left for home at this hour. Or perhaps wandering through the kitchen, searching for food.

"We rescued how many?" the servant asked as he brought a pitcher and cups to the warriors.

"Several women and children," Othniel answered before taking a long draft from the cup. "We have housed them in various homes, including here. They have nowhere to go now that their village burned."

So intent on taking care of her abba, she had scarcely considered that her home might house those in need. And while she would gladly open her door to anyone in need, another issue had to be addressed.

"Othniel, tonight must never happen again."

He glanced at her, his expression unreadable as the servant quickly exited the room with head bowed.

Anger kindled in her as she stared at Othniel. "My abba may be the greatest general Israel has ever known, other than Joshua, but his days of fighting are over. A man in his nineties cannot go out onto the battlefield, even if he slayed the enemy at eighty-four years of age. Younger men need to take his place. And if there is no one to take his place, then I truly fear for our country. Are there no men left in the tribe of Judah? Or must the women take up the swords?"

Othniel said nothing, but his gaze slid from hers. His shoulders slumped forward, perhaps from exhaustion...or perhaps from her tongue-lashing.

She folded her arms across her chest, pacing back and forth on the woven mats. "For years, Abba has all but begged our tribe to secure the borders and deal with the threat lingering around our land. No one listens until it is too late."

"We have all waited for your brothers to take the place of our general. They fought beside him and received his blessing and the best of his training," Othniel said slowly as he set the cup down on a small table.

"Well, they will not fulfill their duty. You know this better than most," she snapped as she continued to pace across the mat. "They are too busy enjoying the fruits of their gardens to remember the wilderness Abba came from."

"You are not being fair. Elah came tonight. As did Iru," he reminded her, his voice even.

Her anger only boiled hotter. "Indeed? Did they do anything of use tonight? If they had done more in the years past, we would not have this crisis on our hands. No, Othniel. It is too little, too late. And now Abba must pay the price for the weakness of others."

A long sigh escaped Othniel as he rose to his feet. Again, she noticed the gouges and nicks from blades across his arms, despite the leather armbands.

"Do you need salve?" she asked as she touched his arm.

A wince crossed his features, but he shook his head all the same, his gaze half-lidded, leaving her to guess at his thoughts.

He brushed her away. "It is nothing I cannot tend to myself. It would be better if you stay with your abba. I fear the stress of the evening overcame him."

"He has always been so strong. So demanding. But now, though I fear treating him like a child, I cannot allow him to leave again, no matter how strongly he demands it. We must tell him no when he thinks of himself as a young man who can do as he pleases."

"Agreed," Othniel said, much to her surprise. "None of us wanted to tell him no, but you are right."

She wasn't used to men telling her she was right. She stopped pacing, startled by Othniel's quiet agreement.

"Where is Eli? Did he...did he get hurt as well?" How breathless she sounded. Wholly focused on her abba, she had not noticed the weaponsmith's absence until just now. In her mind, she envisioned Eli leading the charge to free the captives.

"The weaponsmith, *again*? You want to ask me about Eli?" Othniel asked, his tone suddenly rough.

"Yes, of course," she said, faltering beneath his glare.

"Your Eli survived with nary a scratch," Othniel said as he stepped away from her. A muscle flexed in his jaw. That cryptic tone—what to make of it? Before she could ask more, he heaved another ragged breath and quickly exited the room, leaving her alone.

The sound of footsteps echoing from behind her distracted her from thinking about Othniel's strange expression when she asked about Eli.

Elah, who had exited the kitchen, motioned for the basket on the table. "I will take some of the salve, Sister. Where is Othniel? I heard you giving him a tongue-lashing from halfway down the hall."

"He left," she admitted uneasily.

"Hmm. No sense in clashing with you, I am sure. Do me a favor and grant that man a little grace. Othniel's done more to secure our borders than most."

Swallowing a retort, she reached for the nearest jar of cedar-wood salve and handed it to her brother. "Was the mission a failure? Abba seems to think so."

Elah shook his head as he reached for a large glop and smeared the oily paste over his freshly cleaned forearm. "Not at all. We rescued several people taken from the villages, but it is clear Abba must stay home from now on. For too long, we let him decree every single step we have taken, as if we were but small children instead of grown men with families. That said, I am of half a mind to agree with Iru and Hur. We must settle and plant our barley. If we fight on behalf of all of Israel, we will lose everything in the years to come. Are we priests to receive a portion of the crops for our services? No, Achsah. Israel will drain each of us until our family has nothing more to give. Look at how they drained Abba."

He rolled up his other sleeve and slapped more of the paste onto his opposite arm while she watched. Like Othniel, a pattern of scars, new and old, traced a pattern on Elah's skin. He was older too—nearing fifty-one years of age. Of all her brothers, Elah remained the most reasonable and the most obedient. But if he too no longer wished to fulfill her abba's dream of claiming Kiriath-sepher and chasing out the giants, then there was truly nothing she could do.

"If you will not help Abba capture Kiriath-sepher, then at least Eli will do so," she answered sharply. "I saw him by Abba's side at the wedding. At least Eli will prove young and strong enough to guide the men to victory."

Elah's bushy eyebrows nearly shot to his forehead as his fingers hovered over the cuts on his arms. "Eli, eh? No, it was not him. He would have run under the cover of the night and abandoned the captives to their fate. It was Othniel who led the charge."

Her brother's answer left her unsettled, long after the house returned to silence in the evening's hush just before dawn. Why had

Othniel so meekly taken her flung accusations about the weakness of the surrounding men with barely a murmur or a protest? Why hadn't he said much of anything to her?

A sickening dread suffused her that perhaps she had crossed a line with one of Abba's most faithful men. Her temper had gotten the better of her once again.

CHAPTER TEN

Three Weeks Later

Wind tore at the powdery bluffs on either side of the road as Achsah and Bel traveled to Rebekah's new home. While most newlyweds lived with the groom's family until a house could be built, Dov had the great fortune of escorting his bride to his lavish estate, constructed long before the wedding took place.

The ride, which would take much of the morning, provided her with plenty of time to think about past events. Bel rode beside Achsah, equally silent, although struggling to keep upright on her mount. Ari and another young guard, Amittai, kept pace behind while monitoring the bluffs for any enemies.

Achsah saw little of Eli in the days that followed her abba's collapse. Nor did she see Othniel. His absence, somehow, lingered more within her mind than Eli's. Abba had explained that Othniel was spying near the area of Kiriath-sepher, probing into the rumors of the enemies' possible plans for revenge. The entire region buzzed about the wedding and the recent attack. While she expected the men to hunt for more survivors in the hamlets and villages near Kiriath-sepher, she found that she missed Othniel's presence. He was like a brother, after all. Part of her wished he would return, even if for her abba's sake. As the silence stretched, she feared that she had greatly offended him.

As she rode, Achsah couldn't help but picture both Eli and Othniel. Or the disappointment she felt that neither visited Abba nor her.

Abba improved, slowly, but he remained a husk of his former self. Whatever had happened to his chest seemed to plague him. He complained of weakness in his arms and limbs, his breath came shorter, and sometimes, he would brace a fist against his heart as if it ached still. His speech never fully recovered, the syllables garbled when he tired.

For days, he slept. And slept. The man who never rested, who never took time to truly enjoy life, was now confined to his chambers like a captive. Truthfully, she had little time to think about anything else than to be his nurse and feed and care for him. All thoughts of marriage withered in the days that followed the wedding feast. She would never choose to leave her abba's side now. He needed her too much, and the wives of her brothers cared nothing for him.

The old fire in his eyes had been snuffed out. Despite the recent triumph, the threat of the sons of Anak lingered. When would the giants strike again? Would they grow bolder and take their revenge at long last for Caleb's capturing Hebron and slaying the Baal priests within the walled city?

She adjusted her head covering against the blowing dust, her limbs already sore from the day's travel. The servants, Ari and Amittai, pointed out the house. It gleamed white beneath the harsh sunlight. Surrounded by cliffs and the beginning of an olive grove, the site promised to be beautiful when it reached full bloom.

"Your niece lives too far from family. You should have listened to your abba's warning about traveling these roads," Bel complained.

She flicked her reins to urge the beast to go at a faster trot. An impossible task with her stubborn horse, who snorted his disdain.

Achsah didn't answer. Yes, Abba had roused himself from his pallet to argue with her. But she couldn't rest until she saw that her niece and only childhood friend was safe and well taken care of by Dov. The image of Rebekah being dragged away by her new husband wouldn't leave Achsah. She could scarcely sleep for worrying about her niece. Would Dov hurt his bride?

The ride had proven mostly uneventful until she drew closer to the plastered wall enclosing a courtyard. A clay box protruding from the ground caught her attention as she swayed in the saddle. She slipped off her horse, handing the reins to Ari.

"Mistress, we should not stop," he warned.

She ignored him. As she approached the clay vessel set by the side of the road, her sandals slid in the soft dirt. Dread suffused her as she drew close. Holes lined the clay box and forbidden images of Yahweh frolicking with a plump goddess showed a scene of fertility and new birth.

She sucked in a horrified breath through her teeth.

Plenty of Israelites meshed worship of Yahweh with other gods and goddesses, entwining both into a strange brew of Levitical practices and pagan rites. Yahweh replaced El, the father of Baal. Had Dov or Rebekah placed the box as a marker? No Canaanite would place such a marker on the road.

As a child, she remembered hearing about Moses carrying the stone-chiseled Ten Commandments from Mount Sinai, only to dash them to pieces when finding the Israelites prostrating their half-clothed bodies before a golden calf. Later, he had placed the second set of commandments inside the golden ark of the covenant as a testament to Yahweh's law.

You shall not make for yourself a carved image, or any likeness of anything that is in heaven above, or that is in the earth beneath, or that is in the water under the earth.

"Mistress, come back!" Bel's voice, most insistent, raised to a shout.

She almost obeyed except for a glimpse of something in the trees.

Achsah grasped a handful of her tunic and climbed the slope to the cypress jutting from the hillside. Her heart nearly leaped out of her chest when she spied one tree in particular, stripped down of branches and leaves with the bottom of the trunk unaltered, and the rest carved into the spindly form of a grotesque woman with her chin lifted high to the heavens.

Asherah, the female consort of Baal, and favorite deity of the Canaanites, stared back with vacant eyes. A fertility goddess who demanded horrifying methods of worship to satisfy her whims. An unnatural silence blanketed the grove, as if even the birds dared not make a nest in the twisted branches of the surrounding trees, nor the field mice be brave enough to scamper across the pebbled ground.

Leave this place. The warning circled over and over in her mind as she gaped at the carved pole. Death waited among those stark trees, and the goddess took life as she pleased, in any form or sacrifice.

Achsah stumbled backward, nearly tripping on a loose branch lying on the ground. So pervasive was the sense of evil, from the voluptuous mouth grinning to the unclothed form, that bile rose within her. She pivoted on her heel and marched down the hill to her servants.

Oh, Rebekah. What has Dov allowed in your new home?

How could Dov so readily abandon what Moses had taught them? She reached for the reins held by her guard, Ari, and hoisted herself onto the horse.

"You look pale," Bel fretted as she urged her mount to move forward. "What did you see in the trees?"

"An idol." The very word brought a crest of panic. For with idols came unclean spirits.

Bel frowned, but her grip on the reins tightened until the skin stretched tight across her knuckles. Her voice dropped to a whisper. "Perhaps it is an idol left over from the previous Canaanites who inhabited the area before we drove them out? I cannot imagine your brothers allowing such an atrocity."

"I cannot speak for the Asherah pole, but I saw a marker for Yahweh and Asherah together," Achsah answered as she flicked her reins against the donkey's side, yet the sense of bile clawing at the back of her throat did not abate. Did her brothers know what Dov had done? What must Rebekah think?

Bel said no more, and both of them looked over their shoulders more than once, while the urgency to reach Rebekah only increased with each plodding step Achsah's horse took.

When Achsah dismounted from her horse, the door to the grand house flung open and Rebekah dashed down the steps with her arms outstretched wide. She glowed as she enveloped Achsah in a tight hug.

"I am so glad you came to visit me. Not that Dov has not been as wonderful as wonderful can be. Did you see the bangles he brought me?" She held out a dainty wrist where a plethora of carved bangles gleamed beneath the sunlight. "And my necklace. See what love he lavishes upon me?" Her hand touched the wealth of coins looped around her neck and collar.

So much silver that it seemed Rebekah would be destined to tinkle and make music whenever she walked.

Achsah smiled at her niece, holding her at arm's length to study her. Rebekah wore new kohl around her eyes, and her mouth, stained crimson, made her appear lovelier than ever. And the layered tunics, covered with a linen edged in silver, so delicate, the threads gleamed. An expensive gown that must have come all the way from Egypt.

"Marriage seems to become you," Achsah admitted slowly as she scanned her niece's face for any signs of ill-treatment, especially considering how Dov had exploded at the wedding.

"And soon for you. I saw you with Eli at my wedding feast. He could not take his eyes off you during the dancing." Rebekah laughed as she enveloped Achsah in an exuberant hug.

Had Eli noticed her? Warmth stole through her chest at the idea of the weaponsmith singling her out for attention. "I enjoyed what dancing I could before the raiding."

Rebekah didn't seem to notice the statement, already directing Achsah's servants to water the horses at the well outside her property.

She gestured with her finger. "Come, see the house Dov built for me. I have been hoping you would visit. Dov said you would not dream of it, but I know you better than most. Nothing frightens you, Achsah."

Achsah glanced at Bel, who raised her eyebrows, both of them sharing a discreet look that Rebekah seemed to miss as she pointed out the unique features of the house.

Certain things brought a stab of fear. She pressed her lips as she dutifully glanced about the courtyard, searching for more idols. Rebekah motioned for Achsah and Bel to follow her through the door into a spacious hall. To Achsah's surprise and relief, a *mezuzah* lay within an elaborately carved hollow.

"Where is your husband?"

Rebekah toyed with the coins about her neck. "He left for trade business and will return within a fortnight."

"Left you already? That hardly seems fair to a new bride," Achsah commented.

With a delicate shrug, Rebekah offered a weak smile.

"Do you fear living so close to Kiriath-sepher?" Bel asked as she scanned the room, her movements echoing Achsah's.

Rebekah gestured to a pile of saffron pillows with tassels. She sank down onto the rug in a cloud of perfume. "No. Dov brings peace wherever he goes. He knows exactly what to say to prevent hostilities from breaking out, and he has settled many a disagreement between the tribe of Judah and the Canaanites. We are quite safe, I assure you."

Surely an exaggeration of Dov's abilities, thanks to the bride's infatuation.

Inside the coolness of the house, the great room provided a welcomed respite with tapestries hanging from the wall and ornate grilled windows filtering the afternoon light into pleasing patterns on the floor. They sank down onto the woven rugs, chatting about mundane things, and Rebekah called for a tray of dates and honeyed wines. All the while, the obscene image of the carved woman among the trees flashed through Achsah's mind.

To ask questions might jeopardize her relationship with her niece. But to remain silent...

She held up a hand, refusing the plate of figs Rebekah offered.

"I saw a pole in the hills," Achsah said after a long pause, ignoring Bel's hissed intake of breath and her servant's barely perceivable head shake, full of warning. "Did Dov make it along with the house?"

Rebekah's eyes widened as her hand again fluttered to finger the necklace dangling from her neck. "You saw that thing in the forest? Please say nothing to our family. I am certain that the Canaanites who lived in the area left the pole. Dov assures me it will not cause any harm."

Achsah studied her niece, whose cheeks had pinked considerably. "He will not cut it down?"

"I am sure he will, when he has a free moment. It is just a pole, Achsah. It means nothing to me. I am sure I am not the only Israelite to have something of the sort. When we conquered the land, the Canaanites left many temples and groves. How can we possibly destroy all of it when we can put the buildings to good use?"

The protests rang false.

"Abba would demand you cut it down immediately."

Rebekah pressed her lips into a thin line at the rebuke. "I have a household of my own, and while you may be content to follow every single decree Grandfather makes, Dov promised that we will decide for ourselves. You would not have me go against my husband's decree, would you? Besides, Dov feels that if he is to establish new trade routes, he needs to blend in better. Do you not think some of Moses's decrees are ridiculous? We cannot eat certain foods. We must avoid combining linen with other materials such as wool. Honestly, we are laughed at for our strange rules."

Achsah leaned forward to clasp her niece's hand. "Asherah is the mother of Baal. I do not need to remind you what goes on in those groves at night, do I?"

Rebekah paled as she snatched away her hand. "We would never do such things. Never. But there are many other Israelites, even within the tribe of Judah, who no longer see Asherah as a threat. What if she is the wife of Yahweh and Baal is their child? What if Yahweh is really the god El? What if Moses taught us wrong?"

The Canaanites believed that Asherah and El had formed a turbulent union to create the god of storms, Baal. The Prince of the World, he had been nicknamed. Achsah rose to her feet, heartsick at what she had just heard from Rebekah. "I cannot believe what my ears are hearing. How can you and Dov be so foolish? You cannot be that naive to think you can worship a goddess who demands prostitution and child sacrifice and not become as wicked as the Canaanites!"

"You reek of judgment, just like Grandfather. For too long, you have lived beneath his rod of iron. You cannot see anything different because he will not let you think for yourself. His views will always be extreme. More and more Israelites want something different, instead of constantly clamoring for some sort of moral superiority. Are we really better than our neighbors? Shouldn't we find things in common with them to live in peace? Is peace not a good thing?"

Achsah's mouth dried. "What you describe is not peace. It is compromise, with evil no less."

Bel also rose, albeit stiffly, her expression anxious as she reached both for Rebekah and Achsah as if somehow to draw them closer together. Achsah had planned to stay overnight and enjoy visiting, but all thoughts of staying dissipated with the tension in the room.

"I am truly sorry, Rebekah. You have been my dearest friend. More like a sister to me than a niece and closer to me than any of my brothers. But I fear for you—perhaps more so since you have known the truth and now choose to reject it."

"Caleb tells his version of what he calls truth. Perhaps there is more than one way to honor Yahweh. I still worship our God. But I will do it as I see fit. You saw the mezuzah in our doorway. I will always be loyal to our tribe."

How quickly one generation forgot all that Yahweh had done when calling Abraham out of Ur to form a new nation, providing for the Hebrews, rescuing them out of the hand of Egypt and the hands of wicked kings lying in wait in the Promised Land. How quickly Rebekah dismissed everything Moses had passed down from Yahweh.

"Our God is a jealous god. He says to have no other gods before Him. When we run to the false spirits, like the men in the wilderness, shaping a golden calf to worship, we quickly abandon the One who created us. We cannot serve two masters."

Rebekah jutted out her jaw. "We will speak no more about how to worship Yahweh. Perhaps I disagree with Moses's interpretations. After all, how do we really know that Yahweh said those things about worshiping Yahweh alone? What if Moses exaggerated the laws to suit his own purposes? I want you to leave. I have heard enough."

Achsah wanted nothing more than to envelop her niece in a hug, but Rebekah turned her back on both women, murmuring excuses about tending to something in the kitchen. Achsah waited in the great room, hoping that her niece might change her mind and they could find some sort of resolution. But when Rebekah didn't return, the message was clear.

"We must leave while we still have daylight to travel," Achsah whispered to Bel as Rebekah's tight-lipped servant cleared the platters from where they had shared dates and conversation.

"We will not arrive home until late at night. I do not care for the idea," Bel whispered back.

Perhaps Achsah had been foolish to insist on coming for a visit, but now that she saw the extent of Rebekah's foolish choices, she knew her friend had chosen a far different path. A path Achsah could not tread.

Her stomach growled as she left a farewell message for Rebekah's servant to deliver to Rebekah, and when she and Bel stepped out into the courtyard, the shutters to the windows closed with a decided click, effectively barring Achsah. Perhaps forever.

"It would seem that I have said too much, once again," she admitted ruefully, climbing onto her mount as her guard, Ari, and another escort, followed suit. Regret and anger washed over her as she looked at the magnificent estate again. The more she tried to follow Yahweh's decree, the more she felt separated from others, including those who claimed to follow Him. She had so few friends as it was. Must she lose the love and respect of Rebekah too?

Bel, already astride her saddle, puckered her mouth as if tasting something sour. "You say things as you see them, mistress. I would rather have a woman speak the truth to me, even if it wounded a little, than layer thick honeyed lies on the sweetest bread. Perhaps your niece will listen after she has licked her wounds."

They rode out of the grove and down the dusty road where the forest lay to the right, swathed in shadow, including the tree carved into a goddess. Ari led the way, his piercing whistle to the horse underscoring the urgency of Achsah's desire to flee.

After they had traveled a short while, Bel jerked on the reins, halting her horse as her gaze remained pinned by the grove hovering above, lining the hills. A visible shudder flitted across her shoulders when Achsah forced her horse to stop alongside her.

"There are some memories I wish I could banish altogether," Bel murmured, her eyes suddenly wet with unshed tears. "Your imma and abba rescued me, a slave, twenty years ago. I never told you the story of Hebron when your abba took over the city from the giants living there. I too, as a non-Israelite, experienced being taken as a child and forced to serve a man I hated. I had all but given up hope during the years of my captivity until I saw your abba burst through the city gate, removing all the corruption and filth from the city. Your niece will learn soon enough that she cannot serve other gods and expect Yahweh's protection, but I pray it will not be too late for her. I have seen and experienced the lies of those deities, and I want nothing from them. Beneath all of your abba's fierceness, beneath all his dedication to the law, lies a kindhearted man who would see all of Israel thrive within Yahweh's will. Never forget that, no matter what people like Rebekah or Dov try to tell you."

Achsah studied her servant, who had been like a nursemaid and a second mother and had now become a steadfast confidant.

"Oh, Bel. I cannot imagine what you went through."

Bel smiled through her tears, dashing them aside with a sun-spotted hand. The scar on her wrist appeared as her sleeve fell away, but she made no move to hide it. "Do not pity me, child. I am a free woman these days, and I am more than content to live in the general's house and help his headstrong daughter, however much she will let me."

"My dear, dear friend," Achsah said, her throat tight. "I am grateful Yahweh caused our paths to cross. Perhaps we shall be two old maids, content to pester each other for the rest of our days."

Bel chuckled at the suggestion, her eyes crinkling at the corners.

Achsah felt her eyes water in response as she clicked her tongue, urging the horse forward while the sun glowed hot in the sky.

Thank You, Yahweh. For reminding me that I am not completely alone.

As soon as the prayer of thanksgiving flitted through her mind, a cloud of dust whirled on the horizon. She shielded her eyes against the white sun to see better. Before long, a caravan appeared in the distance.

"We should take another path." Amittai spoke first.

"Agreed," said Ari as he fingered the handle of the sickle sword strapped to his side. "Mistress, please, we must leave!"

Achsah leaned forward, shielding her eyes with her hand and squinting against the bright light. The forms of men and beasts wavered in the shimmering distance as they marched ever closer to her small group. She had paused too long, studying the caravan and the shapes of the men looming unnaturally over the beasts. Giants? Were those the descendants of the sons of Anak her abba had fought?

A tremor rippled through her.

Ari slapped his reins just as he reached her side. "Mistress, we cannot wait. Those might be Canaanites traveling through this way, and we dare not stop to see if it is a slave caravan."

A warning perhaps too late as she coaxed her horse to follow her men.

CHAPTER ELEVEN

A horn blew in the distance. The horse's hooves pounded the dust beneath Othniel as he galloped across the rock-strewn landscape. He dug his heels into his beloved companion, hating to cause pain to Qulal, who more than lived up to his name, "fleet of foot." Despite his rapid pace, Othniel's sense of urgency only increased as the terraced barley fields, budding vineyards, and newly planted groves of olive trees flashed past him in a blur.

This morning, when he stopped by the great house to check on Caleb and provide a report of the surrounding area, he discovered that Achsah had left to see her niece Rebekah at the estate near Kiriath-sepher.

The news proved more than enough to make him break out into a cold sweat.

"I told her not to go," Caleb protested from his pallet, trying, and failing, to prop himself up on one elbow. "But you know my daughter. With a will of iron, determined to do things her way. She is afraid for Rebekah and wants to ensure that her niece is taken care of properly."

The irony—the headstrong Caleb warning his daughter not to wade into trouble without a thought for her safety—was not lost on him.

Othniel knew full well Achsah's iron will. He had already endured her chastising for allowing Caleb to walk into battle, despite his age. Both abba and daughter remained near twins in their temperament and their concern for the affairs of others, even if they hid it behind a gruff exterior.

Hearing about Ari and one other servant providing escort didn't bring him much peace either. Othniel had no desire for her to cross paths with the giants as he had. And so he urged Qulal to go faster.

Kiriath-sepher lay three *parasangs* from Hebron, an easy enough ride with a powerful horse. He only hoped he would encounter her before trouble came. He took a shortcut through a freshly harvested barley field and raced southwest toward the estate.

Part of his scouting included the area of farmland situated near the city of giants. He had plenty of reason to doubt Dov's motives for moving his house so close to the infamous "city of books."

As Qulal crested one hill, a blast of a horn echoed in the distance. Heart nearly stopping, Othniel spied a cloud of dust near the junction where the two beaten paths met, one leading past Dov's house before heading into Kiriath-sepher.

He whistled sharply to Qulal. The horse pricked up its ears and increased its long-legged stride, tearing across the earth beneath its churning hooves. A caravan of camels and horses stretched across the road, but from his position, which gave him a bird's-eye view, Othniel saw two groups. One fleeing. One pursuing.

And the fleeing group had only four horses. A groan escaped him. *Achsah.*

Qulal darted forward, narrowly missing obstacles that could cripple a lesser horse. And though Othniel had no desire to see his beloved horse fall prey to an accident, he let Qulal have full rein, letting him choose the terrain.

A prayer for Yahweh to intervene on behalf of Achsah and her traveling companions, and to keep Qulal safe, flashed through his mind. He could only trust that Yahweh heard his pleas, even though, as of late, it seemed Yahweh felt distant. The prayer had scarcely left his lips when one of the four horses fleeing stumbled on a rock, nearly tossing the rider off of its back.

He was close enough to see that the rider was Bel, the older servant who doted on Caleb.

Ari and his fellow guard pulled their horses short, providing a barrier with their swords already drawn. In the distance, the caravan riders thundered, shaking the earth while blowing on their horns.

Ari reached Bel first; her weathered face blanched white as her horse limped a few steps.

Reaching out a hand, he leaned over in the saddle and shouted to the older woman. "Quick, come onto my saddle!"

Qulal came to a shuddering halt beside the injured horse, his flanks quivering as he whinnied. Othniel reached with one arm and hoisted the servant onto his mount. He feared she would struggle to find her balance, but, quicker than he expected, she scrambled with the ease of a younger woman to swing her leg up behind him and threw her arms around his waist, clinging tightly.

"Follow me," he ordered Achsah, who nodded, her eyes wide as she clutched her reins. Together, they raced, while Ari and the other man waited to handle any threat. He hated to leave the men and the injured horse, but he simply couldn't risk taking a possibly lame creature and risk capture. He also couldn't help but fear for young Ari, who put his life on the line for Caleb's kin.

They fled past several fields, not daring to look behind. Achsah's head covering had fallen off somewhere in the field and now her brown hair streamed behind her as she galloped next to him, keeping pace as she bent low in the saddle.

When they reached the halfway point between the road that ran by Dov's house and the fields terraced with crops, he came to a halt. Bel's arms around him tightened. He felt the older woman shake behind him and he covered her hand with his own.

Glancing behind him, he offered Bel some comfort. "We should be safe now."

Still, he tensed all the same when two riders appeared on the horizon, following close behind. Caleb's men, he hoped.

"It is Ari," Achsah rasped as she patted the neck of her horse.

And indeed, it was. Ari and the other man maneuvered across nearest the field, hurrying while leading the lame horse, but with no signs of giants or any other Canaanite tribe in pursuit.

He glanced at the sky, gauging how much time they had till darkness fell, and exhaled a shuddering breath. "Good. Let us get you both safely home. Your abba is nearly beside himself with worry."

Achsah frowned, a tiny series of lines forming between her brows, but she didn't argue with him. They rode again, albeit at a more tempered pace, until at last, the mud-brick walls of Caleb's estate appeared in view. The courtyard doors swung open, and he rode in, mentally checking himself before he would say something he regretted.

He offered the older woman his arm as she easily slid off his mount. Bel whispered her thanks, to which he offered a comforting smile. As he dismounted, he released a long, pent-up breath. Then he pivoted to Achsah, who still sat astride her bay horse. Clenching his teeth, he reached for her to help her dismount, his hands on her tiny waist…

He swallowed hard as she placed her hands on his shoulders, her touch soft. Yet he still felt it, even when she stepped away from him. His anger, however, did not abate.

"I think you might need to take your own advice," he said gruffly, despite every intention of hiding his exasperation with her. Thankfully, Bel had already entered the house, shutting the door behind her and leaving him and Achsah in the courtyard. "Whatever possessed you to risk traveling to visit your niece? Especially now, when so much danger surrounds us?"

She massaged the back of her neck, apparently at a loss for words at his challenge.

He pressed further, albeit more gently this time. "You and your abba are so alike. He has been worried for you this morning, fretting about your safety—just as you feared for him when he led the last excursion. Who can talk to either of you once you get an idea in your head? I would not normally argue about the need to travel to Hebron or any village or household, but not now—not when we have had so much trouble with Kiriath-sepher. You endangered your hand-maiden and your young guards."

A sigh escaped her as she tucked a strand behind her ear. "I wanted to see Rebekah for myself. Dov moved her out of his abba's home to the farthest outskirts of our settlements, far from family. I know Iru will not listen to my concerns. I cannot help but worry about her. I have never liked Dov, especially after he allowed Haim to dissuade the remaining Israelites from following Abba during the wedding."

"Haim said such things?" That was news to him, but of course, he hadn't returned to the wedding feast. Fresh alarm coursed through him at the idea of Haim spreading dissension.

"Yes, and far more concerning, Dov has an Asherah pole and grove near his home, including markers with Yahweh and Asherah together." Achsah paused. "I had to speak with my niece about this travesty."

He folded his arms across his chest as he regarded her. "What did she say, exactly?"

"She told me to leave and never return after I had told her in no uncertain terms how I felt about that pole and Dov's activities. I will never darken her door again. She has chosen her path, and she will walk it alone."

Blunt and to the point, as always. Yet he heard the wounded note in Achsah's voice all the same.

Silently, he prayed to Yahweh for patience and wisdom. "Achsah…"

Her amber gaze flicked to his, and he felt the resulting spark clear to his toes.

"I appreciate and honor your zeal for Yahweh's commandments and for His way of living. It is the right way. And you are right to question Rebekah and point her back to Yahweh. Yet those who receive our message will recognize whether we convey it in a spirit of grace and mercy or with pride and judgment, lacking respect for the listener."

Her mouth rounded, her lips moving, but no sound came out. Not even a squeak.

He took a deep breath before adding, "We serve Yahweh because we *love* Him. After all, He teaches us to care for others, through the law, no less. But none of us can keep it perfectly. He had the power to set our people free. Neither you nor I can control what Rebekah or Dov choose to do next. We can only choose how we respond. Let Yahweh work in Rebekah's life and pull her back to Him. Do not be so quick to shut her out completely."

Achsah's frown reappeared, and he knew that his words, even if carefully measured, hurt. He saw her suck in her cheek, as if chewing it in thought.

"Give your niece time to think about what you said. Maybe she will reconsider. I know I have thought long and hard about your challenges to me, even if your words pinched."

A lovely color washed over her cheeks. Something that made his chest beat all the harder.

Achsah cleared her throat. "You say a great deal, Othniel, son of Kenaz. I am actually surprised to hear such a speech from you, but as good as I am at speaking my mind, I *am* listening. I never meant to hurt anyone. You have seen what it has been like for me as the only sister with strapping brothers as opinionated as Abba."

He understood, and he had long admired how she held her own against such powerful men, carving out a place for her voice. Before he could stop himself, he blurted, "Perhaps you and I are like iron sharpening iron."

A slow smile spread across her face at his comment, stealing his heart yet again even though he had vowed repeatedly to release her to Eli if that was what she truly wanted.

"Perhaps," she admitted just as the gate to the courtyard flung open and Ari and Shaphat rode in, both men breathing hard.

Mesmerized, Othniel stepped toward her, so many other thoughts swirling within him, each one begging to be said...but with Ari's return, the moment wasn't right.

Her mouth still quirked with amusement, she left Othniel in the courtyard. Her unveiled hair billowed loose as the wind caught the strands in a fresh gust, but he forced himself to turn away. With a sigh, he turned to speak with Ari about the strange caravan.

He kicked himself for not telling her that her challenge for him to rise and do more, to lead rather than to hide in the shadows as a spy, had penetrated into his deepest core. For too long, he had assumed other men would fill Joshua's role, or Caleb's. Wounded that evening from her admonishment, he had hurried home to lick his wounds, but her impassioned speech had set a fire in him. To do more for the people of Israel.

If only she hadn't made her preference for Eli so startlingly clear.

───

Abba certainly expressed his displeasure when Achsah returned home. He called for her to come to his chamber, demanding to know the details of her visit with Rebekah and why she would do such a thing without his consent.

"Perhaps you and I are more alike than we realize," she reminded him primly as she lowered herself onto the mat, thinking of

Othniel's rebuke only moments before. "I am a grown woman of twenty-one years. Since you trust me to run your household, trust me to decide when I visit my family. However, considering the present danger, I will discuss it with you. You need not fear for me."

"I did not worry as much since Othniel went after you," Abba said with a loud harrumph. "Perhaps *you* should trust me when I decide to leave the house as well."

She quickly changed the subject, describing Dov's lavish home and the wealth stored inside the vast estate.

Abba's probing questions, however, brought out the tale of the goddess pole tucked within a sacred grove and, more disturbing, the mixing of worship of Yahweh and Asherah.

"Yahweh will never be El," Abba said with a wheeze as his hand pressed against his chest. "To say so is blasphemy. And dangerous too, mixing such ideas together."

El, the god consort of Asherah, was the chief of gods to the Canaanites.

"A terrifying lie," she agreed. No longer did the mezuzah at Dov's doorpost bring her comfort. Instead, it felt more like mockery. An outward sign, no different from a talisman, hung on a neck, with no genuine commitment to Yahweh. Yet Othniel's challenge to not give up on Rebekah and to let Yahweh intervene in her niece's life brought a check to the emotions roiling within her.

Abba motioned for her to come closer. "Find a papyrus, my reed, and an ink box," he commanded. She rummaged for the tightly woven papyrus in a basket on the table and grabbed the sharpened reed, along with the pot of black ink.

"Shall I write for you?" she asked. She sank down beside his mat with the scrolls, a pot of ink, and a reed.

"No," he said as he propped himself with an elbow, his hair wild like a lion's mane. "I can write. I am not a complete invalid, Daughter."

Regardless, she offered him her arm and helped him ease into a more comfortable sitting position. Then she untied the papyrus and unrolled it, smoothing it for him. He dipped the sharpened reed into the paint jar and pulled it out with a shaking hand, dripping ink mixed with olive oil onto the mat and the expensive papyrus.

"You need not watch me," he said as he licked his cracked lips, his brow furrowed with concentration. "In fact, turn around, child."

She huffed a laugh while folding her arms across her chest. What an incorrigible pair they made. Scooting backward across the mat, she waited, but she refused to turn around. She couldn't read his indecipherable note as he scratched the reed across the brittle scroll.

"Abba, do I sense yet another plan for Israel's most esteemed general?" She kept her tone light and teasing, even as she watched him furtively beneath her lashes. He paused midstroke to rub his chest again, inhaling deeply through his nostrils.

"You ache," she blurted.

"Yes, I do," he replied after a long pause, his voice reedy. "I ache over many things, including my selfishness keeping you so close to my side when you ought to have a home by now with plenty of children running outside to play in the dirt. I ache over my sons and how my eldest has not the good sense to protect his daughter, Rebekah. And I ache for the tribe of Judah and all of Israel. I pray

I am taken like Moses before I see this land devoured by false teachings."

He resumed writing, the scratch of the stylus and his winded breathing filling the hush.

She folded her hands, the calm gesture at odds with the tension coiling inside of her. "Bel told me that you rescued her from Hebron when you cleared the first city of giants."

"I did."

"She said she is not an Israelite."

"She chooses to be one, and Yahweh bid us not to turn away the stranger who wishes to be adopted into the tribes. We are to provide a place of safety for the widow. She never married, but your imma and I treated Bel as a widow and offered her a place in our home. When she told your imma of the terrible things that had happened in the temples, I could scarcely believe my ears, despite my years of battle. The sacrifices of infants and children burned alive. The temple prostitutes— where the young women are forced to serve until they are too old, sold by their families to cover debts. I witnessed evil things in Egypt, but nothing as depraved as the Canaanites or the Philistines. So you see, when Yahweh commanded through Moses that I give Hebron to the Levite priests, how could I refuse? A city of darkness turned into a city of refuge. A place for justice and life instead of death."

"How is it that Bel understands Yahweh's mercy and not Rebekah? How is it that a foreigner such as Bel values the teachings of Yahweh, and not a daughter born into our family?" Her questions must have pierced Abba, because he flinched and dropped the stylus, splattering more ink onto the floor.

"I do not know. I have had hours to spend on this cursed mat and do nothing but pray and think and ask forgiveness for my failures. Did I not spend enough of my days teaching my sons about Yahweh? How did I fail them? What will happen to my children if they walk away from God?"

He stooped over, his shoulders hunched—weakened perhaps from the entire exchange. His entire frame shook, as if sobbing silently. She slipped an arm around his back and eased him back down onto the pillow.

"You have not failed, Abba. You have taught me to love Yahweh. And Bel too. Do not give up hope yet."

He gripped her arm. "No. No, I will not give up, my precious daughter. Take my message to Othniel as soon as you can. He will know what to do. Promise me this, that you will let that poor man read the papyrus in peace without your interference."

The frisson of worry kept her from snapping back an acidic answer. Instead, she smoothed the white hair from her father's brow and cupped his cheek. "For once, Abba, I will obey."

Othniel's farm lay the farthest from Hebron. Unlike her brothers' abodes, Othniel's dwelling comprised a modest two-story home with a flat roof to sleep on when the nights sweltered with heat. Surrounded by an equally unimpressive courtyard, the entire structure blended in with the brown hills. Unassuming. Plain. Just like the man who lived inside.

Then why did her pulse beat so fast the closer she drew to Othniel's courtyard?

She slipped off her horse and instructed Ari to wait for her. When she pushed on the door and entered the narrow courtyard, she fretted that she might have missed him. So often, he was away for the fields or scouting missions. Indeed, if she needed him, she often had only to look at her table and find him eating with Abba. In fact, she had not seen Othniel's home since she was a small child.

Everything about the property suggested respectability but not wealth, unlike Dov's abode or her brother Iru's estate. The bleat of a few sheep and two goats, kept safe in their pen, greeted her when she crept toward the door of the house. Running her sweating palms down the sides of her indigo tunic, she searched for some sign of life within the house. Since his sister had married and his imma moved to be with the grandchildren, it appeared Othniel lived alone.

Why had he never married?

She straightened the satchel carrying the papyrus, now rolled and tied with a string, and told herself to march toward the door and knock on it. How strange that Abba would ask her to visit Othniel after chiding her about her visit to Rebekah. Any servant could have delivered the message. Yet since the wedding feast, she had felt a strain with Othniel and she wanted to make amends. The blistering sun above reminded her to get on with the duty and see it to completion. She rapped her knuckles on the door as loudly as she could. Only a bird flew from the top of the roof in answer.

"Now what?" she said as she propped her fists onto her hips. "I suppose I shall have to go to the fields to find him."

"Find who?" A deep voice said from behind her.

At the edge of the courtyard, Othniel entered his property, his expression almost wary as he came to a halt in front of her.

"You," she said, feeling somewhat foolish at being caught speaking her thoughts for anyone to hear. "I am to find you."

She opened her leather satchel and pulled out the papyrus, thrusting it into his dirty hands. Yes, he had come from the fields, no doubt. But her anxiousness stripped away her manners. "It is Abba."

He stared at her, his eyes widening.

"He is fine. Resting at home and as restless as a gazelle. He asked me to give you this message as soon as possible, and so, here I am."

Her tongue felt somehow twisted as she continued holding the papyrus at arm's length for him to take. At last, he stepped forward and reached for it, his fingers brushing against hers. He fumbled with the string then yanked it free and unfurled the papyrus, his eyes roving back and forth as he rapidly skimmed the symbols.

Moses had taught Joshua to read. And Joshua insisted his top men learn to wield more than the sword. Her abba, a man not much for the finer activities, absorbed the basics, passing his knowledge to her. She could read and she could write. Perhaps she shouldn't be surprised that Caleb had passed what little he had on to Othniel as well.

Regardless of the unintelligible scrawl—and she had admirably resisted all urges to read the message, no matter how much Abba had piqued her curiosity—Othniel's face paled considerably as he hastily rolled up the scroll and stuffed it into his woven belt.

"You seem upset," she prodded, wishing again she knew what those symbols commanded.

He swallowed hard, his Adam's apple bobbing up and down as if something large lodged in his throat.

"Do you know what is in this letter?" he demanded suddenly.

"No," she said slowly, now slightly miffed that Abba didn't take her fully into his confidence. "But I cannot deny that I would like to read it. Abba wept this morning, and you know him better than most. He never sheds a tear. Whatever troubles him, I want to see his burden eased. However, he gave me explicit orders not to peek, and certainly not to pester you."

A muscle ticked in Othniel's jaw. "Tell Caleb that I will do as he asks. And I alone will deliver his message to the rest of the tribes. I will leave this very day."

"We are going to war," she breathed, her pulse picking up speed. "Even from his sickbed, Abba plans one last campaign."

Othniel held her gaze evenly, his amber eyes now darkening like a thunderstorm. "Yes."

She sensed something more lay between the lines on the papyrus, but the rigidity of Othniel's posture kept her from prying for more information.

Instead, she placed a hand on his arm. His skin jumped beneath her cold fingers.

"Thank you, Othniel, for always being there for Abba. For always watching out for my family. When my brothers ignored Abba, you listened. In many ways, you are a better son to him than anyone else. I do not always express appreciation, but I want you to know…" She faltered beneath the intensity of his gaze. Suddenly shy, she withdrew her hand, conscious that even though he had always felt like a brother to her, he most certainly was not, and she had the witness of her servant standing outside the courtyard to hear this awkward exchange. "To know that we—that is to say, *I*—truly value you."

She wasn't used to giving impassioned speeches in which she praised someone, but the color returned to Othniel's cheeks as he studied her. The lopsided smile made an appearance. A charming smile, she had to admit.

"We will speak again," he said with a decided nod. And his hand absently brushed against his belt, almost as if to reassure himself of the papyrus crinkling beneath the belt.

"Good," she said, matching his smile with her own, uncertain what he meant but determined not to cause offense this morning.

He held out a palm, helping her mount her horse. His grip lingered a moment longer on her hand before he withdrew it.

"We *will* speak again," he repeated, so softly that she thought she might have misunderstood him.

Before she could blink, he had already taken several long-legged strides across the beaten dirt of the courtyard, flinging open the door to his house as if a fire had been lit beneath his feet.

Oh Yahweh, what has Abba planned now?

CHAPTER TWELVE

Days stretched into two long fortnights of waiting for Othniel's arrival. Abba said nothing regarding his missive. But Bel had coaxed him to move off the mat with the use of his cane. The chest pains did not return, and bit by bit, Abba regained some of his strength, though as the days passed, it became apparent that he would not return to the way he once was. But never did he have a more tender nurse than Bel, who hovered over him, allowing Achsah to take much-needed breaks.

In the meantime, Achsah kept her fingers busy with the loom as she worked on a length of olive-hued cloth. The thread frayed to lengths dangerously thin, with one weight snapping. She felt the same as she carefully retied the string to the weight. Her gaze traveled to the window that overlooked the courtyard and the road beyond.

No sign of Eli. No word from Rebekah or Dov. Her world seemed to shrink as she stayed close to her abba's side.

As she reached for the fabric, intent on finishing one more section before starting the evening meal, she spied someone just outside the courtyard. The top of a man's dark-haired head. At first, excitement shot through her as she jumped to her feet and rushed to the courtyard. But no one entered through the gate. She hurried outside, but the retreating back of a man on horseback along the faint road running past her villa sent a cold stab of disappointment through her.

"Did you see who passed our courtyard?" she asked Ari, who accompanied her everywhere these days. This morning, he had allowed her some breathing room, sharpening her abba's collection of swords with a whetstone. Preparing each weapon for battle.

He held one such bronze blade in his grip when he stepped outside the gate to stand beside her. The bleak horizon stretched on, a mirage floating in the distance. She had to strain to see the stranger.

Surely Eli hadn't ridden past without saying hello. She didn't think Othniel would attempt such a slight either.

"It was Haim," Ari said after a moment, his relief evident when he tossed the blade and caught it in his nimble grip. "He came yesterday too."

She frowned, studying Haim's retreat. "Did he try to speak with Abba?"

"No. He rides by the property and never speaks with any of us."

The hair on the back of her neck rose as Haim disappeared over the hill. The road shimmered like the Sea of Salt, making her doubt what she had just seen.

"Why would he travel our road? He lives far to the east of us."

Her guard shrugged, perhaps ignorant of how much Haim's family hated hers.

She couldn't possibly imagine what would possess Haim to ride past her family's abode, not once, but twice.

Achsah's heart pounded when she heard Bel's voice calling for her to come to the great room. Rushing as fast as she could, she greeted an older man, a servant, who passed a missive to her to take to Abba.

"Is Othniel with you?" she asked the messenger.

"No, he remains at Jerusalem. The representatives of each tribe are to gather immediately."

"Gather where?" she demanded, her anxiety mounting with each heartbeat.

"Here," the messenger said with a slight scowl, as if she ought to know the news.

"Here?" she repeated stupidly. Delegates from each tribe coming to her courtyard?

Abba, of course, appeared unfazed by the news. Today, she had encouraged him to shuffle to the great room, where a plethora of feather-stuffed cushions waited for him.

"Abba, what have you planned? How am I to feed so many?"

Even while lounging on cushions, her abba wore a cunning expression, one that made him seem almost pleased with the news. "Your brothers' wives will help. Yahweh has blessed us greatly these past years. We will have more than enough food. If not, we will send the lot of them to Hebron. Stop fretting and see what the Lord will do. Our future lies in His hands, yes?"

She pinched the bridge of her nose in frustration, the idea of the courtyard packed with servants and hungry men clamoring for water or stew overwhelming. The future these days appeared more precarious than ever. And she hated cooking, truth be told.

Abba's question caught her off guard as he motioned for her to fill a cup. "You have not heard from Eli, have you?"

"No," she answered thickly, ducking her head to hide the heat of shame spreading across her cheeks. She had been so sure about his intentions that his latest absence brought a fresh stab of doubt. "And I take it from your question that you have heard nothing either."

At that moment, Bel appeared in the doorway, saving Achsah from any further troublesome questions or answers. "Mistress, we have need of more olive oil."

An understatement, considering the horde of warriors about to descend.

At least Achsah could bury her disappointment in work, especially with the help of a woman who had proven to be loyal and caring, despite her gruff exterior.

───────────────

Within a month, the peaceful hush of the courtyard was exchanged for the braying of animals and the jovial shouts of men from across the land, just as Abba had requested. Achsah rose to the challenge, directing the guests where to best pitch a tent and sleep for the night and overseeing a large spit of roasted meats for a feast later. Everywhere, from inside her home to the gardens and courtyard, she could scarcely escape the press of men, some wearing armor and others dressed as simple farmers. Once, she thought she saw Eli's stocky form amid the crush of horses and donkeys. Resisting the urge to call out to him, she watched him disappear into the men clustered near Abba's famed armory.

On the morning of Abba's planned speech to the assembly, she helped him step outside to the plain beside the massive courtyard, where everyone could gather and listen. At the edge of the property, she spied Othniel. He looked in her direction, his steady gaze unreadable. As she helped her abba sit on a chair positioned before the assembly, she glanced over her shoulder. Othniel still watched her—or perhaps Abba.

Her brothers also maneuvered themselves close to the front of the immense group, dressed in their very best robes. Iru held himself straight as if he were a king about to receive his court. Elah, Hur, and Naam jostled for the closest position beside Abba.

"Over a hundred men—maybe more—representing each tribe, including many volunteers from the tribe of Judah," Abba told her, sounding very pleased. "They are Israel's best warriors, the sons of those who had served alongside Joshua and me."

Despite the spark in his eyes, he still heaved a sigh, as if nervous. She patted his shoulder for comfort. Just as she withdrew her hand to duck into the shadows with the rest of the women, he reached up and snatched her wrist, holding her firmly in place.

"Stay with me, Achsah. Stay by my side."

Iru bristled at Abba's command. Achsah's eldest brother leaned over to whisper in Abba's ear. "It is unseemly to have your daughter to your right during a war council. Let her appear appropriate for once in her life." He reached for Achsah, his hand heavy on her shoulder, like a vise. "Do you know what Abba has planned?"

"No," she whispered, jerking free of her brother's grip. "But we will know soon enough."

"Perhaps age has addled our abba," muttered Naam. He cleared his throat and spoke louder. "Go, Achsah. Our guests will be hungry soon."

How could she possibly feed every single person standing in front of her family? She refused to budge, her feet pinned to the ground despite the weight of so many staring. Instead, she let her abba hold her hand while turning to Naam. "I will do no such thing."

Elah blew out an exasperated breath as he scanned the crowd. "Abba, have you called *all* the men of Judah to our home?"

"Yes," Abba said, his mouth curving into a slight smile. He explained nothing more, leaving Achsah's brothers to shift with discomfort.

As the brilliant sun slid across the azure sky, more men joined the assembly. A commotion at the back occurred when a few men argued about where to place the donkeys and the wagons. To her surprise, someone called for Othniel to settle the disagreement. It was easy enough to follow his tall frame as the crowd melted away for him. Once the matter was settled, Abba let go of her hand and raised both of his arms.

She knew Abba had aged, but in that moment, she realized it so clearly. The sun shone on his skin, highlighting every wrinkle and spot. He had lost weight these past months, and his robes hung limply on him. His arms trembled as he kept them raised until the men of Israel and Judah hushed.

When Abba spoke, though his speech slurred and his voice no longer rang with power, the men listened. "Men of Israel. Men of Judah. I have led you into battles and witnessed the mighty hand of God at work. He led us from captivity into this land, as He promised. He told us to secure Israel, but we have not finished the work. The land God promised us remains in the hands of wicked men. Our enemies lie in the middle of Judah and taunt us. The giants of

Kiriath-sepher and the Philistines to the east wait for our demise. We grew soft in our wealth. We grew complacent and beat our swords into plowshares. And we forgot the commandments of Yahweh given to Moses from Mount Sinai in thunder and lightning. I have heard it said that some of you worship idols. That you wish for peace with our neighbors. But they will destroy you when you least expect it, and you will step away from the goodness of Yahweh, who has protected you through the wilderness."

He paused to take a deep breath before continuing. "I have sent reports to you of the raids. If you shut your eyes to the suffering of your people, you will be lost. I would lead you again, but my days shorten, along with my breath. I am an old, old man. I took Hebron at eighty-six years of age. Now, I ask you to rise as warriors and chase out the last of the giants who plot to oppress the tribe of Judah."

A roar rippled through the great assembly as Abba reached for Achsah's hand again, his grip tight.

"How can we betray our God, who freed us from bondage? Will we go back to that same bondage?" he cried.

The men shouted, some raising spears or bows into the air. "Lead us, Caleb! Lead us!"

She groaned. Her abba would surely die if he did so. Couldn't they see how frail he was? How could he keep working when the younger men refused to take responsibility for their communities?

Abba raised his left hand once more to quiet the crowd.

"Let him speak! Let our general speak!" a man cried out.

Abba motioned for Achsah to give him her arm as he leaned on it and stood, rising to his full height.

"I have prayed that Yahweh would raise a new leader who loves the Lord with all his heart. One who will be courageous and unflinching in protecting Judah. Whoever conquers the city of giants will get my daughter's hand in marriage, and I will give her the wilderness of Negev as her inheritance."

He sagged against her just as a startled cry escaped from her mouth. Along with the mouths of hundreds of other men, their mouths gaping with shock. As one, they stared at her. Her!

A red haze floated in her vision, and her ears rang as she nearly fled, but for the need to help her abba sit down again.

"You are worth fighting for, Daughter," Abba told her, squeezing her fingers again before releasing his grip. "A worthy man will come forward. One who is bold and loves Yahweh."

She resisted the urge to duck her head and hide. A deep fear suffused her. What if the wrong man volunteered to slay the giants? One who had more in common with her brothers, in the desire for riches, than her abba, who longed to follow Yahweh?

Then again, a more humiliating thought made her cringe. What if *no one* wanted her or the trouble it would take to marry her?

"I will do it!" a man shouted as he pushed his way through the assembly to stand before Abba. *Othniel.* He stood before Abba and her, his shoulders moving up and down as if he couldn't quite get enough breath into his lungs. Then he straightened and looked her in the eye.

"I volunteer to take Kiriath-sepher."

The men cried out again, raising their fists into the air, and suddenly, more warriors moved toward the front of the assembly, including Eli who, beaming, stood shoulder to shoulder with Othniel, until at last an immense line of men offered themselves to take the city of giants in exchange for her hand. Was it the promise of Negev that drew the men to fight for her?

But a shiver rippled through her at the way Othniel stared at her, and only her, even as he addressed her abba.

She could scarcely tear her gaze from him.

"Take the city," Abba ordered, pointing to the men. "The shadows of the sons of Anak, Sheshai, Ahriman, and Talmai have haunted us long enough. We will show no fear. Not even when their grandson, Marduk, vows revenge upon the tribe of Judah."

Caught staring for far too long at Othniel, she turned her head just in time to catch Eli's impudent wink at her.

"You ask the impossible!" another voice cried out, hoarse and full of fury. Haim also pushed his way to the front of the assembly. Dressed in an embroidered tunic and finely tooled leather belt, he appeared more the courtier to a king, so unlike the surrounding men who stood sweating and dirty from their travels.

"My grandfather, Eshkron, tried to warn Moses. But Moses refused to listen. Instead, we found ourselves mired in a war that we or our children will never win. Do you want to incur the wrath of the Philistines at Ashdod and Ashkelon? Shall we forever be fighting, passing nothing to our sons and daughters but a legacy of death? Or can we have peace by arranging for treaties between our regions? Do you want to follow the Father of Destruction on one more vanity quest, because he was promised that city? Promised by whom? Yahweh? What a convenient claim to make by a man who has so much to gain from our spilled blood."

Unease rippled through the crowd, and Abba, though he didn't shrink, visibly shook at the challenge. None of Achsah's brothers said anything. Iru folded his arms across his chest while Elah stepped back, whispering to Naam. Even Hur moved away from his abba, the message clear that he no longer supported his father's quest.

There was only one thing she could do. And that action might offend others. So be it.

She positioned herself in front of her abba. "Men of Israel and Judah, must I remind you that you found freedom through the efforts of my abba and Joshua? When no one else would fight, they led the charge as men in their eighties. Repeatedly, they laid down their lives to secure the land given to us by Yahweh. Land which you now enjoy but remains threatened by Marduk. Your abbas were slaves in Egypt. Now you are free, but your freedom will always come at a cost. It is earned, not inherited. Will you so easily give up your villages and your fields because the sons of Anak wish to crush you? Yahweh told Moses to take the land. How many miracles and wonders do you need to see before you believe in Yahweh's word?"

The crowd cheered again, even as Iru spoke loudly, "Our family paid our dues, and we will not pay with our blood, fighting for all of Israel."

Haim scowled, his cheeks red, but even he could do nothing against the will of the soldiers, many of whom loved Abba. In the meantime, Othniel called the men closest to him to make plans.

How easily he fit into her abba's role. Indeed, it seemed as if he had been preparing for it most of his life. She hadn't seen what was in front of her the entire time.

He cared enough to battle a city of giants for her hand, volunteering first. The thought felt strange. And yet...

Her heart pounded like a drum at the idea, leaving her breathless.

She stepped back toward her abba's side. He smiled at the assembly, but with the drooping of his shoulders, he could no longer stay outside, even if the men demanded it.

"Come, Abba." She held out her arm for him to take. "Your work here is done."

CHAPTER THIRTEEN

Later, as she dressed for the evening meal, putting on her best earrings and a dab of musk at the base of her neck, she inhaled deeply to steady her nerves. Bel hovered near, offering a polished metal disk to serve as a mirror.

"You are beautiful, Achsah. Truly, an ornament, as your imma named you."

"I want to be more than just a glittery armband to ornament a man's arm. I want to be of some use."

Bel thumbed away a stray tear as she brought forward a comb to work out the curls cascading down Achsah's back. "You are more than a decoration. I listened to your speech from the edge of the courtyard, and I have never been so proud of you. I had no say as a child and later when I was enslaved, but to see you, a woman, standing by your abba's side, defending him before some of the greatest men in Israel…"

"I always wished I had been born a son," Achsah said wistfully as she submitted to each brush stroke.

Bel paused, holding a handful of hair. "No, child. Yahweh made you just as you ought to be. Today, a woman stirred the men to action. Because of a woman, they will fight to cleanse Kiriath-sepher and set the captives free."

The figure in the metal mirror appeared a stranger by the time Bel finished. Achsah touched her cheek, remembering Othniel's intensity and Eli's wink. She would be given to the one who conquered the city. What if neither man conquered it in the end? What if one of them lost his life? What if…

Her stomach roiled as she allowed Bel to fuss over the sash at her waist.

"You have lost weight. Worrying about your abba, I believe."

"I fear he does not have long to live and I will lose the person dearest to me."

Bel nodded, her sigh making it clear that she felt the same. "You will not lose me. And, I believe you stand to gain something precious with this future husband. Your abba has seen to it. He fears what will happen to you if you move in with Iru's family."

"I am a little afraid. Hard to admit, I know, especially as Caleb's daughter, but I am afraid of an unknown future. I do not know who will take the city, or if our people will emerge victorious. I cannot imagine leaving Abba's side, even though I have longed for children of my own."

Bel placed a comforting hand on Achsah's shoulder. "Then you must trust Yahweh to provide. All He asks is that we continue in faith, even when the task seems impossible."

The words were true and comforting as always, especially coming from one who had tasted such sorrow. A subtle challenge to her mounting doubts.

The sounds in the courtyard rose while bonfires dotted the brown landscape outside the courtyard. Predictably, Achsah didn't have enough to feed everyone, but for those she could, she offered the best, serving roasted lambs on spits, and raiding her garden for leafy greens and leeks. By morning, she would be completely out of supplies. Iru's wife grumbled when asked to help, bringing in baskets of round loaves.

Everywhere Achsah went, she felt the weight of stares following her every movement.

"That is Caleb's daughter."

"Truly, she is…"

She hurried past the men sitting cross-legged in her courtyard, unwilling to hear what assessment they might cast upon her. Somehow, despite her fine tunic, the earrings dancing in her earlobes, or the bracelets tinkling at her wrists, she felt strangely inadequate. Nor did she fully like being the prize.

In some ways, the evening mimicked a wedding feast instead of a call to battle. When she ordered the pithoi opened for serving extra wine and fresh water, she bumped into someone large. A hand reached for her, steadying her. Othniel's mouth quirked when she raised her head to see him near her.

Suddenly tongue-tied, she tried to think of something to say, but all the words seemed to scatter in her mind like chaff blowing in the breeze.

"I—" she started, but when he removed his hand from her shoulder, all she could think of was the absence of his warmth. "Thank you for easing my abba's burden. I know it will mean a great deal to him to see the city freed."

He opened his mouth to answer when Elah and Naam surrounded him, pulling him away. "We need our spy to plan the route of attack," Elah threw over his shoulder. "I am sure you will understand, Sister."

She understood, especially growing up with an abba who left her alone in the house for seasons at a time.

"Are you sure you want such a woman as Achsah? Her sharp tongue can slice a man to shreds," Naam joked loudly as he slapped Othniel on the back. Sputters of laughter echoed among those near enough to hear Naam's caustic remark.

"She has spirit, like her abba," Othniel readily answered.

"And the great Negev to her name. No doubt that will sweeten the deal," another man laughed. "You will need all the payment you can take to live with one such as her."

Her heart nearly shriveled with the cruel jest. Nor could she hear Othniel's answer to the stranger, who thought he knew her so well. Was that why Othniel volunteered? His land, his house, everything he owned paled compared to what Abba held. Had she misread his intentions? Was his volunteering truly motivated by power and wealth?

Anger bloomed on her cheeks and she wanted nothing more than to march over to that stranger and give him a piece of her mind. But as she took a step forward, another familiar voice called her name.

Whirling, she saw Eli approach. With a flourish, he reached for her hand, bringing it to his lips. The kiss, an ostentatious gesture for all to see, pressed, lingering against her knuckles, yet it only left her cold while the men hooted. For well over a fortnight, she hadn't heard from Eli, and now he refused to let go of her hand. Embarrassed, she tried to withdraw, but he held on all the more tightly, his handsome face creased with a wide grin. The dimples on his cheeks didn't elicit the same sense of charm this evening.

"I will claim you, Achsah, by the end of the week, and all of Judah will come to our wedding and celebrate," he vowed loudly for all to hear.

Helpless to pull free, she caught sight of Othniel's frown as he glanced over his shoulder.

"We shall see," she said curtly, finally withdrawing her hand.

Eli's laughter, loud to her ears, drew even more attention. "Next time I see you, I will kiss more than your hand. I will kiss any objections from that lovely mouth of yours."

She left then, too irritated to linger in the courtyard and serve the guests. Inside the cool of the great room, more men sat on the rugs, discussing the number of Benjamites with slingshots.

"Take all the archers and slingers to distract the enemy at the city gates," a man to her left said. "No swordsman can breach the walls of Kiriath-sepher, no matter what Caleb says. No one has taken the city, including him. Nine years ago he tried and failed. It will take a miracle to win against the giants."

She slipped through the throng, her ears ringing and her throat tight as she found her abba's room. When she ducked in, he lay fast asleep, already exhausted from the day's events, his beard fluttering with each deep breath. At ninety-four, he deserved such rest. Satisfied he would sleep well this evening, she left him.

But she felt more alone than ever as she ducked into her quarters for a moment of peace.

CHAPTER FOURTEEN

Two Days Later

A t the well, a group of women waited, clutching their pitchers and jars full of water as they watched Achsah climb the hill. Although she had servants who would readily haul water, Achsah took advantage of the early dawn to duck outside the courtyard and bring back enough for Abba and Bel now that the men had left, depleting most of her supplies. Walking gave her a chance to order her thoughts, especially at sunrise.

One of the oldest women in the group, Bilha, with a long white braid, offered a small smile as Achsah approached the well. Others parted for her, leaving her to feel just as closely watched as she was by the men who had flooded her home and courtyard.

She murmured a quiet greeting and yanked on the frayed rope to hoist the water bucket, feeling the unnerving weight of the women's eyes on her. Most of them she recognized, including the gray-haired Simchi, who had tossed accusations toward Achsah during the previous visit to the marketplace. Simchi's cold gaze took in Achsah for a long moment before the sound of hooves pounding the ground distracted the women.

Simchi pivoted, breaking the stare. "Look at who rides on the trail this early morning."

Relief poured through Achsah as the women tore their attention from her to a figure riding past the well. He broke into a gallop, urging the horse to fly along the beaten road, scattering plumes of dirt beneath the churning hooves.

"Isn't that Haim?" one matron asked.

Another left the well to peer closer. "I believe so. He leaves so early these mornings. I pity that horse of his. A fine creature. My husband, Jared, says Haim whips his beasts."

Achsah held her breath as she poured the water into her jar. Did others see Haim's treachery as she did?

"You know he trades with the enemy. He has built himself quite a caravan, bringing in goods through enemy territory," a younger woman confided as she stood on her tiptoes to view Haim better.

"No wonder the sons of Anak leave him alone," the other woman replied with a sneer.

Bilha, the woman with the long white braid whose smile had been so welcoming, glanced at Achsah. "I heard that the daughter of Caleb gave the Israelites quite a lecture."

Achsah nodded. "Haim wants the men to pursue peace with Marduk."

"Of course he does. He visits the Canaanite innkeepers with his friend in tow."

The image of Rebekah, isolated out in the wilderness, surrounded by the budding pagan groves and the twisted tree carved into a goddess, brought a pang to Achsah. Was Haim's friend Dov? Or someone else?

"I heard your abba will offer your hand in marriage to the man who conquers Kiriath-sepher." Simchi chuckled, her voice dry, as she drew closer to Achsah. "Did Eli, the weaponsmith, volunteer? He has been telling everyone in the village that he will be the first to return to you."

She would have welcomed such gossip only weeks prior—a final reassurance of Eli's intent—but the passing days had only heightened her sense of unease.

Another woman answered before Achsah could. "I heard Othniel volunteered first. My husband was so shocked when he heard the news. He said Othniel hardly speaks, so this must be something indeed serious. I told him he must be mistaken."

"And to have the Negev as a dowry! Why, how many men would dream of owning such land? A wilderness, yes, but the potential! You will be the richest woman in Judah, Achsah," someone else exclaimed. "No wonder he found the courage to act."

The women all fluttered around Achsah, exclaiming in surprise and delight while she cringed inwardly. She didn't want to be the richest woman in Judah. She didn't want to be a prize to be fought for, even if the idea of the men battling for her hand might turn any woman's head. What if the Negev was the sole reason that Othniel and Eli and all the other men finally fought, after years of watching her grow older?

She stuffed the mortifying thought deep inside and instead focused on the women. Her pride, although bruised this morning, must not stand in the way of Yahweh's will.

"You each know what is at stake if we do not take the city of giants. Othniel understands the risk better than any of us. For years, he has searched for a young girl, now a woman my age, who was taken long ago from one of our farms. When he could not find her, he sought the others who had disappeared over the years. No one else has protected our borders as well as Othniel while we enjoyed our vineyards and barley crops."

"My, what a defense of Othniel," someone whispered with a giggle. "Perhaps Eli should be worried."

Achsah brushed aside the comment. Why discuss such personal matters with the gossipers at the well?

To her surprise, Bilha nodded. "I agree with Achsah. I remember hearing about my grandfather, who worshiped the golden calf outside of Sinai. The devastation it wrought to our family when he turned from the worship of Yahweh to a false god! He died shortly afterward. My abba vowed we would never slip into the same bondage. We would do well to remind the men of what lies at stake. Give the enemy a corner, and soon they will devour us like bread."

Dawn brightened into morning as the sun tracked across the sky. Achsah found her abba sitting in the courtyard, watching the servants sharpen the weapons from his armory.

"I melted my first plow into a sword," he said from the cedar bench. "I always assumed I would refashion it into a plow, but Yahweh had other plans."

She sat beside him, enjoying this moment of companionship outside his chambers. It felt almost as if her life would return to its normal rhythms. "I remember your story."

He grunted, folding his blue-veined hands over his stick. "Our tribe has few weapons. They melted the metals to form farm tools as soon as we had a glimmer of peace."

"What about the slingers and the archers?" she asked. The Benjamites were especially renowned for their skill at hitting targets with precision.

He shrugged, his mouth pulling down at the corners. "A sling is for the light infantry and long-distance attacks. It is useless in hand-to-hand combat with a sword. I will be sending every weapon I have from this house, Achsah. It is the least I can do."

"Will Eli donate anything?"

"He will. He has been most persistent in his efforts to secure your hand, but I have set my terms and I will not budge. Capture Kiriath-sepher to marry my daughter."

He slanted her a look to gauge her reaction, but she pressed a hand against the fluttering in her stomach. Fear once again rose within her, but how could she admit it to Abba?

"You are silent, Achsah. How unlike you."

She fidgeted with the tasseled edge of her sash. "Why did you put my hand up for marriage in such a manner? I felt like a horse at the market, ready for the highest bidder. I am shocked none of the men asked to inspect the condition of my teeth."

He chuckled and leaned into her just enough to nudge her with his shoulder. "My darling girl, who is no longer a girl, even if I will always see you as one, I know you love Yahweh with all your heart. For the past six years, I have watched you reject men of lesser qualities because they could not, would not, commit to God the way you desired. The man you marry will certainly shape your fate. And you, his."

She nudged his shoulder back. "None of them compared to you, Abba."

His lips curved, but the smile remained sad. "You flatter me. There are better men than me out there in Judah. Men who will hopefully spend more of their days at home than I ever did. Men who will do a better job of teaching their children to love Yahweh. I want such a man for you, and one who will fight for you and cherish you all your days."

Her heart swelled at the love her abba so freely offered. A love that Yahweh offered as well.

"Do not be afraid, Daughter. You must let Yahweh choose your husband. And we must trust, together, that He will deliver Kiriath-sepher. I have tried for so long to control everything, and now, as an old man at the cusp of his twilight, I am left in the uncomfortable position of letting others fulfill the God-ordained mission. We must trust Yahweh will provide for the Israelites and for you."

The sun shone down on her face, warm and comforting, as she let Abba's words sink into her heart. Could she completely let go and trust? Did she doubt Yahweh's words like the fickle Israelites around her?

"I rather like Othniel," Abba said with a touch of humor. "He loves Yahweh as you do."

Her mouth dried at the idea of Othniel raising his voice to volunteer to fight for her. For so long, he seemed like just another brother. Another mouth to feed at her abba's table. And now? She understood Abba's ploy of sending her with that very letter, right to Othniel's doorstep.

"I should like to know what you wrote to Othniel. You were quite cruel to leave me in the dark."

Abba laughed. "One day, I hope you will know the truth of it."

She inhaled deeply to steady the fluttering in her chest. "We do not know who will take the city, or if they can even do so, Abba. Kiriath-sepher has long proved a thorn."

"True enough," Abba agreed as he motioned he would like to leave the bench. "I shall have to comfort myself with my words. Sometimes, I struggle to release my fears to Yahweh, even if I appear to have all the answers."

She rose to her feet and looped her arm beneath her abba's arm, allowing him to place his weight on her as he slowly pushed away from the bench.

Anything could happen. And yes, those unknown possibilities terrified her. Her abba had waited so long to enter the Promised Land. He had spent the last years of his life fighting nonstop instead of enjoying that land.

Would Othniel also have the same life—always away from home?

CHAPTER FIFTEEN

As the moon slid across the sky, Achsah stood in front of the massive gates guarding Hebron. She felt a presence behind her, and when she looked over her shoulder, the faceless man waited in the shadows. Despite the cold moonlight, she couldn't decipher his features no matter how hard she tried.

She shivered as she turned her attention to the terraced fields in front of the Levite city. In the distance, a harsh wind gathered speed, pushing against the heads of barley, forcing them to bow to the ground.

She braced herself against that wind, remembering the dust storm from before.

Why did she guard the gates? An unnatural moan brushed against the walls and tore at her hair and clothes. Something else spread on the horizon, a black blight creeping through the fields. Trees, hundreds of them, sprouted from the dark soil, with branches twisting and writhing to take the shape of women. Asherah poles as far as Achsah could see.

Such a grove had trapped Bel, causing untold agony. Abba had sacrificed his entire life to fight against such idols and depravity. What could she do? Why did the man beside her stand as if carved of stone? Why didn't he do something? Was he afraid, like her? She was only one woman, and she was tired, so very tired of standing alone for the truth, especially when others, including her own family, hated her for it.

I made you with the heart of a lioness for what will come. A voice resonated deep within her, one that filled her with so much love. She positioned herself in a defensive pose, leaning forward on the balls of her feet, her fists balling at her sides.

Achsah, be bold. Do not be afraid of wicked men. Do not be silent when injustice sweeps across this land.

Her eyelids fluttered open. The cooing of a dove greeted her as she sprang from her mat. Morning light filtered through the cedar grille covering her window. She rubbed her arms, chasing away the prickles. A second dream. Surely, Yahweh wanted to prepare her for some future ordeal.

Outside the window, a man shouted from the courtyard. She dressed quickly, throwing on the clean tunic left by Bel the night before. Stepping to the windowsill, she spied her abba's servants rushing about the courtyard. Ari gestured to the gate, his movements jerking as if propelled by rage.

"Tell the master and be quick about it!" he yelled. He held up a satchel as though it were a trophy.

She dashed outside the room, down the hall, and through the great room into the brilliant sunshine outside. A cluster of men huddled together as Ari spied her and hefted the bag. But when she reached him, he didn't relinquish the satchel as she expected. The young servant's brow creased as the others pressed in close around him, everyone eager to see what lay inside.

Ari raised his head to meet her gaze. "Mistress, I heard a sound at dawn outside our courtyard. A whinny of a horse. When I investigated, I saw a rider fleeing east. A man with shoulders as big as cedar trees. I have never seen such a horse. A monstrous beast."

"Haim?"

Ari shook his head, his jaw working. The other servants grew silent.

"You saw a giant?" she demanded.

"Perhaps." Ari nodded, his face pale as he opened the satchel. "Hard to say. He moved so fast, and there was not much I could do. But I found this by the courtyard wall."

Her servant had never been the sort to display fear, yet he visibly flinched as he reached in and pulled out the ugliest carving she had ever seen, of an elongated face wearing a ridiculous cone-shaped hat with its left arm raised to strike a death blow.

A chill swept through her at the sightless eyes.

Ari grimaced as he held it up for everyone to see. "It is Baal. Asherah's son. And it is a warning of what is coming. For what other reason would someone leave an idol at the general's door?"

Mesmerized, she reached out a finger to touch the grotesque visage, snatching her hand back to her chest just in time.

She finally found her voice. "If the Canaanites feel emboldened enough to wander through our fields in the middle of the night, then we are truly in danger."

Ari nodded, his lips pressed into a thin line.

The idol taunted Achsah as if to say, *"You cannot stop us."*

CHAPTER SIXTEEN

"Why do you pace so? You will wear grooves into my floor." Othniel's imma smiled at him from her position on the floor where she was grinding barley into flour, while his sister Rachel held a hand up to her mouth to cover a grin. Despite Rachel's efforts, laughter escaped her slim fingers.

He huffed, glaring at his sister, which made her sputter all the harder. Meanwhile, his nephew, Ben, crawled toward him, reaching with chubby hands to grasp the edge of Othniel's tunic. Ben pulled himself up with a toothless grin, lifting Othniel's cheeks as well.

He picked up the child, now a year and a half old, and swooped him into the air. Anything to avoid Imma's probing questions.

She rolled the millstone over the barley kernels, crushing them into a fine white powder. Yet her observant stare never left him, no matter how hard he tried to deflect the question.

"You have not been to Caleb's house since the assembly," she said flatly as the millstone rasped beneath her white-knuckled grip, stone scraping stone.

Not unlike her questions, rubbing raw against his pride.

He set Ben down, and the boy reached out again to be swung high into the air. Shaking his head at his nephew, his heart clenched.

"It has only been a few days, Imma, while we gather supplies before striking the city of books."

Ben reached for him, his chubby fingers wiggling as he made cooing sounds.

He wanted a son of his own. He wanted a wife to pull close in the middle of the night and feel her warm form next to him. He wanted a companion to fill his lonely house with chatter during the middle of the day and chase away the loneliness that had only grown over the years. He wanted...

He wanted Achsah.

Had always wanted her, if he was honest with himself. And the reasons only grew as the years passed; her bravery, that inner fire that made her eyes spark whenever she looked at him. When he couldn't think of something to say, she never let the silence fall between them. More than anything else, he admired the way she loved her abba, defending Caleb when his sons withdrew. And the way she clung to Yahweh, never afraid to speak her mind no matter what the others said or did, it inspired him to do more. Be more.

Yes, she was strong. Untamable, Elah had stated. Othniel had never cared for meek or simpering women, always blushing and stammering around him. It made his own stammering all the worse.

"It is Caleb's daughter, Imma. Look at Othniel." Rachel pointed to him before she grasped another heavy satchel of barley and carried it toward their imma, dropping the bag with a plop. "He cannot say the words, but I can see the stark longing in his eyes as he mopes around the house."

"I do not mope," he said through clenched teeth.

More girlish laughter filled the room as Rachel smirked at him, but Imma shook her head as once again she dragged the millstone, the rhythmic sound filling the small but tidy room. "You know full well Othniel does not mope. He does not show any emotion, just like his abba." She peered up at him, her braided hair threaded with white. She remained one of the loveliest, kindest women he had ever known. "Have you spoken with Achsah now that you have volunteered to take Kiriath-sepher in exchange for her hand?"

His sister glanced from Imma to him and then clapped loudly, bringing Ben to clap his dimpled hands. "I wondered when you would finally reveal your intentions," his sister added slyly.

He shoved a hand through his thick hair. Five years ago, when Achsah was sixteen, he had watched her turn down man after man, loudly proclaiming no one lived up to her abba. And he agreed. Very few would ever reach the legendary fame of Caleb. Then, over the years, the line of men had dried up like a straggling creek. Still, Othniel visited the great house outside of Hebron. Partly to learn from the man who was like a father to him…and partly for her.

He had no wealth. No name proven in battle. He had nothing. He was of no consequence. And she…she grew lovelier and stronger each year, soaring like the eagles ever higher while he could only watch with secret delight.

"I am not the only man who volunteered," he admitted slowly, his neck flushing as his family stared at him. "Eli, the weaponsmith, says he will fight as well, along with a host of others from the tribe of Judah and beyond."

Rachel snorted as she snatched up her son before he dipped his fingers into the growing mound of flour and made a mess. Ben wriggled free and ran to his grandmother, peering at the millstone. "So? Perhaps it is time to rise to the challenge."

Imma pressed a kiss against Ben's head. "Rachel, would you take Ben out and clean him? I smell a whiff of something most unpleasant."

Ben stuck two fingers into his mouth and blew bubbles while Rachel held him up and sniffed. Wrinkling her nose, she sighed. "Tell him, Imma. Tell Othniel that he cannot stay in the shadows any longer, even if he does not feel worthy."

Watching his younger sister sweeping out of the room with her son, Othniel allowed himself to exhale.

Imma scooped up the fine flour and poured it into a clean vessel. "Your sister is right. You have never felt worthy enough, as though you could never match our general's valor or your abba's example. I remember how your abba came home after hearing one of Caleb's impassioned speeches. How he glowed. He could talk of nothing else after watching Caleb and Joshua at the Jabbok River, outlining the plans to defeat King Og. Moses, Joshua, and Caleb led our people through great trials. They were great men, chosen by Yahweh."

He nodded, his throat tight with regret that he had never known his abba, who had died in battle. At twenty-five years of age, Othniel felt that he had so much to learn yet, and Caleb, in his nineties, had not much longer to live. Israel had no true leader, especially after Caleb's injury, which had left the general more often at home than traveling through the land allowed to the tribe of Judah.

"But I am of mixed blood," he protested, his answer so soft that he doubted his mother had heard a word.

The rasping of stone halted. Imma stared at him, quelling his urge to pace. "Othniel, Caleb also came from the Kenezite blood, and yet he found himself adopted into the tribe of Judah. Joshua broke free of Egypt's rule, his slavery a thing of the past. And Moses? Moses, at the age of forty, found himself banished from Egypt. A former prince forced to be a wanderer. A failure, by every estimation. Yahweh uses those who wish to serve Him. He equips those He calls. All you need to do is obey."

"I will fight the giants," he said thickly. "Not just for *her* but because Yahweh told us to inherit the land He gave us. Even if I do not take the city, I will give everything I have to see Caleb's decree fulfilled."

Imma kept her flour-coated hand on the millstone, but she made no move to grind the grain. "A wise decision, my son. Do what you can for the Lord and leave the results in His hands. It is all any of us can do."

The grinding resumed as Imma turned her attention to the plump kernels. But her next comment threw him off balance, showing that she wasn't finished with him yet.

"I have also heard gossip at the well that Caleb will give Negev to the groom."

"Yes," he answered after a pause.

"There will be many men who dream of such a prize. I wonder how many of them will truly see the jewel that Achsah is?"

He worried too. Worried so much that his chest throbbed.

"Which leads me to ask," Imma went on, "why are you still here? Shouldn't you at least take her a gift before you leave for battle?" She glanced at him, shooing him away with a sprinkle of flour. "You cannot fear risking your heart more than facing the giants. Let her know you do indeed care for her. For her, Othniel. Not Negev."

"I am not good at talking," he said under his breath.

"Then give her a gift that shows your affection," Imma said with an hint of exasperation as she wiped her hands on the side of her tunic.

He gulped, but Imma and Rachel gave good advice. And he had been silent for so long, hoping that somehow Achsah would eventually notice him. For too long, he had let his insecurities keep him tethered. For too long, he had feared she would reject him like the others, and so he did nothing. If he didn't do something quickly, Eli would certainly make a move.

Othniel carried his abba's dagger, the most prized possession in his home. The bronze blade, newly shined as Othniel blew steam on it and rubbed the cold surface, now glowed in the evening sun before he wrapped it carefully in soft leather. Delicate carvings of Egyptian hieroglyphs told a story long since forgotten. But the ancient blade sliced sharply enough to draw blood from the tip of his fingerprint. He smiled to himself, remembering twelve-year-old Achsah practicing with her abba's sword in the courtyard, her thin arm barely able to hold the heavy weapon. How she had answered her brothers, all defiance and fire when they tried to put her in her place.

The gift felt somehow appropriate, as lovely and as fierce as she.

His spirit lifted as he thought of her, and his pace quickened until he jogged across the winding landscape to the enormous house perched on a rocky hill. The sound of men talking stole his enthusiasm when he reached the whitewashed wall, but he pushed on the courtyard door, nodding to the young man, Ari, who guarded the family.

"Get in line." Ari jerked his head toward the great door of the house. "There have been plenty of men coming in and out all day to pay their respects to the general and his daughter."

Othniel tamped down his dismay and eased his features into what he hoped was an emotionless picture. But his chest beat faster when he spied the stocky weaponsmith waiting near the house. Arriving or just leaving?

Eli folded his arms across his chest, his expression smug.

"Greetings," the weaponsmith called out, sounding far too cheerful for Othniel's liking. "I have been told Achsah cannot be disturbed, and Caleb, apparently worn out from all the visiting, needed a rest. When she will appear, who knows? You need not waste your time, if you do not wish to wait."

"I will stay," Othniel said coolly, but his fists balled all the same.

Eli unfolded his arms, pushing away from the mud-brick wall. "I will conquer the giants, Othniel. I know you and I have always been friends, but I will not relinquish Achsah so easily." He had the audacity to hold out a hand to shake with Othniel. Othniel ignored it. He caught the sour scent of wine on Eli's breath.

How could he forget how tears had sprung to Achsah's eyes when she asked her abba about making a match with Eli over an evening meal? A conversation Othniel had no desire to overhear.

It was exactly as Imma had predicted. Men coveted the southern Negev and its strategic position bordering Egypt. Bounded by the Sinai Peninsula and the Jordan Valley, the Negev limestone and chalk deposits, along with portions of pastoral land, offered so many possibilities for immense wealth.

It was also a desert. And, like Achsah, untamed.

The door opened, creaking loudly. Both Othniel and Eli jumped, but instead of Achsah, Iru shut the door with a scowl on his face.

"You may as well go home. Abba is in a fine temper this afternoon."

"Why?" asked Othniel, his curiosity piqued.

"I felt it was my duty to warn the men about the giants." Iru tugged at his unruly beard. "I told a group this morning, 'Imagine swinging your sword against a man six cubits tall.' The arm swipe alone is nigh impossible to parry. And those arms are strong, with enough force to knock a man's teeth clear out of his mouth. Nor can you outrun the iron chariots, nor their warhorses trained for battle, unlike our donkeys, who bolt at sudden noises. Even if you can approach the city wall, the sheer number of arrows and slingshots will blot out the sun."

"If the sun is hot and shining in my eyes"—Eli shrugged with an impudent grin—"I may not dismiss a touch of cloud cover."

A flippant answer, bolstered from drink. Othniel clenched his fist even tighter around the bundled dagger.

Iru arched an eyebrow. "Were you not there at Kiriath-sepher when Abba's last campaign failed?"

Eli's cocky expression dissipated like the morning dew. "It has been so long, I cannot quite recall the details."

But Othniel remembered every detail of that disastrous night when he had made a promise to Achsah that he would protect her abba. The foolish promise of a seventeen-year-old youth yet to be tempered by life's demands.

"Nine years have passed since that night. We will do better," Eli said, regaining the color to his cheeks. "We cannot allow failure this round, or we really will have a war on our hands."

Iru snorted. "Take the city for all I care. It is a foolish quest, and we will lose more lives. I secured Hebron with Abba, and what good did it do any of us? Yahweh demanded we give the city to the Levites. All that work and for nothing. Do not be swayed by Abba's fanaticism. He would ensure that Israel continue with endless wars. It is all he knows. Do not throw away your life for nothing. The tribe of Judah has had peace and prosperity for nine years."

Do not throw away your life for nothing? Did Iru care nothing for the hamlets and farms raided by the giants? While Iru's bitterness did not shock Othniel, this new callousness did. He had heard Iru's grumbling comments for years, but even Eli appeared surprised. Regardless, Othniel had learned long ago not to waste his breath on Iru. Arguing now would not change the eldest's mind.

A window opened, the shutters flung open to the cool evening air. Othniel thought he saw long brown hair and a slim arm lined with tinkling bangles. He straightened, the rapid beat of his pulse even stronger—as if he were about to go into battle. As the door opened again, he palmed the back of his neck.

Iru slanted him a curious look, partly amused. Partly pitying.

But Othniel had no opportunity to dwell on deciphering Iru's expression. Instead, he watched as Achsah stepped out of the house, her frown clear. "I can hear you outside, and I wanted to warn you to speak softer…especially now that Abba is sleeping."

Her chiding made no dent to Eli's grin, so large, it nearly split his face in two. He kept beaming, flashing a row of straight, white teeth. Belatedly, Othniel realized Eli had dressed for the occasion, wearing a tunic edged with embroidery. And his curls and beard appeared neatly trimmed.

Othniel grimaced as he looked at his dusty outfit. He had thought to bring a gift, not to change his tunic.

Eli took the lead, angling himself in front of Achsah.

"I must admit that you are worth the wait," Eli said in a husky tone. "I wanted to see you before I go out into battle." He puffed out his barrel chest. "I have provided the best of my weapons to Caleb's cause."

"Abba's donated all of his swords as well." Achsah appeared unimpressed.

"Will you have a sword at the house?" Othniel asked quickly. She noticed him, stepping to the side so she could view him better.

"Ari will have his sword and three servants. They have refused to leave the house ever since someone left an idol at our courtyard gate."

Ice seemed to harden in Othniel's veins. "An idol?"

"Baal," she answered in a flat tone, her gaze swiveling to him. "A hideous, skinny version of Baal with the largest nose you ever saw."

Her limp attempt at humor only exacerbated his fear. Pressing his lips together, he glanced over his shoulder to see what Iru thought of the news.

Iru shrugged. "An idle threat, perhaps. There are Israelites who are angered about more conflict. I would not be surprised if one of them left it."

Othniel pictured Haim's protest after Caleb's speech. Yes, Haim and a small group of men resisted the idea of being drawn into another skirmish. Then again, what if it was someone else?

He frowned. "But to leave something so close to the general and Achsah? Perhaps we should leave others to guard your abba's home."

"I will remain close by," Iru said, his chilled voice brooking no disagreement. "I will not let anything happen to my family."

"Have no fear, Achsah," Eli soothed as he reached for Achsah's arm. "We will not let a little statue hurt you. Nor will we allow the Canaanites to step near Hebron."

When she didn't answer, the metalsmith tried a different tactic. "Will you not invite me inside?" Eli pleaded, twin dimples carving either side of his cheeks.

She nodded curtly and motioned for them to enter, but Othniel felt a meaty hand pull on his shoulder, pinning him in place.

Iru scowled as he kept his grip firm. "Think about what I said, Othniel. I do not want you to throw your life away like your abba did. I know the power the general has on other men, although that influence is finally ending and most of the Israelites want something other than the battle cry of a shofar. It is a season for new leadership. We must have allies, not enemies, if we are to survive." He released Othniel, the warning clear. Disturbed by Iru's advice, Othniel watched the older man walk away. Iru would rather compromise for a sense of security than to engage in Yahweh's calling. A hard but righteous calling.

A man's low chuckle from inside the house sent a frisson of alarm skipping down Othniel's spine. He pivoted back toward the house and flung open the door. Two steps inside, and he found himself confronted with an unpleasant scene, with Eli tipping rather close to Achsah.

To worsen matters, Eli had reached for a lock of Achsah's silky hair, capturing it between his fingers. "Have I told you how beautiful you are? I have dreamed of nothing else but you these past nights."

Once again, Othniel's throat seized up as he stood in the doorway. Achsah appeared mesmerized by the weaponsmith, her mouth slightly parted. Her shocked expression, however, did not suggest rapture.

Neither of them seemed to notice him. Especially, Eli, who puckered his mouth in the most ridiculous manner. Dread coiled within Othniel as he pondered what to do next, while rote instinct warred to take over. What if Eli truly was her choice? What if he had misread Achsah these past few days? Yet he could hardly flee and leave her with a man who had been drinking too much.

Without a word, Othniel set his dagger on the nearby cedar table and with long steps, grabbed Eli's collar, jerking the weaponsmith backward.

"Excuse me," he told Achsah while yanking Eli out the door.

Iru's warnings leaked through the door. Othniel stood on the other side, listening to Achsah's brother's latest complaints. She strained to hear Othniel's reply even though Eli stood next to her. A hand reached for her. Shocked, Achsah could only stare when the weaponsmith touched her hair to draw her attention back to him—the action so intimate...so inappropriate. For once, she found herself speechless, which didn't happen very often.

"Do not worry, Achsah, I will return safe and sound to you," Eli said, mistaking her shock for concern for him. He grasped her by the shoulders, turning her to face him. Tenderness softened his tanned features. "I swear you and I will be married within a fortnight."

Suddenly, his massive hands felt like a prison. She gently untangled herself from his grip, giving plenty of room between the two of them. He followed, taking one large step to place himself in front of her and before she could protest, he leaned in, his eyes closed, his mouth smelling like a rotting vineyard.

Absolutely not. She would not tolerate a kiss. Without even thinking, she pushed him away with as much strength as she could muster.

His eyelids fluttered and a look of hurt chased away the former ardor. "Achsah!"

"You have not conquered Kiriath-sepher yet," she said, not intending to be coy, even though his grin returned, albeit with a touch of hesitancy. "The hour grows late, and I cannot leave Abba alone any longer. I will pray that Yahweh strengthens each man's arm tomorrow and that the Israelites will know victory yet again."

"Future generations will remember this battle. I understand Marduk wants revenge on your abba for killing his grandfather and uncles," Eli said, but she had already stepped into the hall near the door, her hint for him to leave clear.

He said other things, but her ears rang while a scream silently rose within her, rendering his latest attempt at winning her favor useless.

Was the Baal idol, placed outside her courtyard, from Marduk? Or someone closer?

When Eli leaned into her again, his face hardening with resolve as he reached for her cheek to pull her in close for a second attempt, the door opened, and suddenly, Eli clutched his collar, gasping as he swayed backward. Caught in Othniel's grip.

"Excuse me," Othniel said to her, his eyes sparking with something dangerous. Then he pulled the weaponsmith outside the way a man would treat an errant son.

Relief caused her to sag against the door. She leaned against it… satisfied when she heard the clop-clop of a horse growing fainter and fainter. When she dared to peek around the door, Bel's worried voice called for her, drawing her away from the sight of Othniel and Ari at the courtyard gate.

"Achsah! Your abba. He needs you!"

She rubbed her throbbing temples and reconciled herself to yet another sleepless night.

If only Eli hadn't demanded so much of her attention. If only she could have spoken further with Othniel. She should have liked to talk to him about the Baal and Marduk. He seemed to always give levelheaded advice to her abba.

Honestly, she would like to have talked to him about other matters. What would it feel like to have his arms around her? To have his mouth brush against hers?

A groan escaped her as she covered her face with her hands before she closed the door and headed toward Abba's room. A rolled package on the nearby cedar table caught her attention. She reached for it and untied the rawhide strings, flipping back the flap of leather. Her breath caught when a glimmer winked back at her. In her hands, she held a bronze dagger with ivory inlaid into the handle. Such exquisite craftsmanship. As she traced the delicate lines with her fingertip, warmth stole into her heart. Othniel had left her this priceless gift? This dagger meant for an Egyptian prince?

He *had* wanted to talk to her. She hadn't imagined that flash in his eyes. Yes, he had volunteered to take the city. But he had always been a dutiful son, more so than her brothers.

Did he truly desire her? The gift said yes.

Eli had brought no gift. Only his pretty but empty words. Nor had he stopped talking long enough to hear her speak. Instead, he filled the quiet hush of the great room with his chatter, sounding very much like the women at the well or the market. And when he tried to kiss her, she had shoved him away, unwilling to let those puckered lips graze hers.

Eli was nothing like Othniel.

Later that evening, after taking a meal to Abba, she took the dagger with her to her pallet and lay down with the sheathed weapon beside her. The faint hieroglyphics caught bits of moonlight, the language a mystery to decipher. Just like the silent man who had left it on the table. A man who saw her in distress and acted.

Bel took one look at the dagger with a knowing smile. "Othniel came back for you, but you were with your abba."

Disappointment crested through her at the missed timing. As she fingered the sheath, awareness dawned. He understood her. He cherished her in bringing such a magnificent gift with him— perhaps the most valuable thing he owned. For years, he had sat near her. Listening to her. To Abba. And more importantly, to Yahweh.

How humbling to admit that she had been wrong about him, that she had overlooked all of his virtues. And tomorrow, he would head into the most dangerous battle of his life. A shiver rippled through her at the way his lips had pressed together when she had shared with him about the Baal idol left on her doorstep. He said so little, yet she knew he would fight with everything that he had to keep her and Hebron safe.

If only she could have told Othniel that she truly cared for him. What if he died battling the giants, just like his abba? Pain knifed through her at the idea, for the one man she had always ignored was the first one to volunteer his life to save the tribe of Judah. Unlike Eli, Othniel would do what he said.

She reached out to touch the cold dagger to gather some sense of comfort, but all she could see in her mind's eye were the roving shadows of giants stretched across the rocky ground. And Othniel, caught within those very shadows.

CHAPTER SEVENTEEN

Abba refused to eat the broth that Achsah brought. She heard Bel's muttered prayers as the old woman knelt on the other side of Abba.

"Please, Abba, Bel cooked especially for you. It is not too bitter with herbs, unlike my stews. Can you smell the roasted lamb?" She waved the steaming bowl closer to him, but he didn't answer.

This morning, she had found Abba in the most peculiar state, with drool slipping down one side of his mouth. Carefully, she wiped it away while the flame of fear ignited once again. He opened his mouth to speak, but nothing but a low cry, reverberating in his throat, escaped.

Setting the bowl down, she did what she could to make him comfortable while Bel fussed over the blankets. Somehow today he seemed more gaunt, more fragile, like the papyrus rolls kept safe in the cedar box on his desk.

"Abba, please wake up. It is morning, and I saw the pigeons fighting over scraps of bread in the courtyard. Would you like to see them? Maybe the sun will feel good on your back."

"Let him sleep," Bel warned. "We will try the broth later, when he feels like it."

Bel left no room for argument as she tugged Achsah up from the floor. Abba's chest barely fluttered, his breaths so shallow…so quiet.

"You should eat." Bel grasped Achsah's hand. "I do not want to see you fall ill too."

"What is wrong with him, Bel?"

"Age," Bel said, her smile sad as she led Achsah to the kitchen. "Your abba is tired. He is come to the end of a long life. I have seen it before. Some men have an internal attack that steals their speech and movement. I fear your abba had one in the night, much like the attack that happened when he tried to join the other men after the wedding. His heart beats like a lion's, but even lions need rest."

She was so used to Abba recovering. Surviving. Beating any obstacle in his path. The idea of death hovering around him didn't seem quite possible. Except she couldn't deny the pallor of his cheeks or the long bouts of rest.

Placing a hand on his forehead, she felt herself wilt. Heat radiated from him despite the waxen pallor. "Abba has a fever."

Bel touched Abba as well, her expression bleaker than Achsah could remember. "Death comes to our door, little one."

She wasn't little, but Bel's insistence on treating her like a daughter brought a spark of warmth to her chest. "Not yet. While the men battle giants, we will snuff out this illness."

"It is old age, not illness," Bel whispered back.

But Achsah refused to listen. Hyssop might help to purify whatever ailed him. Perhaps she could coax Abba to open his mouth and allow her to dribble water. She left Abba and Bel, the rapid walk to the kitchen where Bel kept the dried herbs in storage taking far too long. She pulled a vial of crushed hemlock mingled with olive oil and mixed the drops in a cup of water.

"Mistress!" Ari's voice came from behind her. "There's trouble."

She nearly knocked the cup over, her nerves all ajumble, when she whirled to see her dusty guard, clad in leather armor, sweating and breathing hard as if he had come from a skirmish.

Alarm skittered through her, making her hands shake.

He grimaced at her reaction, but, without apology, pointed his index finger to the eastern wall of the kitchen, toward the courtyard. "Your niece just arrived. She is beside herself with terror, and I thought it best to come to you directly."

"What brought her to our door?"

Ari's scowl brought even more alarm. "It is Rebekah's husband, Dov. He is missing."

After taking the medicine to Bel and leaving her dear friend to tend to Abba, Achsah found her niece crumpled on the floor, hugging a crimson cushion to her chest. She rocked back and forth on the rug, her wail keening ever higher.

Meanwhile, Ari stood guarding the door, his stiff posture showing his discomfort. Perhaps he felt as helpless as Achsah did.

She sank down beside Rebekah and pulled her into a hug. For a long moment, Rebekah wept until at last her sobs subsided into hiccups. To Achsah's surprise, Rebekah rested her head on her shoulder. Hot tears soaked into Achsah's tunic, but she held Rebekah all the more tightly.

"Dov has disappeared. He said he would return home after a trip, but my servants found no sign along the road. At first, I thought it was nothing. Perhaps he had been delayed in his trading since he ventured closer to the Philistines a fortnight ago. As the days stretched on, I knew something was wrong. When I woke up this morning, I found myself all alone in that awful house. The servants must have heard something, since they all fled in the night."

Rebekah abandoned and left alone so close to Kiriath-sepher?

Achsah grasped her niece by the shoulders to peer into her face. "Did you tell your abba the news?"

"Your house is the closest to mine. And all I could think of was returning to grandfather and how safe he made me feel. I wanted to feel secure again. Besides, I heard rumors that our family went to war again against Kiriath-sepher. Is my abba even home?" Rebekah cried again. Her eyes, swollen and red, shut tight. "I do not know what to do. I am so frightened."

"Iru said he would not fight. If he has changed his mind, he has not told me," Achsah said as she wrapped an arm around Rebekah's shoulders once more.

Ari started pacing by the door, his leather armor creaking. To her dismay, she saw light flash down the edge of his blade. He had already drawn his sword as if expecting danger to come to her home.

"Ari, stop pacing. You are not helping any of us calm down."

He sheathed his sword, albeit slowly. "My apologies, mistress. I cannot help but think I must run to Iru and speak with him about Dov. I doubt Iru knows what happened to his son-in-law." He leveled a look at Rebekah. "It is a shame we cannot start a search party and look for your husband. If we wait too long, the tracks will disappear."

"Go then," Achsah ordered. Although Ari was her best guard, two other men, older but faithful, tended the olive grove and helped her abba as needed. She had Bel. And now Rebekah. "I suspect you will find Iru in his fields. Let him gather my brothers. If Dov was taken by..."

She couldn't finish the thought. If Dov was taken by the Philistines or the Canaanites as a hostage, then his chance of survival would diminish with each passing day.

Ari's hand gripped the pommel of his sword, and he resumed his restless stride across the room. "I cannot leave you. Not after what happened the other day."

He left the incident with the idol placed outside the courtyard gate unsaid. No sense in frightening Rebekah further.

"At least warn Iru and come back. I am certain we can manage for a few hours without you," Achsah said firmly.

Rebekah nodded, sniffling as she wiped her face with the edge of her veil. "Please tell my abba about Dov."

Ari exhaled and then nodded, his jaw set in a resolute line. "I will be back before nightfall."

Iru's farm lay farther west than Abba's land. Abba lived the closest to Hebron, while his sons had scattered across the terraced hills, dividing the land between them. She dearly hoped she would see Ari by evening. The sound of horses' hooves beating the ground filled the eerie silence. The muffled crying from Rebekah resumed, and Achsah struggled with how to best comfort her niece. Rebekah had sunk down on the pillows, pulling her knees to her chest in the most undignified pose, swiveling away from Achsah's view.

"Rebekah, I am sorry—" Achsah began, but Rebekah kept her back to Achsah.

Truthfully, she was mightily tired of this fight between them, one that had been circling the past year, about the right way to follow Yahweh. She reached out and gently squeezed Rebekah's shoulder, just as Abba did to her. "I know we have not always seen eye to eye lately, but you are welcome to stay here."

An intake of breath followed by noisy hiccups, but still no response from Rebekah as she blew her nose.

Sensing her niece needed time to reflect and perhaps rest, Achsah left Rebekah alone in the great room. She snatched a basket and headed outside to the bright sunshine and her herb garden, which provided a moment of solace with the wind caressing her hair and the sun warming her back.

But her mind couldn't entirely banish the thought of Dov being ripped away from his home and family. He had insisted on living as close to the enemy as he could, absorbing the Canaanite culture, and in doing so, left the protection and provision of Yahweh. Such a terrifying consequence to stepping outside the will of Yahweh, who understood full well the cost of rebellion.

Just as she found extra herbs in her garden to add to another pot of broth for Abba, soft footsteps padded behind her. She looked over her shoulder to see Rebekah grasping a sprig of rosemary.

"You must think I am a fool," Rebekah said as she reached next for the leeks, yanking them out in a fistful, leaving the dirt clumps to fall onto her elegant tunic. Rebekah kept her swollen, tear-stained face averted even when she handed the dangling clump of leeks to Achsah to place in the basket.

A thousand answers rippled through Achsah, some biting and acidic, some no doubt far too blunt even if couched in a gentle tone, but she had no desire to wield her words like a sword anymore. Was it perhaps time to use her voice to heal instead? She had always prided herself on speaking her mind. To be a truth teller.

It was one thing to stand for the truth, but she needed to show love—just as Othniel had challenged her prior, his advice stoking a low fire within her. One that demanded removing the dross from her life to become a better, stronger person. Nor would she stop telling the truth, for that could hardly be called compassion.

No, she would speak. Rebekah needed to be reminded of Yahweh's grace.

"I have been worried about you for many nights. I know you think I am overbearing and strict, but I truly love you. When you hurt, I hurt. For so many years, you have been my only sister. My closest friend. I wish you knew how much Yahweh loves you. We have been given a precious gift—a chance to receive atonement for our sins and return to Him, since He is a holy God. How can we worship the fallen gods of the Nephilim? Is that not the greatest of betrayals to the One who delivered us from every evil?"

Rebekah didn't move a muscle.

"He loves you," Achsah repeated. "When our earthy abbas pass, He will forever be our Abba...if we let Him."

"I much prefer your version of Yahweh to Grandfather's version," Rebekah said.

"Abba and I worship the same God, but we cannot be in communion with Yahweh if we turn our back on Him. I know Abba can be intense, but he witnessed the depravity of the cultures surrounding us. He battled against King Og and rescued Bel from what we now call Hebron. He does not want to go back to the old life he left behind."

"He is a warrior, not a farmer." Rebekah's mouth tilted into a half smile.

"If he could leave the house, he would be the first one to find your husband and bring him back home."

A sheen lined Rebekah's eyes before she quickly ducked her head and studied the nearest row of herbs. "Yes, Grandfather would have given his life for Dov's. It is a shame because Dov kept trading with the Canaanites and Hittites. He even had plans for the Philistines, promising me that we would bring prosperity to our people."

Something checked Achsah from saying more, even though she felt a lecture building within her along with the desire to ensure that Rebekah fully understood the seriousness of worshiping idols.

As they gathered more leeks from the garden, she couldn't help but admit that Othniel was right. She couldn't control or change Rebekah with endless lectures or impassioned speeches. She couldn't even save her niece or Dov. That burden alone was for Yahweh to bear.

Yahweh, only You can move Rebekah's and Dov's hearts. Save him before it is too late.

Yet something seemed to shift in Rebekah, marked by a quiet thoughtfulness as they continued to work in the garden. Later, after Achsah made a broth soup for Abba from the leeks, he opened his eyes, if only for a moment, his pupils dilated and focused.

"Othniel," he rasped.

"He has left, Abba. Eli too. The men will take Kiriath-sepher as they promised," she told him. "Now open your mouth for me and taste a few drops. It is the best broth I have ever made."

He tried to obey, but some of the soup dribbled down his chin.

Bel, who had sat by his side in the darkened room, removed a cloth from a basket near the pallet and ever so gently wiped Caleb's face. "He has borne the burden of Israel for so long, his heart can no longer stand the weight of it."

"Will he recover?" Achsah dreaded the answer.

"I wish I knew," Bel replied softly. "You must prepare yourself for change. When he passes away, all of Israel will truly flounder." She fingered the curved scars etched into her forearm, her expression distant. "There will never be another man quite like him."

A small voice whispered a rebuttal inside of Achsah. Othniel was like Abba in more ways than she had ever realized. While Abba slept, his pallor increasing by the hour, she brought three bowls of stew for Bel and Rebekah and herself. She tried to eat, but the chunks of lamb tasted like mush with little flavor.

"Still too much salt," Bel said, with a hint of a twinkle in her eyes.

"Indeed." Achsah tried to smile and failed. "It so happens that I like salt."

But any attempts at lightening the sober mood, which fell as shadows gathered within the room, proved futile.

Rebekah placed her bowl down on the mat. "I overheard Dov speaking with strangers two nights before he was taken. Apparently, the raids have extended all the way south and north along the line of the Tribe of Judah."

"We know as much. We may yet have another full-scale war on our hands," Achsah replied, studying her niece.

"Did you know it is purely for revenge? Marduk swears he will have Grandfather's head displayed on the city gates for all to see. And then he will take Hebron next. Did you also know that he is the champion fighter of Kiriath-sepher? It is rumored no man can best him. The city leaders boast he could pull down the sun if he wished to."

Bel stiffened beside Achsah. The older woman clasped her hands, but Achsah saw the tremble of the gnarled fingers. "Marduk is the grandson of Sheshai."

Rebekah startled. "Did you know Marduk's grandfather?"

"Yes," Bel said thickly. "I was a slave in Hebron before Caleb freed the city, and I belonged to the mightiest of the Anak. His name was Sheshai. He had two brothers, Ahiman and Talmai, who hated each other and spent their days conniving to take over the city and supplant the other. They brought death to the city. Never did the sacrifices to Baal cease, nor did the temple celebrations. No one could oppose the brothers. Sheshai reached seven cubits, and his arm was like a mighty oak tree. But I remember most of all the necklaces heaped about his neck, which was so thick it looked like a column. I was a child, only ten years of age. When I grew older, he gave me to the temple." She raised her arm, allowing the sleeve to fall back and completely reveal the path of sorrow marked into her skin. Rebekah gasped.

Achsah tried to swallow past the low burn in her throat at the idea of someone so young and innocent forced to live with such cruelty.

Bel continued, "I thought I knew what a powerful man was until the day Hebron found deliverance. Your grandfather broke through the city gates while blowing on his shofar. I had never seen a man fight like him before, like a whirlwind in the desert. He struck with the venom and the speed of an asp. I could only gape as I crouched on the temple steps. It was as if Yahweh had made him for such a purpose. While others cowered and bowed before Sheshai, Caleb shouted, declaring Hebron belonged to the Lord."

Achsah looked at her friend and saw her in a new light, her auburn hair, long since peppered with white, a testament of years of unfathomable pain and suffering.

"When the city fell and destruction lay all around, he spotted me frozen on those temple steps. I thought he would slay me right there, at the entrance to the Baal's sanctuary—me, a newly consecrated priestess forced to serve the Prince of the Air. But his gaze softened, and he held out his hand and said, 'Come, child.' I was not a child. I was sixteen. Even though I hated men, I took his hand, and he brought me to his wife, Namir. They took me in and taught me about Yahweh. I had no desire to marry, and instead, they let me stay in their house, treating me as one of their own. Such kindness. Such mercy. I had never encountered so much love and safety in a home. Imagine, a former pagan priestess of Baal serving in the house of Caleb the Kenezite. If Caleb and Namir's way of life was evidence of the power of Yahweh, then I wanted to serve Yahweh too." She turned to Rebekah. "Your grandparents showed me how to live again."

"He never chided you, never berated you for your service to the temple?" Rebekah asked with a puzzled frown.

"No. He is a good man, and it grieves him to see the same threat he tried so hard to remove has now returned. Marduk will seek his revenge."

Bel glanced at Achsah, the message silent. Achsah couldn't help but picture Ari smashing the idol and burning the remains far outside the estate walls, not willing that a single fragment taint the household.

Rebekah grew silent again, wrapping her arms about her knees. In fact, the house seemed far too quiet, with most of the men away except for two older male servants now in their seventies. Achsah lit the lamps, pausing long enough to peer out the grilled window, even though darkness smothered the land. The great room felt especially lonesome now that Bel had excused herself to check on Caleb for the night, leaving Achsah alone with her niece.

"I hoped that the men would have returned by now," Rebekah said as she fidgeted with her braid.

Achsah blew out the taper. "If I know Ari, he will have rallied Iru and your uncles to search for Dov. They will find him, rest assured. No one can track better than my brothers, save Abba. It is what they have been trained to do."

Unfortunately, her brothers had so abdicated their duties, refusing to deal with matters at hand, that she worried the situation might already be beyond repair.

Rebekah stood beside Achsah. "I have been replaying the past several weeks in my mind. I fear that someone betrayed Dov. Someone close to him. Several nights prior, I awakened, hearing a rustle in the next room. I believe Dov was searching for something in his ledgers, but he could not find it, whatever it was. His curses kept me awake. I could not make sense of his mutterings at so late an hour. I wish I knew who he feared so much."

"We will be safe," Achsah reassured as she set the smoking taper on a nearby table, but nonetheless, she pulled the shutters inward, shutting out the cooling night air.

When everyone else had finally stumbled exhausted onto their mats, she checked on Abba and pressed a kiss against his forehead. His breathing had evened, deepening too. A good sign.

"I am afraid, Abba. Being your daughter, I do not like to share my fears, and I have tried to believe in Yahweh's provision. Right now, all I can think of is Othniel caught in yet another ambush." She laid her head next to Abba's chest, the way she had as a little girl. Would she lose not one but two men she cared for?

The lamp left by Bel on a table cast gruesome patterns around the room, like those of giants writhing and striking and taking on the shapes of monstrous demons waiting to devour her and Abba.

She hid her face in her abba's chest and tried to pray. She tried to recall each of Abba's miraculous stories: the Nile turning to blood, the Red Sea parting to let the Israelites cross over, the provision of manna and quail and water when it was needed most, Mount Sinai scorched black from the holiness of Yahweh, and Caleb having the supernatural strength at age eighty to cleanse the land from danger.

"Yahweh, I want to believe in Your protection," she whispered into the folds of her abba's tunic. Help me even though I quake with fear. I am the daughter of a warrior, and yet my strength melts. Please protect Othniel and all the men fighting for You. Save Dov. Rescue that girl who was lost so many years ago. Only You can find them. Deliver our land and people. Do not turn from us when we sin against You."

Her prayers grew bolder, more desperate.

"Bring Othniel back to me. I do not want to lose him. I cannot imagine my life without him. And...he listens to me." A sob mingled with a laugh escaped her. "He loves Abba so. He loves You. Help Othniel become the man You have always intended him to be."

Abba shuddered, his breath quickening. She raised her head, tears dripping from her cheeks, sliding down her neck.

"Yahweh," he mumbled. "Yahweh."

Had he heard her prayer? Did he fret as she did that Othniel and the men might face failure yet again?

"Go to sleep, Abba. You need your rest to gather your strength once more. Who else will greet the man who conquerors Kiriath-sepher?"

Abba's answer was no more than a puff of air stirring his white beard. "*You.*"

She understood. He intended for her to greet the winner.

She might not wield a sword, but at least she could do battle with her prayers.

Yet her resolve felt tested with the sounds of every single creak in the house, the wind moaning against the rooftop, along with Abba's snores as he drifted back to sleep. Three women, an empty armory, and only two older servants to keep watch.

She waited in Abba's room until her eyes burned and she could no longer keep herself from falling over. Ari had not returned. As she crept to her chamber, she found Othniel's treasured dagger wrapped in the buttery rawhide. She took it with her, finally allowing herself to stretch out fully on the mat and let sleep claim her while she gripped the cold metal handle, seeking some sense of comfort.

Her last waking thoughts were of Othniel.

CHAPTER EIGHTEEN

The Day Prior

The city of Kiriath-sepher appeared just as formidable during the harsh light of day as it did in the gloom of evening. To Othniel's dismay, a man appeared on top of the city gate, his massive hands gripping the crenellated battlement as he peered over the edge. Sunlight glinted from his helmet and armor as he studied the road. A gate that remained locked at night.

A sliver of unease crept through Othniel as he hid behind a copse of trees dotting the terraced hills. Once again, he couldn't help but wonder if the giants knew that an attack was all but imminent. Could there be a traitor among the Israelites? Someone who fed a constant stream of information to the enemy?

"We are outnumbered. Hopelessly outnumbered," Eli moaned to the left of Othniel. He and several other archers had slithered on their bellies to join Othniel from the hilltop.

"Yes, they outnumber us," Othniel agreed from his position as he studied the landscape below. A well-traveled road led to the massive city gate, framed with twin towers. The thick walls reminded him of his abba's tales of Jericho crumbling into a heap of rubble and dust. More troubling, Kiriath-sepher's massive walls allowed plenty of room from which archers and slingers could unleash their deadly projectiles.

Nine years ago, he and Caleb had foolishly tried to force their way into Kiriath-sepher, boasting of a confidence in Yahweh to take the "city of books." He had falsely assumed that Yahweh would grant a supernatural victory. Only shame came that day. Shame and defeat.

Nine years had stretched into an interminable wait...for Achsah and for the city.

Were my motives wrong nine years ago? Did I try to win for my glory instead of Yours? Why did You make me wait so long?

That last thought—more a grumbling, if he was honest—immediately brought a prick of rebuke.

Nine years had tested his faith, his endurance, and his resolve, bringing a painful refining, like the sword sharpening against the whetstone, smoothing the blade until it was honed into something worthy.

He had no desire to be a blunt, useless weapon.

So he crouched in the same spot with four other men scouting the city walls. To the east, the rest of the men waited in the cypress trees.

After Caleb had ordered the taking of Kiriath-sepher, several volunteers, including Eli, had jostled for control of the group. Othniel had listened to the men argue over the best way to defeat the giants. He waited for the right moment to step in and share what he had learned while scouting over the years.

"That is Caleb's kin," someone had shouted to the few naysayers. "Listen to Othniel."

He wasn't truly Caleb's kin, but to be considered as such brought a rare warmth to his chest. Despite feeling inadequate, he shared his plan for taking over the city.

"Someone needs to lead." Achsah had challenged him with fire in her eyes.

He hated having her anger and disappointment directed at him, but she was right. He needed to do more than scout. To his amazement, Yahweh's timing proved miraculous, as always. The men listened to him, even if his speech faltered. They followed him.

And now three volunteer soldiers watched to see how he would handle Eli's complaint.

"We cannot attack the same way we did nine years ago. We must use subterfuge. If we enter disguised as merchants, especially since Marduk allows a few Israelites to do business with him, we might enter without being discovered. We need a cart and supplies. And a driver, who will pretend to sell his wares. Six men can hide in the back of the cart and dispatch the guards at the gate," Othniel stated.

One soldier protested, "Those same guards will probably check every single cart that enters Kiriath-sepher."

Othniel had thought of that very issue after he vowed publicly to take the city of books. During a sleepless night, he prayed for wisdom.

"We will hide under supplies, and when the moment is right, we will emerge from the cart and force the guards at the gate to surrender. In the meantime, the rest of the Israelites will wait in the nearby hills for the sound of our shofar. When I give the signal, they will advance into the open city and strike down the soldiers."

"What supplies?" demanded Eli, his brows raised.

"Mats and tapestries," Othniel said with a small grin. "I have Elah buying donkeys and a large cart. Elah also promised me he would arrange for several mats. They should arrive any day now."

Elah, the only son of Caleb to do so, had chosen, even if half-heartedly, to join in the melee at the last moment.

"Someone has to watch your back, Othniel, and return you safely to my sister," Elah had said with a snort. "I refuse to see any other man join our family."

The gruff sentiment had warmed Othniel.

"I have heard nothing so foolish in my life. You will get us all killed before nightfall." Eli spat on the ground. Without wine to likely bolster his courage, the weaponsmith wiped away the beads of sweat forming on his forehead.

Although Othniel had included those trustworthy into his circle of confidants, a nudge of caution made him omit Eli from the planning as much as possible. The weaponsmith grated on Othniel, and it wasn't simply the way the man fawned over Achsah when it was convenient. Othniel had no patience for such faltering, especially when the stakes rose.

"Stay behind if you feel safer. I do not want a timid man with me in the cart," Othniel replied coolly before returning his attention to the wall. More guards strolled across the top of the wall. A heavy air of anticipation lay on the land. Waiting. Watching.

"It is a good idea," the other scout beside Othniel said. "They will expect an attack, much in the style of the Father of Destruction. Caleb was not known for his subtlety. It worked in the old days, to rush the enemy and frighten them witless. But today, we need a different tactic."

To Othniel's relief, most of the Israelites, a combination of farmers and older soldiers, agreed with the plan.

"Who made you leader of us all?" Eli protested as he pulled out one of his weapons to inspect the blade. The action felt like a threat, and Othniel felt his muscles tense with anticipation. He needed unity. Not defiance to his leadership.

"We did," the other scout answered quickly before Othniel could reply. "It is a decent plan. You, Eli, have nothing to offer us." The rest of the scouts chimed in, their agreement enough to make Eli to pause.

"Come back another day, when the giants do not roam the city gates," Eli muttered under his breath as he finally sheathed his blade.

"You will not take the city for Achsah?" Othniel demanded, his temper rising. "You will not do it for Israel?"

"No wife is worth such trouble."

The weaponsmith's answer, though muffled, settled like a stone with Othniel.

He heard a sound of rocks and pebbles scraping behind him, like that of a man scuttling away. Good. A fool like Eli would only bring danger and dissension to the ranks.

A breath escaped him, and he turned his focus to the giants at the gate, silently counting the number of men.

"Is she worth it?" the other scout asked, his voice amused as he crawled closer to Othniel to peer at the city below the hill.

"Yes."

Yes, Achsah was more than worth fighting for. He relished the opportunity to prove his devotion to her. When he and the other scouts returned to the Israelites waiting near a copse of trees west of the city, to his delight, Elah waved. Caleb's son had bought perhaps the most rickety cart in all of Israel.

Othniel encouraged the men, who had gathered around him on one lonely hillside, set far enough from Kiriath-sepher to avoid detection. Eli had returned to the group, but he hung on the outskirts of the archers and slingers, his face cast into a petulant mask.

Encouraged by the response of the Israelites, Othniel pointed to Elah's cart. "If Caleb, in his eighties, rescued Hebron, and refused to let fear keep him from doing all that Yahweh asked him to do, then we too can trust in Yahweh's provision. We can trust that He will bring the victory. It is by His Spirit, not our might, that we will find success."

He prayed out loud for the warriors, and when he opened his eyes, Othniel saw that Eli and a few of the others had slipped away, fading into the terebinth trees to make their escape and return to the safety of Hebron. But a hero's welcome would not wait for them in the Levite city. He felt certain of it.

He focused instead on instructing the best warriors, six in all, to cram into the cart. Elah then covered them with an assortment of mats and rugs taken from nearby houses.

Smirking, Elah approached Othniel and thrust something foul into his hands. "A robe to disguise your armor."

"Smells terrible." Othniel raised the rough-spun fabric to his nose and then coughed as he threw the fetid garment over his head and stuck his arms through the wide sleeves.

"I could not have given you a better gift. No one will approach you close enough to see your features, not when you smell like the droppings in a stable." Elah clapped Othniel on the back before placing a gleaming shofar into his hands.

"Do not even tell me how you procured this foul tunic." Othniel tried not to gag as he reached for the ram's horn, which had been buffed to a perfect sheen and secured with an attached leather strap. It brought a comforting weight as he slipped the strap around his neck.

"The robe will remain my secret. But I can share that you hold the very horn used at the march of Jericho." Elah's gaze sobered. "When you sound the alarm, I will rally the rest of the men and we will rush into the city."

Othniel nodded, his throat tight. His abba had marched around Jericho seven times and taken the city. The story had enthralled him as a small boy, and now he would do the same. Still, he missed Caleb. Missed the old general fiercely.

As if sensing Othniel's changing mood, Elah offered one last encouragement. "My abba will be proud of you. Very proud."

CHAPTER NINETEEN

The faint crash sounded far away.

Achsah opened her eyes, seeing only the black curtain of night. She sat up from her mat, disoriented for a moment. Her heart pounded wildly, as if she had been awakened from a nightmare. Yet she couldn't remember dreaming this evening. Straining, she held her breath as she listened for that strange sound to repeat. Nothing. The hair on the back of her neck rose as she felt among the tangled blankets for her dagger. Her fingers wrapped around the gilded hilt, its weight a comfort. In the room's corner, Rebekah snored, her even breaths soft but steady.

Yet something felt wrong. Achsah scanned the room, her eyesight adjusting to the thick darkness. Just as she loosened her grip on the dagger, the scent of smoke—faint, yet still acrid enough to catch her attention—drifted into the room.

She tried to reason why there would be smoke at such an early hour. She threw off the coverlets and rose on unsteady legs to hurry to the hallway. Nothing drew her attention as she stood in the doorway. The narrow hall was nearly pitch black, and the scent of smoke fainter.

Had Bel left a lamp burning? Abba's room, however, which lay farther down the hall, also remained swathed in shadow with no flickering of an oil lamp to pierce the gloom. She glanced into her chamber where Rebekah slept, the mat positioned against the opposite wall. Had she dreamed of fire?

No, she hadn't imagined the smoke. She rushed to the window and flung the shutters open. There, an orange glow lit up the massive courtyard. Fire danced along the roof of Abba's armory and storehouses of grain and barley.

"No!" she cried.

Abba stored grain in an underground cistern covered by a secret door, but he also had built circular storage units close to the armory. A supply kept overflowing, thanks to his sons.

"What is it?" a sleepy voice called from the other side of the wall.

"Fire. The armorer and grain storage are about to collapse if we do not act. Go wake up Bel and Abba. I will find the other servants."

Startled awake, Rebekah scrambled to her feet. She flew to Achsah's side, her hair mussed from sleep.

"We are being invaded!" She grabbed Achsah's arm and shook it. "The giants have come for us."

Achsah gently disentangled from her niece's panicked grip, sounding calmer than she felt. "No need to fear yet. Get Bel and Abba to the cistern near the garden, and I will see to the storehouses. You will find a wooden trap door beyond my patch of rosemary and leeks. If you leave now, you can hide there safely."

She didn't wait for Rebekah to protest. Still holding the dagger, Achsah threw on a wrap and motioned for Rebekah to follow. Without waiting to knock on Abba's door, she pushed it open to find him awake with Bel sitting by his side. Bel's eyes flared open—as if she had fallen asleep, taking care of Abba.

"Achsah," he said, his voice, though reedy, sounding much clearer than the day before. She hated to share the news with him and cause further stress, especially if Bel was right and Abba's heart had failed.

"I need you to take Abba to the cistern," she said to Bel. Without even blinking, the older woman nodded. For years, they had planned in the case of an emergency to use the cistern, which now waited for a fresh supply of barley following the harvest. Abba had built it belowground with a series of stone steps leading into a dry space. A space mostly empty, providing the perfect hiding spot during war.

Rebekah and Bel looped their arms beneath his armpits and pulled him to his feet. He swayed, tipping toward Bel, who grunted as she supported him.

"Can you walk, Abba? I do not think Bel and Rebekah can carry the full weight of you."

"I can walk," her abba assured her, though he nearly buckled.

"We will manage," Bel said as she supported Caleb. "You must join us, after you wake Kez and Bashan."

Achsah fled. She had no intention of going to the cistern. As soon as Bel and Rebekah left the house with Abba, they would smell the smoke. Bel would understand and keep everyone calm.

A prayer left Achsah's lips as she ran toward the servant quarters on the other side of the house. Both men, older, with gray hair, lay fast asleep on their mats.

"To me, Kez and Basham! We have a fire in the courtyard."

Both men woke, their pupils dilated in surprise at the sight of their mistress standing over them.

"Fire?" Kez said as he struggled to rise from the mat, propping up his lean form with an elbow.

"I sent Bel, Rebekah, and Abba to the cistern, but I need you both with me. Grab a weapon. Anything to defend yourself. We will need to get the rainwater from the pithoi."

Kez found only one sword in Abba's room—the beloved bronze blade from countless campaigns. The Israelites who had volunteered to conquer Kiriath-sepher, had taken the rest of the weapons. Unfortunately, Avi had not returned during the night. His mat and rolled blanket remained untouched, shoved against one wall. Was he combing the hills, searching for Dov with Iru and her other brothers?

She rushed to the courtyard with the men close behind. Intent on reaching the pithoi, she dreaded discovering how low the rain water had fallen. Her recent trips to the well were evidence of an already depleted supply. Her only other option might be to beat the flames with a dampened blanket. Yet the sheer heat emanating from the roaring fire told her such a plan would prove futile.

Her heart stuttered as she ground to a halt nearest the pithoi. At the opposite end of the courtyard, a mighty crack echoed as the storehouse roof beams buckled in the flames. Sparks showered in the gusts of wind, landing haphazardly to kindle new fires.

Had the fires started by accident? A lamp left burning and somehow tipped over? Would Abba lose everything? For a moment, she stood paralyzed with indecision and fear warring within her.

But the heat from the blaze scorched her skin, forcing her to move.

"Quick, Bashan!" Rebekah's voice called from the garden that lay to the left of the courtyard. "We must help Achsah retrieve water from the pithoi. We cannot let her fight alone."

Rebekah's frantic gaze collided with Achsah's. Rebekah had left Bel and Abba to the safety of the grain cistern, choosing instead to join Achsah in battling the flames. A flutter of appreciation stirred Achsah.

"I will grab a pole," Bashan rasped as he squared his shoulders, galvanized into action. "We could pull the sections of burning roof to the ground."

A good plan.

Without another moment to lose, Achsah pivoted on her bare feet and rushed toward the pithoi and the collection of water jugs. As she slid off the clay lid, she groaned, her fears immediately realized. The pithoi reached her waist, and only gaping darkness greeted her inside the jar. A trip to the well would also prove too late. The next pithoi held more water. She dipped her water jar, filling it to the brim, and then Rebekah joined her to do the same.

Smoke stung Achsah's eyes and burned her throat raw. As she prepared to battle the fire, something darted away, melting into the shadows of the house. At first, she thought it was Bashan, but he had just yelled at Kez as they used staffs to pull down sections of the storehouse roof.

She thrust the water jug into Rebekah's arm and darted toward the house.

"Achsah! Wait!" Rebekah cried as she struggled to hold both jars.

"I saw someone," Achsah tossed over her shoulder. She pulled out the dagger tucked in her sash and unsheathed it. Pebbles dug into the soles of her bare feet as she moved stealthily forward, her breath coming in noisy gulps. It was one thing to hear of Abba's exploits. It was quite another thing to live a version of them.

She had seen something. Or someone, to be exact.

Had he seen her too? The front section of the courtyard was brightly lit like an oil lamp, but toward the back of the house, darkness provided better coverage. Abba's hours of training men in the courtyard came back to her, and she pressed herself against the wall, blending in further with the night in her indigo tunic.

To her horror, a glimmer of light glanced off the farthermost courtyard wall. Another fire? This one at the back of the house?

Her fingers tightened around the hilt of the dagger as she ducked around the corner. Her immense garden lay several paces ahead, and beyond that, Abba's secret cistern where he waited, hidden with Bel.

A man stood beside the wall, his smoldering bundle of reeds illuminating the sharp planes of his lean face. Holding the torch high, he pushed on one of the shuttered windows, checking for weak points. A final shove with his fist and the shutter broke, leaving the window defenseless to whatever he had planned.

"Haim!" she cried out, rage bubbling to the surface as she stalked forward, forgetting to check herself. "How dare you!"

He whirled, half of his face in shadows, the other half painted orange by the flickering torch clenched in his white-knuckled fist. A growl ripped through him as he opened his mouth, his lips pulling back like a jackal about to lunge.

She had caught him by surprise. Perhaps he thought the family was asleep, or perhaps he thought he could ensure the greatest damage while she and her servants panicked over the storage and armory.

He intended to throw the reeds into her house.

He intended for her and Abba and Bel and everyone else to burn in their sleep.

CHAPTER TWENTY

Othniel held the reins loosely in his hands, even though he felt his fingers tense right before the fight. His pulse beat with a wild rhythm as he pulled up to the massive gates of Kiriath-sepher.

Yahweh, be our guide. Help us in our hour of need. I cannot do this without Your help.

"You there!" a gravelly voice shouted from the watchtower at the top of the city wall. "What do you want?"

Othniel held the reins loosely, his posture slumped. "I have brought rugs and mats for the market."

"I have not seen you before." The guard peered over the mud-brick wall, his hand massive even from a distance. A bow lay strapped behind his shoulder. And Othniel suspected that a supply of large rocks was stacked at the city wall to throw on unsuspecting heads.

"I had no choice but to come. The Israelites took another city, Ashteroth, and are forcing many of us to find safer places for selling."

"Ashteroth?" the guard demanded, his tone scoffing. At least he seemed curious enough to keep talking with Othniel. "They took Ashteroth from the Philistines? Impossible!"

Othniel swallowed past the dryness of his throat, hoping to sound nervous enough to draw the man to trust him. Not a hard task to sound afraid. "Yes, their patriarch ordered one last battle to push the Philistines into the sea."

"Caleb, the dog." The man spat on the city wall. "We know all about him."

"Then perhaps you will allow a poor trader of mats to peddle in information as well?" Othniel squinted at the man. The donkeys in front of the cart twitched their tails, and a few flies circled around Othniel. He tried not to inhale the stench of the itchy garment thrown over his leather armor. The sweltering heat of the sun brought beads of sweat to his forehead, trickling down his neck and dampening the edge of his tunic.

His sword remained hidden beneath the oversized outer garment. If he didn't move too much, hopefully, the outline wouldn't be visible until too late.

The guard on the wall seemed to consider Othniel's offer. Finally, the enormous man nodded, tempted by the promise of news. "You will need to see Marduk. He's at the temple, offering a sacrifice for the victories to come and asking for Baal's protection."

Victories to come?

A breath escaped Othniel as the implication sank in. Marduk had more atrocities planned.

The gate creaked open slowly to reveal a contingent of four guards waiting for Othniel. He flicked the reins, careful to make his expression neutral while the cart rattled behind him.

The rest of his men remained hidden on the nearby terraced hill. As the cart jolted forward, the shofar bumped against his waist, also covered by the foul robe. Mentally, he calculated four guards to disarm. The one guard at the top of the wall would prove a hard target, but Othniel hid a slinger beneath the mats, a man from the tribe of Benjamin famed for his deadly aim.

The Rephaite men, the sons of Anak, known for their long necks, overshadowed the cart as they approached. Othniel tensed when one held out a huge spear, indicating the cart must stop. Othniel flashed him a grin, pleased when the giant, who reached at least six cubits, leaned over, then flinched when he caught a whiff of the foul robe.

The guard's nostrils flared. "I hope your wares smell better than you, merchant. Why not try the services of our innkeepers? Padriya will give you a bath and a clean tunic for a fair price."

The other guards snickered as they kept a healthy distance from the cart.

Othniel kept his tone light. "The fairest Philistine maidens wove these mats and rugs. You will smell nothing but their perfume. But you are right, I have no need for this robe when the sun warms my back."

The nearest guard grunted as he ran a hand down the side of the cart. Othniel peered over his shoulder, one hand on the reins and the other slowly inching toward the hem of his robe.

Any moment now.

"Beautiful rugs," the Rephaite said, with a hint of approval. "Take them to the center of the city where you will find the market. But first, what is this we hear about the Israelites making war with Ashteroth?"

"It is not just Ashteroth that will feel the wrath of the Israelite's God," Othniel replied calmly as he pretended to scratch an itch in his side. He let the reins sag loose in his hand and forced his beating pulse to slow. The guard near the back of the cart frowned as he looked at Othniel for further clarification.

With one smooth motion, Othniel let go of the reins and threw off his robe, tossing it at the nearest guard. "It is here as well."

The next several moments blurred as he sprang forward, pitching himself from the cart with pure instinct guiding each sword thrust. A vicious jab to the guard on the left, who tried to tear the filthy tunic off his head. The guard sank to his knees, clutching his side. In the meantime, the rugs flew upward and six men leaped into position with swords already drawn.

"Up, to your right!" Othniel shouted to the slinger, who spun the leather sling in a hissing arc over his head. The stone whined as it launched, yet Othniel couldn't wait to see if the slinger hit his target. Instead, he dived to his right, parrying with another giant. The swords clashed, the sound ringing throughout the city entrance, the sounds of fighting broken only by the guard on top of the wall tumbling over the edge. The precise aim of the Benjamite slinger had proved all the legends true.

Othniel's sword arm shuddered from contact with the last guard, but he ducked under the outstretched hand of the enemy, lunging at the right moment to pierce the man's exposed thigh. Another thrust of the sharpened blade did its work, slicing through layered leather armor above the enemy's knee. The man stumbled backward with an anguished cry, and Othniel batted the sword out of the man's grip.

Speed counted as much as strength. Fumbling for the leather string at his neck, Othniel snatched the shofar and brought it to his lips. The shofar blasted the call to arms, singing a clear note that ran through his blood.

Today, they would free Kiriath-sepher.

The donkeys, startled by the shofar, jerked forward with their ears pricked. Othniel ran beside the cart and swiped the dangling reins. Snapping them hard, he sent the cart careening into the heart of the city. Three of his men, having finished off the guards, sprinted alongside the cart before grabbing hold of the edges and pitching themselves into it. To his relief, the slinger flung himself into the back of the cart, barely pausing to fish out another round stone to fit in his sling.

"Marduk waits at the temple," Othniel called over his shoulder to the men who rode with him. "Shall we answer his prayers?"

They rattled down the street, keenly aware of the stares from the rooftops of mud-brick homes. The cart wasn't an iron chariot, but it would provide a level of protection. Children darted out of the way, and a few women paused at the edge of the street, dropping their clay water jars when the cart shuddered past, the Israelite warriors brandishing swords.

Another shofar blew, and then another and another, until the city filled with the sound of the Israelites pouring through the city gates like a mighty wave crashing against the shore.

In the center of the city stood the temple to the goddess, its mud-brick walls painted a brilliant white, with smoke billowing from twin bowls of fire set at the bronze-plated entrance. He had never once entered the inner sanctuary of Ashteroth, but Caleb had shared the singular tale of his battle in the incense-drenched interior of the pagan temple. Her followers' appetites for evil were insatiable, and hopefully, Marduk would be easy enough to find.

"Strike the head of the asp without hesitation," Caleb had told his sons during training. Othniel had listened then.

By now, the city dwellers ran in every direction as Othniel's men poured into the streets waving spears and swords. Arrows flew, tearing through the awnings that covered the market wares. Women screamed, and men shouted in panic. The marketplace at the heart of the city appeared like a wasp's nest, with people shoving each other to get out of the way, overturning tables and diving for cover. Elah ran with his sword in hand, accompanied by a hundred men. Eyes bulging and his streaked beard flowing, he resembled a younger version of Caleb.

"The victory belongs to the Lord!" Elah cried as he held his sword aloft.

"It is the Father of Destruction!" another woman shrieked from a merchant table. Someone cut the strings holding the awning in place and she became engulfed in the billowing fabric.

Othniel tore his attention away from the melee behind him. He jerked on the reins and pulled the donkeys to a sharp halt. His men bounded out of the back, eager to rush the temple steps, but Othniel felt someone staring at them from the depths of the temple.

He motioned for the others to head toward the pillars.

A quiver coiled in his chest as he crept into a vast, cool space, his feet making no sound against the paved stone floor. Bowls of incense cast long fingers of smoke into the sickly sweet air. And a bronze statue of Baal, the Prince of the Earth, stood with arm raised as if to strike. On either side of the temple walls, lurid paintings of Baal and his sister Anath dancing together, and later siring a bull, stretched from one end to the other. Thick pillars stout enough to hide a man, placed at even intervals, supported the massive roof above. Black smoke stained the ceiling—a testament to the sacrificial fires burned before the idols. Othniel gulped at the sight, his stride faltering for a moment. A sense of evil, so thick and pervasive, brought nausea bubbling up his throat in the unnatural hush.

A shuffle of sandals whispered from behind one of the painted pillars.

He motioned with two raised fingers, indicating his men to fan out on either side. With his right hand, he lifted the sword into a defensive position and lunged toward the nearest pillar.

But instead of a giant, he found a quivering woman with unbound tresses and a sheer veil covering her features.

She raised both hands in submission and lowered herself to her knees, her linen gown pooling on the stone floor. Jewelry tinkled at her wrists and neck, but her eyes above the veil appeared nearly dead, as if she had witnessed Sheol itself. Was this the priestess?

Her whisper startled him, halting his next step.

"Do not kill me, my lord. Please..." Her hazel eyes scanned him from head to toe. "You are of the tribe of Judah."

He paused, studying her face with no sense of recognition at first, and then shock sent a ripple tingling through him... Where did she learn to speak the Hebrew language with an accurate dialect?

"I am Othniel, son of Kenaz. How do you know we are from that tribe?"

"I heard the faint sound of the shofar and recognized it immediately. I escaped my cell while the priest burned incense. I needed to find you. Someone kidnapped me from my parents nine years ago, when I was only twelve years old. Take me home, I beg you. Let me return to my family."

Before he could answer, she pointed to a door behind the idol. "There is a secret entrance leading out to the courtyard. My master, Marduk, heard of your arrival as soon as the shofar blew. He snuck out that door. It leads through a corridor, past the chambers reserved for the priestesses. If you hurry, you may find him heading toward the city armory and the soldiers' barracks."

Wordless, Othniel could only stare at the priestess.

Was this the child he had searched for, among the others, so many years ago? Now a woman, shaking before him?

He pointed to the slinger, a younger man, before choking out an answer. "Stay with the Benjamite. He will see you home again."

The dead eyes sparked with life and just as suddenly flooded with tears. He saw one teardrop escape, forging a trail of kohl that disappeared behind the veil that marked her as the property of Baal and Marduk. Her thanks was so soft he barely heard it before she ducked from behind the pillar and joined the slinger, hiding behind the Israelite's lean form for protection.

The door to the secret entrance opened, and rooms big enough for a cot lay on either side. Only tasseled curtains provided any sense of privacy. As he jogged down the crimson corridor, he felt the weight of stares from inside those cells. He heard the horrified gasps from women not unlike the Israelite he had just stumbled upon. The incense seemed to burn hotter and thicker, filling the cramped space with an overwhelming stench.

Bile rose again in his throat as he pushed on yet another door, which led to the bright outdoors. He blinked and regained his senses, clearing his nostrils of the foul air.

He was in a courtyard, a garden, reserved for the temple priests. Pots of lush plants lay staggered at intervals and another sculpture, one of a woman, stood in the center. A seductively carved Asherah pole set among an artificial forest of potted palm trees.

At the end of the wall, a man waited, his left hand poised on the gate latch. A very tall man.

With an oiled and braided beard adorned with golden beads, the man stood seven cubits tall, indeed matching the tales spread about him. His bare back and chest, lined with chiseled muscles, gleamed in the sunlight, as if freshly anointed. He slowly turned around, holding a sickle sword, the weapon reminiscent of those Egyptian warriors wielded.

"You are Caleb's son," the man said in a voice that sounded like thunder. Yet hesitation and dread marked the man's demeanor, as if he was deathly afraid and intent on escaping through the back door reserved for men visiting prostitutes in the middle of the night.

Othniel gritted his teeth. *Yes, I am Caleb's kin.*

The presence of Yahweh filled the pagan courtyard with a blinding light, promising Othniel imminent victory, ensuring that the enemy, no matter how fearsome and huge at first sight, actually quaked with fear before the Lord.

Othniel didn't hesitate, nor did he answer. Instead, he raised his sword and charged.

CHAPTER TWENTY-ONE

Achsah had thought that evil lived among the Canaanites and Hittites and the Philistines, tucked away in their sacred groves and Asherah poles. But to come face-to-face with it in a fellow Israelite, somehow that treachery felt even more profane.

"Why would you set fire to my abba's property? Why would you try to kill us?" Her challenge rang in the air.

Haim appeared equally captured by her presence as she was by his. He thrust the torch in her direction, as if he couldn't quite believe his eyes. He stared at her, and then his jaw clenched as he swiveled.

That anger, which had brought her plenty of trouble in the past, now raced through her limbs, urging her to act. She charged him just as he threw the burning torch through the open window.

A scream erupted from her throat as she rushed headlong, the bronze dagger in her hand jutting outward. She ducked just as he swung out at her, and reached upward to slice his chest. The knife rent through the thin tunic. A cry escaped from Haim as he stumbled backward, shock registering on his narrow features.

She had only grazed him, but the rage shining in his eyes proved she dare not miss again. He lashed out at her, snagging her wrist in his hand, twisting it painfully until she cried out. Her dagger fell to the ground with a clatter.

Spittle flew from his mouth. "You ask why I burn your land? Your abba shamed my grandfather and ensured that Eshkol would never enter the Promised Land. Nor did my family get the full allotment of the land promised to each family among the tribe. We are of the tribe of Judah, not your abba, who will always be a Kenezite."

She bit back a wince as he continued to push back on her wrist, stepping behind her and forcing her arm at an unnatural angle against her back.

"Your grandfather made his choices, as have you. Yahweh honors those who obey Him," she panted while struggling against him. "Was it you who left the idol at our gate?"

She twisted her head to see his expression.

He finally ground out, "No, I did not."

Who left it then? Was it a threat or a warning?

"Haim! Let my daughter go."

Achsah raised her head to see her abba standing upright, with Bel close behind. He placed one palm against the wall of the house, breathing hard. But never had Achsah seen her abba appear so fierce. How hard had it been for him to climb the steps of the cistern? Had he mustered his last vestige of strength to save her? A strangled sob escaped her.

"Caleb!" Haim exclaimed, but he made no move to release Achsah's wrist. Instead, his grip only tightened until she cried out loud. "I will take from you what you took from my family all those years ago. I should have this farm. I should own Negev and everything surrounding it."

"It is not too late to serve Yahweh." Abba waved away Bel's supporting arm and put one foot in front of the other, albeit slowly. "Be free of this bitterness. It will not serve you."

"I make my own path," Haim retorted. "I have had no choice but to seek my interests, since no one else has cared for my family."

Haim's anger was misplaced. A shame that the grandson echoed the grandfather's rebellion. A sound cracked in the air and suddenly Achsah felt her wrist released as Haim crumpled to the ground, face-first.

Strong arms looped around her, pulling her to her feet. She heard her servant Kez's reassuring voice in her ear. "My lady, I believe this man will suffer quite a headache in the morning. Perhaps that will deflate his enormous ego, if but for a moment."

"My thanks." She smiled at Kez, her relief at seeing him making her shoulders slump. She straightened, remembering Haim's intent to harm her home. Pointing to the open window, she said, "The house may be on fire. I saw Haim throw a torch inside it."

Rebekah and Bashan rounded the corner, their gazes caught by the sight of the man lying prone at Achsah's feet.

Kez glanced at Haim's back, perhaps reassured by the sight of the enemy, vanquished for the moment. "I will check on the interior." He bowed to her and to Abba before jogging away.

She stepped over Haim's limp arm and headed toward her abba.

"Abba!" She wrapped him in a big hug, noting how frail he felt in her arms. He had lost far too much weight this past month.

"My heart felt as though lightning had struck it when I heard you scream. How could I let my beloved daughter come to any harm?"

"But your chest? How could you walk?"

He rested his forehead against hers. "My chest hurts. My days are shortening like each breath I take, but perhaps Yahweh gave me just enough strength for this day."

Bel looped her arm around him, allowing him to lean on her. "What will you have us do, my lord? Do you want to rest?"

"Bah!" he cried, "I have done nothing but rest for days on end. Take me to the storehouse you were moaning about earlier."

Bashan cleared his throat. "My lord, perhaps we should tie Haim in case he awakens?"

The storehouse burned to the ground, with ashes and embers whirling in the wind, floating higher and higher to the pink sky. The first blush of morning tinted everything in hues of rose, and with it, enough light to see the extent of the blackened destruction.

Achsah wept when she saw Abba's beloved armory completely burned to the ground, along with the grain and barley storehouses. But Abba, though pale, didn't appear as fazed as she thought he might be.

"Yahweh will make a way for us as He always has," he told her. "What has He not provided these past years? He gives, and He takes away. We will still praise Him."

She wiped away her tears with her soot-covered hands. All their efforts to combat the fire had failed, but at least the house stood. As she helped her family clean up the courtyard, with Haim now secured, thanks to Bashan, and slowly waking despite an enormous bump on the back of his head, her thoughts drifted to Othniel. Did he survive the night as well?

Haim glowered at her, wiggling to free himself of the restraints. She ignored him, his threat now impotent. He refused to answer any of her questions about his trading with the Canaanites. Perhaps one of his cohorts had placed the idol to frighten her and Abba away from Hebron. The frightful thought snaked through her, bringing an anxiety she had never known. Would Yahweh grant Othniel victory on this occasion? Nine years ago, her abba nearly lost his leg because of the giants. Would Othniel fare worse? Was it possible one of the Israelites would betray him?

As she cleaned the courtyard with her family, now facing the ruins of lost wealth, nothing seemed so important as seeing Othniel's face again. The dark hair, the broken nose, the quiet hush he brought with him whenever he stepped over her threshold. The way he challenged her with a hint of teasing and compassion. Iron sharpening iron, he had said.

What if she lost him forever, before she told him that she loved him? How could she live without the man who had been so much a part of her life? She would be bereft without his daily presence. She had disregarded him, sometimes resented his closeness to Abba, and had even taken issue with his silence. But where could she find a stalwart heart, like Abba's? Where could she find a more patient man, who, as Abba had stated, listened to her. Where could she find another man who loved Yahweh wholeheartedly?

Fear fought to overcome her, threatening to consume her as the fire had consumed the armory. A ragged sigh escaped her as she swept away the lingering ash from the path leading to her front door. She couldn't control the outcome of her life, no matter how hard she tried. Like the Israelites, she must trust in Yahweh's goodness, even when life brought crushing disappointments. She prayed as the morning sun flooded the courtyard with fresh light, bringing with it fresh hope.

CHAPTER TWENTY-TWO

Two days later, Iru marched through the gates of Abba's land with his servants. He dismounted from his horse, brushing the dust from his tunic, his gaze lingering on the ruins of the courtyard. Achsah watched him speak with Bashan and Kez.

To her delight, Ari returned, looking worn out from his days spent hunting for Dov in the surrounding villages. The men, however, appeared grim as they gestured to the lost armory.

Her rejoicing at seeing her guard and brother safe soon turned to swift dismay. Where was Dov? She welcomed Iru into the main room. He blinked with surprise when he saw Abba sitting upright again, cushioned with many pillows and waving away Bel's bowls of soup with an irritated smile.

"Abba, you have returned to us."

"I never left you," Abba said, resembling his old peevish self. "Did you find Dov?"

Iru paused before sitting down cross-legged before Abba. He stiffened when he saw his daughter, Rebekah, tiptoe into the room, her face wan.

"We do not have Dov. I fear it is worse than we thought. He was not captured, as we had been told. He ran away to join with the Philistines. Dov is a traitor, selling secrets, even to the sons of Anak.

And he sold our people, even if a few at a time, to our enemy. He is not just a merchant, Abba, he is a slave trader."

Rebekah gasped, covering her mouth with her hands. "No, that cannot be true!"

"It is true," Iru added grimly. "I did not realize the extent of Dov's treachery. His abba swears he has nothing to do with his son's crimes, but we will test those claims in the days to come."

"You will be interested to know that Haim paid us a visit, actually set our property on fire," Achsah added. "Perhaps Haim will answer your questions. He refuses to answer mine."

Iru leaped to his feet and withdrew his sword so fast it sang. His eyes bulged as he looked wildly about the room. "Show me the murderer and I will end his life right where he stands."

"He is sitting, tied at the moment," Achsah said wryly.

"Sit down, Iru," Abba said, sounding tired again. Iru obeyed, though he did not sheath his blade. "I do not want you to kill him."

Iru scowled at the command. "I will speak with him. I heard rumors that Dov had accomplices, including younger Israelites, working with him. But we heard from the village of Jattir that Dov was the one to lead the operation."

Achsah remembered the slave caravan that she and Bel, Ari, and the other guard tried to flee. Perhaps that slave caravan had been intended for Dov's home after all.

"I did not know," Rebekah said as she sank down beside her abba. "Dov hardly came home, but I thought it was for a noble pursuit. I thought—" She bit her bottom lip with her teeth and averted her gaze.

"I will kill him," Iru stated again, his voice grating like a millstone. "And Haim, for that matter."

For once, Iru had been moved enough by tragedy to threaten action. He would kill Haim before the sun set this very day. Not so long ago, Achsah would have readily agreed with her brother's desire for vengeance.

Now, she shook her head. "Why not send Haim to Hebron for justice? If he is guilty of slave trading, the priests will ensure that he remains locked up. We do not have proof other than that he burned our storehouse. Allow the city of refuge, Abba's former city, to act as Yahweh intended. Yahweh will bring justice, and if Haim can be redeemed, then the priests and Yahweh will see to it. That way, the blood of revenge will not stain your hands."

There was a season to fight and a season to seek peace. She couldn't let Iru's bloodlust separate him from Yahweh. Already, her brother and niece had wandered too far. Even though her heart cried out for retribution and the freedom to unleash her anger to the fullest, she couldn't deny the wisdom of letting cooler heads prevail.

"Wise words, Achsah. We bring justice when necessary, and mercy when needed," Abba agreed from his pile of pillows. "I knew when Yahweh commanded me to release Hebron that I would not regret it, not when the priests promised to put that city to good use."

"Will you hunt for Dov?" Rebekah asked as she folded her hands in her lap to control the visible trembling.

"I must," Iru stated. "For your sake and mine. Until I find your husband, you will return home with me." Then he cupped his daughter's cheek. "Rebekah, truly, I am sorry. I thought only of the comfort Dov would bring you. I should not have handed you over to such a man."

"Nor should I have agreed, even though I saw things that were not right. I did not want to believe he could hurt me," she whispered.

A bitter end, to be a bride without a groom.

Iru rose to his feet and Achsah joined him. He glanced down at her, his expression surprisingly contrite, considering his former pride. "I was wrong to dismiss the idol placed by the door. I thought it nothing, but now I realize it was intended to frighten our family."

"Haim says he had nothing to do with it," Achsah said as she studied her brother.

Iru leaned forward, his voice low. "I shall have many questions for both Dov and Haim when I see him. You did well to save the house and keep Rebekah safe."

Rare praise coming from Iru.

"I am grateful Yahweh led her to our door. I needed her just as much as she needed me."

Iru blinked after a pause. His throat bobbed with effort and then he sheathed his sword. "Lead me to Haim, and I will escort him to Hebron." He added after a noisy exhale, "I will obey you, Abba."

"It was Achsah's idea," Abba said, closing his eyes. "Give the honor to her."

Already Abba had tired and now would need sleep. She felt somehow that this reprieve of improved health had been a gift. A blessing. But who knew how long it would last?

Iru tilted his head in a show of respect to Achsah. "I hope a man of valor will come to claim you, Achsah. It would appear that the lady made of iron guarded Abba after all."

There was not one hint of disrespect in his tone, and she couldn't help but grin in return, especially when she caught the rare twinkle in his eye. But when she said goodbye to Rebekah, that sparkle changed to tears.

"I will always be here for you, Rebekah, no matter what happens," Achsah promised after an embrace.

Rebekah squeezed Achsah's hand, her voice raspy. "And I, you."

Something had changed in Rebekah during her visit. A softening. A humbling. It brought Achsah a sense of peace to realize that broken relationships could be whole once again. Yahweh would draw Rebekah to Him in His manner and choosing.

Two long days passed. Still no sign of the victor. Had trouble occurred and Kiriath-sepher, once again, proved a trap for the Israelites? Achsah could scarcely sleep, even when holding Othniel's precious dagger at night.

The more she thought of that dagger, the more she realized he truly cared for her. Yes, she would bring Negev, the desert inheritance, a prize enough to entangle any man. But Othniel, ever shy, had come to her over and over, despite his fears. He had borne her sharp personality with good humor. And he had been the first to volunteer to fight for her hand. He had told her of his love in a hundred ways except for words.

She sat by the window in her spare moments, her loom long forgotten. The sounds of rebuilding the storehouse could hardly distract her. Bel even teased that Achsah could not tear her gaze from the gate. Hours passed, long and painful, as she waited in silence.

And then it happened. The courtyard door swung open, rousing nearly everyone from their tasks.

A dust-coated man limped through, his gait exhausted but sure. She ran from the window, past Abba who reclined on his pillows, barely missing Bel who brought a tray of honeyed pastries studded with nuts, past the other servants and Ari who grinned at her, and flew out the door to come to a skidding halt in front of the one man, the only man she had ever truly wanted.

A bruised Othniel stood in front of her, caked with dirt and smelling like...

But she didn't care.

He raised his head to meet her gaze, his eyes flaring with delight. He opened his mouth to speak. Before he could say anything, she flung her arms around him and pressed her lips firmly against his, stealing any speech he might utter. The kiss expressed everything she longed to say...her love for him. Her joy in seeing his return. It contained everything she had held close to her heart.

He froze beneath her touch, and then, just like the previous fire in her courtyard, an ember lit within him and he kissed her thoroughly in return, chasing any lingering doubt away. Indeed, he kissed her for a very long time.

"You slayed the giants," she breathed, when she finally pulled away from him long enough to get a gulp of air.

He nodded, a slow grin carving twin lines into his whiskered cheeks. "For you and Israel, yes. But mostly for you."

A laugh escaped her. She knew he was teasing. But when she laid her head against Othniel's chest and heard the quickening thump of his heart and felt his arms band about her, she thanked Yahweh for giving her a man who loved his people and Yahweh so completely. And one who loved her enough to wait for her heart in return.

CHAPTER TWENTY-THREE

Four Months Later

Achsah held Othniel's hand as they entered the courtyard. Her husband squeezed her fingers. "I am not sure I can ask your abba for such a request."

She chuckled at Othniel's shyness. He had slain one of the most famous giants, Marduk, and captured a city of giants that had eluded her abba. Yet, today, following the heady celebration of the most wonderful wedding in the history of the tribe of Judah, and a subsequent move to a tiny mud-brick house at the edge of the desert near a wadi, her new husband could not ask for a field of wheat to sustain them while they lived in Negev. A field they needed dearly. For the past several weeks, they had tried to do everything within their power to shape the homestead into something livable. When she asked to return to Hebron, to see her abba, Othniel had readily agreed, even if it meant leaving his latest irrigation project.

"Abba loves you, Othniel," she jested, tugging at his hand. "And he will be pleased that I am so pleased by you."

Othniel palmed the back of his neck, his face burning bright red, but his answering grin brought a spark of joy to her. She envisioned many happy years being married to this man. But…but, sometimes, his reticence needed to be honed into something that would serve him better.

"Iron sharpening iron," she whispered to herself. She would help her husband claim what was rightly his.

"What did you say?" he asked, raising a dark eyebrow.

"Nothing," she answered with a playful smirk. "Just come with me and let me do the talking."

Abba remained in his chambers these days, his strength slowly ebbing. Bel took over the household duties, serving as a nurse and as Caleb's housekeeper.

The older woman greeted Achsah with a hug, her smile soft. "My darling girl, come back to visit us at long last."

"Four months, Bel."

But in the four months, something had changed for Achsah, and she could hardly wait to share her news, if only she could keep the nausea at bay.

Her hand strayed to her middle, which remained flat enough, but Bel caught the gesture and gasped. Joy flitted across the older woman's features while Achsah raised a finger to her lips.

"I will not say a word," Bel murmured, "but your abba will be so delighted. He has spoken of nothing else but his children. And now he can truly rest, seeing you, and with child, no less."

The immense joy of bringing a new life into the world was tempered with the reality that another would leave soon. Abba, like an old lion, had watched over his pride until, at long last, he had come to the end.

She sank beside Abba to kneel next to his mat. Othniel and Bel entered the room and knelt with her. Abba's translucent skin revealed the blue veins tracing a path along his arms, like the winding rivers and desert paths of Israel.

"Abba," she choked out, leaning forward to raise that frail hand to her lips. She pressed a kiss against the dry skin.

His eyes fluttered again, stirring him from his slumber. "Daughter."

"I have come to share good news. I am with child. Perhaps a strapping son to bring honor to you and Othniel."

"A daughter," Abba breathed. "A daughter would be fine enough."

Tears fell as she held her abba's hand, stroking his withered fingers. "I shall be very pleased to share with her, or him, all the stories you have told me."

He smiled slowly, as if the act drained too much energy. And though she wanted nothing more than to bury her head into the folds of his tunic and weep, she knew she must speak on behalf of those she loved.

"My beloved abba, we ask for fields. We cannot live without grain or barley and secure the desert for the tribe of Judah. Will you give Othniel what he needs to survive in the Negev? We promise to protect the land with our lives."

"Done," Abba breathed.

She kissed his hand again, her tears falling freely. "And Abba, will you give us the springs to water our livestock?"

A bold request. One that drew a sharp gaze both from Bel and Othniel. Women never asked for land. They most certainly never asked for water rights. To do so would give her and Othniel tremendous control over the area, but it would also secure her husband's future. And that of her child.

"Done." Abba sounded so feeble, but Achsah could have sworn that his eyes flickered with amusement.

"See, I told you, Othniel. You only needed to ask Abba." She turned to her husband, dashing discreetly at the tears pooling in her eyes.

But Othniel wasn't looking at her. His face sobered, and she quickly shifted to examine her father again.

A reedy sigh escaped from Caleb. "My children, never stop loving Him. Yahweh promised me that Othniel, with my sons, will protect Israel. I dreamed...I dreamed..."

He closed his eyes, as if caught in that vision that had taken his breath away. Prickles skittered across her skin as she recalled her dreams not so long ago. Of a man standing beside her, to guard Hebron and all of Israel against the gathering storm and against the rise of idols.

"He is so tired these days," Bel murmured. "The lion finally sleeps."

Achsah and Othniel sat by Abba's side, each holding his hand and whispering of their love to him, letting him at last go into the fading light that called him home. Her brothers and Rebekah returned, each one equally moved as they said their farewells to the great general, who had guided Israel. And when dawn broke, Joshua's and Moses's faithful servant had passed from one world into the next.

She wept that morning, comforted only by Othniel's arms about her and his hot tears falling upon her neck as he grieved with her. He held her, murmuring of his love. And when he could offer no more declarations, he kissed her wet cheeks and then her lips.

The family buried Abba in one of the nearby caves outside of Hebron. Abba would forever be a part of the land he had fought to secure.

After the period of mourning, Achsah said goodbye to her family and invited Bel to return with her. Bel, thankfully, readily agreed to live in Negev and act as a grandmother. As she oversaw the packing of the donkeys for the long journey, Achsah spied Iru and Rebekah waiting for her in the courtyard.

"Where is your husband?" Rebekah asked as she glanced about the courtyard.

"He wanted a moment alone." The more days Achsah spent with him, the more she unraveled his unique personality. His need for silent contemplation gave him a strength she was only beginning to understand. A quiet man but by no means a shallow one. And a man she could trust implicitly.

With a tremulous smile, Rebekah handed Achsah a satchel filled with freshly baked loaves. "I will visit to help with babe as soon as I can."

Although no one had located Dov, Rebekah had rediscovered peace in Hebron and safety within its walls. More importantly, she had returned to all that Abba had taught her.

Achsah embraced her niece, grateful that Rebekah had found some measure of joy again. How good it would be for her, Bel, and Rebekah to fuss over a baby. "You would be most welcome."

Iru cleared his throat. He offered no hug, but he jerked his head toward the terraced hills outside the courtyard where Othniel waited on a nearby hilltop. "Your husband will make a fine leader. I told him that whenever he needs me, I will come."

Wonder at Iru's change filled Achsah as she said goodbye to Iru and Rebekah and went to join Othniel. She saw his strong outline on a nearby bluff. Feet braced, arms folded across his chest. A picture of strength. Climbing the hill, and feeling winded because of her condition, she joined him, huffing for air.

He smiled when he saw her and wrapped an arm around her waist to draw her close. Othniel glanced down at her, his expression tender. With one look, he could melt her.

"Are you ready to say goodbye?" he finally asked, his voice husky.

She nodded, her throat too tight to speak. Leaving Hebron and burying Abba felt like losing a piece of herself, yet she couldn't deny that the desert called to her. Life waited among the craggy rocks and desolate stretch of land bordering Egypt. Her wadi, though strange and full of danger, held so much promise, especially with her husband and a child by her side.

Othniel turned his gaze to the faint blue horizon. "I cannot imagine no longer sitting in the great house, listening to him speak of the old battles and of Yahweh. He was family to me."

"You were always his son, Othniel. Always. He believed in you. Loved you."

Othniel's eyes were shimmering when he looked at her. A ragged sigh escaped him. "I pray that I never let either of you down."

"You never will, my love."

Caleb's dream of Othniel leading Israel...well, she dared not bring it up quite yet. One day soon, she would speak to him of the need to guide the tribes. Her husband would prove to be as tempered and wise a man as Joshua, and as fierce and loyal as Caleb. Othniel had been shaped for something far greater than either of them could understand at the moment. Abba's vision confirmed the ones given to her.

Her husband pressed a kiss to the top of her head. They stood together in comfortable silence, surveying the sweeping Promised Land. A hillside covered in brown soil and littered with far too many rocks, weeds, and asps. But to her, and to Othniel, it was truly a land flowing with milk and honey. The land in which she would raise her children to know the freedom that only Yahweh could bring.

Storm clouds gathered on the horizon, bringing a cool wind. She shivered with the breeze, grateful for the firm arm about her. Together, with Yahweh's help, they would face the future without fear.

FROM THE AUTHOR

Dear Reader,

I knew I wanted to write about giants when asked to contribute to the Mysteries & Wonders of the Bible series. Many of us have heard of David's fight with Goliath and of the mighty men of old, the Nephilim, who existed before the Flood, but Othniel's story is lesser known, although equally important.

The Old Testament describes a race of men, both spiritually oppressive and physically intimidating. King Og had an iron bed of nine cubits—appropriate for a man needing fourteen feet of length and six feet of width for comfort.

Interesting archeological research hints at settlements built for extraordinarily large individuals with the remains of houses significantly larger than those in other archeological sites. The Gilgal Refaim, otherwise known as the Wheel of Giants, can be toured today near Golan. Some scholars wonder if the Wheel of Giants represents the final burial spot for the infamous King Og slain by Caleb.

The Israelites met Og at Bashan, known as the "place of darkness," which may also mean "the mountain of the gods." If Sinai represents God's glory, Bashan became synonymous with evil. Although Othniel routed out the giants in Kiriath-sepher, David, too, would face a remnant of the giants known as Goliath. Repeatedly, the

Israelites faced hatred and the threat of destruction, relying on a holy God to rescue them or send a deliverer. David's last battle with the giants, as an older king, would likely have killed him but for the intervention of his mighty men.

Fantastical tales of giants abound all throughout the world, some rooted in archeology such as the massive Stone Age tools recently discovered in England, and others considered a fabrication, such as the mythological stories of redheaded cannibal giants who plagued the Paleolithic Native Americans. When separating truth from legend, the Old Testament makes it clear that the Israelites encountered a tribe of fearsome men who were compared to the Nephilim.

Is it possible that some kind of genetic mutation created men of unusual size? The most well-known genetic condition associated with excessive growth is caused by overproduction of growth hormone. This can result from a noncancerous tumor on the pituitary gland, leading to an excess of growth hormone secretion. The condition that develops before the closure of the growth plates in the bones is called gigantism, while after closure, it is referred to as acromegaly. It's crucial to note that these conditions are relatively rare.

Scholars are divided as to whether the giants were truly the Nephilim or described as such to give the impression of a terrifying enemy. Scholars continue to debate who the Nephilim actually were. Some say the sons of Seth (Adam's son) intermarried with Cain's daughters. Others suggest something far more chilling—fallen angelic beings intermarrying with humans.

Although Caleb and Joshua trusted that they could take the new land as promised by Yahweh and settle it despite the threat of the sons of Anak, unfortunately, the other ten spies refused to enter the

Promised Land. Caleb and Joshua fought their enemies despite being over eighty years old.

While some may question why God called Caleb and Joshua to claim the land, it's important to clarify that the patriarch Abraham purchased the area around Hebron from Ephron, the Hittite, for the price of four hundred silver shekels (Genesis 23) as a family tomb. This transaction marks the first parcel of land owned by the Jewish people in the Promised Land.

Genesis also records the burial of Abraham, Isaac, Jacob, Sarah, Rebekah (from the Bible, not from Achsah's story), and Leah near the area. Jewish tradition also notes that Adam and Eve are buried near Hebron.

In the years that followed, the Canaanites took possession of Hebron, formerly known as Kirjath-arba, which translates to the "city of four," perhaps referencing the former rulers. Interestingly, Hebron means "friend." Caleb graciously allowed Hebron to be returned to the Levite priests to act as a sanctuary city that would provide justice for those accused of murder or manslaughter. The city served as a protection against revenge. Years later, Samuel crowned David as the king of Israel at Hebron. Today, people can tour Hebron, one of the oldest cities in the world.

It did not take long for the Israelites to abandon the way of worship so carefully prescribed by Moses. Archeological digs have encountered a blending of worship of Yahweh with Asherah, merging both religions despite Moses's and Joshua's warnings to avoid syncretism, the term for blending different religions and beliefs. The book of Judges describes the Israelites repeatedly absorbing the culture and religions around them.

Othniel, as the first judge, led the people for forty years until his death. Later came Ehud, ending with Samuel, the last judge and the first prophet before the arrival of the kings. Unfortunately, only a remnant of the Israelites kept the truth consistently alive during the period of the judges and kings.

Although little is said about Achsah, some key verses offer insight into her character and that of Othniel's. She stayed with her abba and never married until, at last, he offered her hand in marriage to whoever slayed the giants and freed the city. Her father esteemed her highly, both in her name and in the inheritance of a massive swath of land.

The bride had no qualms asking for land and water rights—an unheard of request from a woman. Caleb's ready acquiescence demonstrated his great love for his daughter. I couldn't help but imagine a strong woman who loved Yahweh but didn't mind bucking tradition.

Othniel and Achsah's story still resonates today. Othniel faced danger and relied on God's strength to accomplish what others viewed as impossible. Othniel's and Caleb's faithfulness demonstrates that we must trust God when He asks us to do difficult things. He gives us strength when we have none. God also demonstrates a willingness to forgive when we repent, as seen in Othniel's deliverance of the Israelites in Judges, chapter three.

Finally, only God can bring lasting peace. No matter how troubling or broken our circumstances, He alone is our protector and defender.

Blessings,
Jenelle Hovde

TOWERING FIGURES OF FAITH: EXPLORING THE GIANTS IN GOD'S WORD

By Reverend Jane Willan, MS, MDiv

The Bible is filled with captivating stories that have intrigued readers for centuries. Among these narratives are the accounts of giants—mysterious beings of great stature and strength who walked the Earth in ancient times. As people of faith, exploring the mystery of these giants can enrich our understanding of God's Word and the historical context in which these stories unfold.

The first mention of giants in the Bible appears in the book of Genesis, where they are referred to as the Nephilim. Genesis 6:4 states, "The Nephilim were on the earth in those days—and also afterward—when the sons of God went to the daughters of humans and had children by them. They were the heroes of old, men of renown." This cryptic passage has sparked much debate among scholars and theologians.

One theory, suggested by the Jewish historian Josephus in the first century AD, is that the Nephilim were the offspring of human women and angels who had turned away from God. Josephus wrote, "For many angels of God accompanied with women, and begat sons that proved unjust, and despisers of all that was good, on account of the confidence they had in their own strength" (*Antiquities of the Jews*, Book 1, Chapter 3).

However, not all scholars agree with this interpretation. Some interpret the "sons of God" in Genesis 6 as referring to the godly descendants of Seth, while the "daughters of men" are seen as the unrighteous descendants of Cain. They see the emergence of the "giants" as a symptom of the moral and spiritual decline of the time rather than focusing on them as a separate race of beings or supernatural entities.

Regardless of their origin, the Nephilim were depicted as mighty warriors, "the heroes of old, men of renown" (Genesis 6:4). Their presence on Earth was one of the reasons cited for God's decision to send the Great Flood during Noah's time, as it was believed that their existence threatened the purity of the human bloodline and the fulfillment of God's plan for humanity.

Giants are also mentioned in other parts of the Old Testament, particularly in relation to the Israelites' conquest of the Promised Land. In Numbers 13, when Moses sends spies to scout out Canaan, they return with reports of encountering the Nephilim, who are described as being of great stature. The spies exclaim, "We saw the Nephilim there (the descendants of Anak come from the Nephilim). We seemed like grasshoppers in our own eyes, and we looked the same to them" (Numbers 13:33).

This account highlights the Israelites' fear and intimidation when facing these formidable foes. The presence of giants in the Promised Land was seen as a significant obstacle to the Israelites' possession of the land God had promised them.

Other notable giants mentioned in the Bible include King Og of Bashan, whose bed was described as thirteen feet long and six feet wide (Deuteronomy 3:11), and the Anakites, a race of giants living in Canaan (Numbers 13:28). These accounts reinforce the idea that giants were a real and significant presence in the ancient Near East.

While the physical descriptions of giants in the Bible are certainly impressive, it is important to consider their spiritual significance. Theologians emphasize that the presence of giants in the Promised Land tested the Israelites' faith and trust in God, serving to reveal the true states of their hearts and minds.

The story of David and Goliath, perhaps the most famous account of a giant in the Bible, serves as a powerful reminder of how faith in God can overcome even the most daunting challenges. Goliath, a Philistine warrior who stood over nine feet tall and was clad in heavy armor (1 Samuel 17:4-7), struck fear into the hearts of the Israelite army. However, young David's unwavering faith in God and his skilled use of a sling and stone led to a stunning victory, showcasing how God's power can be manifested through the most unlikely of individuals.

To fully appreciate the significance of giants in the Bible, it is essential to consider the historical and cultural context in which these stories were written. Biblical archaeologists have sought to shed light on this by examining ancient Mesopotamian texts that contain similar narratives. By examining cuneiform tablets and other archaeological finds, researchers are trying to connect these stories to the wider myths of the Near East. This helps us better understand how people in the ancient world saw these legendary creatures, and how they fit into their beliefs and culture.

The discovery of the Epic of Gilgamesh, a Mesopotamian epic poem, has led to understanding that the biblical accounts of giants may have been influenced by the oral traditions and legends of the surrounding cultures. Gilgamesh is described very much like the giants in the Bible. He was a heroic giant, possessing superhuman strength and courage. He was thought to be two-thirds god and one-third human, making him an unparalleled warrior and leader. The story of Gilgamesh explores themes of heroism, friendship, the quest for fame, the fear of death, and the search for eternal life.

Just because giants are found in mythology as in the Bible does not diminish the importance or integrity of the biblical narratives. Rather, it highlights the way in which God's revelation to humanity often intersects with the cultural milieu of the time.

Another scholarly interpretation suggests that the giants in the Bible might have been men of great power, influence, and military might as well as those of enormous stature. Moreover, the English word "giant" as used in the Bible is translated from Hebrew words denoting those same qualities or attributes. This view adds depth to how we understand giants in the Bible. It pushes us to think not just about their physical size, but also about what they meant for the society and spiritual world of that time.

The enduring mystery of the giants in the Bible serves as a testament to the timeless power of these ancient stories to capture our imaginations and inspire us to seek a closer relationship with our Creator. The fascination with the biblical giants reflects the human interest in stories of beings and heroes beyond the ordinary, a theme that spans cultures and epochs in human history. Exploring the diverse perspectives and scholarship surrounding these narratives can only serve to enrich the study of the Scriptures and deepen an appreciation for the complexity and richness of God's Word.

The presence of giants in the Bible can serve as a metaphor for the spiritual battles we face in our own lives. Just as the Israelites had to confront the giants in the Promised Land, we too must face the "giants" of fear, doubt, and temptation that threaten to inhibit or destroy our spiritual growth and relationship with God. By placing our trust in Him and relying on His strength, we can overcome these challenges and emerge victorious.

JENELLE HOVDE

Jenelle writes gentle stories filled with redemption and hope. She lives in Florida with her husband, close to the ocean for quick writing breaks. When she isn't scribbling on scraps of paper, you can find her in used bookstores perusing antique romance novels and historical journals. Her other biblical fiction novels with Guideposts include: *The Dream Weaver's Bride: Asenath's Story*, *A Harvest of Grace: Ruth and Naomi's Story*, and *The First Daughter: Eve's Story*.

REVEREND JANE WILLAN, MS, MDiv

Reverend Jane Willan writes contemporary women's fiction, mystery novels, church newsletters, and a weekly sermon.

Jane loves to set her novels amid church life. She believes that ecclesiology, liturgy, and church lady drama make for twisty plots and quirky characters. When not working at the church or creating new adventures for her characters, Jane relaxes at her favorite local bookstore, enjoying coffee and a variety of carbohydrates with frosting. Otherwise, you might catch her binge-watching a streaming series or hiking through the Connecticut woods with her husband and rescue dog, Ollie.

Jane earned a Bachelor of Arts degree from Hiram College, majoring in Religion and History, a Master of Science degree from Boston University, and a Master of Divinity from Vanderbilt University.

*Read on for a sneak peek of another exciting story
in the Mysteries & Wonders of the Bible series!*

SEEKING LEVIATHAN:
Milkah's Story

BY VIRGINIA WISE

Milkah sat stunned and silent in the doorway of her mud-brick house. A warm breeze swept up from the barley fields, carrying the scent of wet dirt. Sunlight fell across her bare feet and bathed the hard-packed, earthen courtyard in a golden yellow glow. She pulled her feet closer to her body, into the shade of the house, and wrapped her arms around her knees. The jangle of her copper bracelets seemed too loud in the solemn quiet.

This house had never been silent before. There had always been the laughter of her younger sisters, the low murmuring of her *imma* and sister-in-law as they lit smoky fires and stirred a pot of lentils, or the good-natured shouts of her *abba* and older brother as they jostled for the last piece of flatbread at dinnertime.

Milkah had not bothered to light a fire today. She had not soaked the lentils or ground the barley into flour. The morning's goat milk sat untouched beside the hearth, beneath a circling fly.

She had no appetite. How could she, when everything she had known and loved was gone?

The funeral rites were completed, the dirt floor smoothed flat over the graves where her family would lie together forever, beneath the home they had loved. Now she did not know what to do but sit and wait. Wait for what, she did not know. "Show me what to do, God," she whispered. "Show me that You are still here, with me."

A shadow blocked the sun, and Milkah looked up. Her neighbor, Shiptu, stood in front of her, a serious expression on her face. "I did not hear you coming," Milkah said, then looked down again.

"Your thoughts are elsewhere, I imagine." Shiptu adjusted the coarse fabric of her single-sleeved tunic that covered one shoulder and left the other bare, squatted on the ground near Milkah, and sighed. A donkey brayed in the distance. "You cannot stay here, you know."

"Yes," Milkah said without looking up. "I know." She turned the bangle on her wrist in a slow circle. The metal felt familiar and comforting against her skin. "I have never been farther than a half day's walk from the village."

Shiptu hesitated. "No one here will marry you now. They do not want any part of this."

Milkah's eyes flashed as they shot up to Shiptu. "Part of what?"

Shiptu frowned and made a vague motion with her hand. "This..."

"Just come out and say it, Shiptu."

Shiptu grunted. "That is no way to talk to a woman who has known you all your life. I have been a friend to your mother since she first arrived from the coast—"

"Please, just say what you are thinking," Milkah asked in a softer voice.

Shiptu lifted her hands in a gesture of helplessness. "Since you insist. You know how people are. With the gods turned against you—"

"Not 'gods.' My family still worshiped the One True God." Not many people did anymore. Memory of the old times faded with each generation, blotted out by the lure of new gods that could be seen and touched and understood. The great cities had glorious ziggurats soaring toward the heavens so the gods could come down the pyramid steps to their people. The educated men living behind the glistening city walls believed that the new ways were better, more advanced, and felt sorry for the country folk who clung to their myths of a lost garden, remembered a righteous ancestor they called Noah, and taught their children there was only one God.

"Either way. There is not so much difference between them, is there? They all need to be placated. Whatever you have done to offend them..." Shiptu shook her head. The blue beads and copper ornaments in her headdress rattled with the movement. "Well, no man will risk a god's curse coming on his house."

"My abba always sacrificed burnt offerings for us at the family altar. We welcomed every guest who came our way. We never turned anyone away. My abba—my entire family—feared God and did right. We followed the old ways."

Shiptu reached out and patted Milkah's arm. "Even so, dear. Even so." She shifted her weight. "Sometimes we offend a god without knowing it."

"I only serve the One True God."

"Then you must have offended Him. Offer a better sacrifice. Promise your firstborn child."

"Never. My God does not ask that."

"How can you expect the favor of any god when you refuse to do what they require? When we offend them, we must pay. Then they will turn away their anger, and all will be well. It is not complicated."

"We did not offend Him."

Shiptu pinched the bridge of her nose between her thumb and forefinger. "Milkah, you are not making this easy."

"Please. I just want to be left alone." Milkah moved her gaze beyond the small courtyard, to the fields and the long, narrow irrigation ditch lined with date palms. Their green fronds swayed in the breeze. Sunlight sparkled against the muddy water. Milkah had looked at those fields, those trees, those waters, every day of her nineteen years on earth. She could not imagine a life anywhere else. This land was in her blood. Her abba had been born here, and his abba before him. And they had all faithfully worshiped the One True God.

"You know I cannot do that."

"I need more time."

"You do not have time. You have no father, no husband, no brother. You cannot stay here, alone."

"I will go to Nahor's family. They might take me in."

Shiptu did not respond.

"I waited all those years for them to afford the bride price my abba set. We should have already been married when he was killed."

"'Should have' counts for nothing in times like these."

Milkah stood up so fast it made her feel woozy. She remembered she had not eaten that day and pressed a hand against the cool mud wall for support. "I will go talk to them now."

"Come with us, Milkah," Shiptu said quietly. "We have a place for you in our boat. We pass right through your mother's hometown. We will find her people there."

"We cannot be sure they are still there. My imma left there to marry my abba twenty-five years ago, and she never went back."

"No, no, they are still there. You have a few cousins, at least. We pass through there every year, so I would know. And anyway, I would never steer you wrong. You know that, do you not? You can trust us. Your mother always did. The entire village does. We always come back with a fair trade for their goods, do we not?" Shiptu caught Milkah's eye. "Your father trusted us to trade for him." She let the statement hang in the air.

Milkah turned away. Her bare feet pounded the earth as she hurried across the courtyard. "I have to try," she said without looking back. The path to Nahor's house was as familiar as her own body. Her feet knew every stone, every curve, every palm tree along the way. His family worshiped the One God too, so her abba and Nahor's abba had arranged their marriage from a young age. It grew harder every year to find like-minded families to marry into. Milkah had been especially fortunate because she had liked Nahor. He had been quick to joke, and his smile lit up his entire face. He never raised his voice to her. He was kind to animals. He was a good man who had offered the promise of a good life for both of them.

Milkah's future had died with him.

Three women stood chatting beside the dirt path as Milkah hurried past. One of the women held a baby in a sling, his big, dark eyes following Milkah's movements. She knew these women, had grown up alongside them, gone hungry with them when the crops failed, celebrated with them when there was a marriage or birth in the village. Milkah and her sisters had brought figs and honey when the baby had been born. They had sat with his mother in the cool of the evening, whispering and giggling as they admired his tiny hands and feet. Now the women fell silent as she passed, and the young mother made a sign against the evil eye.

Milkah pretended not to notice. Nothing they did could be worse than what had already happened. Her life had ended even though she still walked through the village alongside the living. Before the Terrible Day, she had walked in peace with the One God, trusting that life would go on as it always had, following the predictable rhythms of village life. Good begot good, and evil begot evil. This was the way the world worked. Life might not always be easy, but it would be good, and it would be secure with the One God—the just God—watching over them all. Milkah had kept that knowledge deep inside her since childhood, and it had filled her with a quiet, steady warmth.

Now, fearful questions that she had never before thought to ask boiled within her. Did the One God really have power over her life? And if so, did He actually care enough to intervene? Ever since the Terrible Day, she had become consumed by a growing, gnawing terror that life was nothing but a series of random events.

It had all started on an ordinary morning, with shouting in the fields. Her abba's panicked voice had pierced the still, dry air, followed by the growl of a dog. More shouting. Milkah, her imma, sister-in-law, and two younger sisters had flown from the house, leaving a pot of lentils to burn. It was only when they drew closer that they understood her abba's words. "Do not leave the house!" he had screamed. "Stay away!"

The women had stared, confused. The men were shouting as they tore through the barley toward them, trampling the stalks as if it didn't matter. And in the end, it hadn't. There was no one left to eat the harvest now.

"Get back in the house!" Milkah's older brother had shouted, his face locked in an expression of shock and fear. "They are mad! All of them, mad!" His wife had stood for a moment, watching, before she turned and ran, mud splattering up from her bare feet. Then three dogs had erupted from the barley field, eyes wild, mouths foaming, and chased Milkah's sister-in-law as she fled. Milkah had stood frozen, watching but feeling as if she were not really there—that none of this could be happening—then closed her eyes and covered her ears when the dogs reached the woman.

And then the dogs had wheeled around and descended on the rest of them.

Somehow, in the chaos, Milkah had not been bitten. She, her abba, and her four-year-old sister were the only ones of her family spared. Nahor and Milkah's sister-in-law had not survived the attack. As for the others, they all knew that nothing but a miracle could save a person from the bite of a mad dog. Milkah's abba had offered their finest goats as burnt offerings to the One God as they pleaded with Him to intervene. After that, the ones who had been bitten could do nothing but wait, day after day, huddled on the reed mats in the stifling heat of their one-room house, watching each other for the first sign of the sickness to come. Eventually, the madness that brings death took each of them.

Afterward, Milkah and her abba tried to make sense of it all. He offered another burnt offering at the family altar, seeking the One God's protection and restoration. The three survivors had prayed and held each other and had tried to remember how to go through the motions of normal life. During the night, Milkah's little sister would scoot onto Milkah's sleeping mat, snuggling close in the stillness, and Milkah would feel that she could go on because she was still needed and loved.

Then, less than a week after her family had been buried, Milkah's abba had offered to take her little sister down to the river to play. "Rest," he said to Milkah. "You do not sleep anymore. Your sorrow is too heavy. Lie down and forget for a while."

Milkah had nodded, numb with grief, as she settled onto her sleeping mat. She watched her sister smile for the first time in days as their abba lifted her to his shoulders and strode through the courtyard, toward the muddy riverbank beyond the fields and date palms.

Milkah did not know how long she slept, but when she awoke, groggy and disoriented, she wandered outside to see her abba and sister in the middle of the distant river, splashing and laughing. Milkah shaded her eyes from the sun and smiled. Perhaps life would go on after all, and those who were left of her family could find their way back to happiness. But then her abba's hand jerked to his chest, and his expression changed to one of confusion then pain. He fell, dropping his small daughter alongside him. Both of them disappeared beneath the muddy water. By the time Milkah reached them, it was too late.

Now she had no one left.

Ever since then, the villagers had kept their distance. An entire family attacked by a pack of mad dogs? Then the survivors drown in the river? Bad things happened sometimes—that was life—but this was too random, too senseless. It sent a ripple of fear through the village that was best soothed by the reminder that this couldn't happen to them. This kind of thing only happened to those who deserved it somehow.

Even Nahor's family had retreated, despite the ties that had bound them for as long as Milkah could remember. Her stomach churned as she approached their house. She straightened the fabric of her tunic where it draped from her shoulder, and whispered a prayer to the One God that Nahor's family would take her in. The prayer had escaped automatically, and she wondered if she meant it. Her eyes cut to the muddy river that had swallowed her abba and sister. How powerful could her God really be? She wanted to believe in His power and love—with all her heart she wanted to—but a pang of doubt gripped her like the iron jaws of the mad dogs. Perhaps they had bitten her after all, in a strange sort of way that could not be seen by human eyes but left her wounded nonetheless.

The front door opened before Milkah reached it. Nahor's mother stood in the cool shadow of the interior. Her eyes were red and swollen, and she wasn't wearing any kohl or jewelry as she normally did. "Stop."

Milkah froze.

"Have you come to bring more death to our house?"

Milkah opened her mouth then closed it again without answering.

"Who is there?" A deep voice boomed from behind Nahor's mother. His father appeared in the doorway. The man's face hardened when he saw Milkah, and he stepped protectively in front of his wife. "We trusted your abba," he said. "With our son. Our only son." The last sentence carried so much quiet rage that Milkah took a step back.

"It was not our fault. The dogs came out of nowhere—"

"And killed no one else in the village."

"If my son had not been betrothed to you, he would have been spared. God's wrath fell on him only because he was bound to your house."

Milkah shook her head. "No."

"God does not punish the innocent."

"This was not punishment."

"Then what was it?"

Milkah took a step back. She didn't have an answer for that.

"Leave us," Nahor's mother said from behind her husband. She made the sign against the evil eye.

"But what will I do?" Milkah held up her hands to them. "Where will I go? I have no one."

"Would you have God strike us too? We cannot help one that He has seen fit to cast out. You are on your own."

A NOTE FROM THE EDITORS

We hope you enjoyed another exciting volume in the Mysteries & Wonders of the Bible series, published by Guideposts. For over seventy-five years, Guideposts, a nonprofit organization, has been driven by a vision of a world filled with hope. We aspire to be the voice of a trusted friend, a friend who makes you feel more hopeful and connected.

By making a purchase from Guideposts, you join our community in touching millions of lives, inspiring them to believe that all things are possible through faith, hope, and prayer. Your continued support allows us to provide uplifting resources to those in need. Whether through our communities, websites, apps, or publications, we inspire our audiences, bring them together, and comfort, uplift, entertain, and guide them. Visit us at guideposts.org to learn more.

We would love to hear from you. Write us at Guideposts, P.O. Box 5815, Harlan, Iowa 51593 or call us at (800) 932-2145. Did you love *Among the Giants: Achsah's Story*? Leave a review for this product on guideposts.org/shop. Your feedback helps others in our community find relevant products.

Find inspiration, find faith, find Guideposts.

Shop our best sellers and favorites at

guideposts.org/shop

Or scan the QR code to go directly to our Shop

If you enjoyed Mysteries & Wonders of the Bible, check out
our other Guideposts biblical fiction series!
Visit https://www.shopguideposts.org/fiction-books/
biblical-fiction.html for more information.

EXTRAORDINARY WOMEN OF THE BIBLE

There are many women in Scripture who do extraordinary things. Women whose lives and actions were pivotal in shaping their world as well as the world we know today. In each volume of Guideposts' Extraordinary Women of the Bible series, you'll meet these well-known women and learn their deepest thoughts, fears, joys, and secrets. Read their stories and discover the unexplored truths in their journeys of faith as they follow the paths God laid out for them.

Highly Favored: Mary's Story
Sins as Scarlet: Rahab's Story
A Harvest of Grace: Ruth and Naomi's Story
At His Feet: Mary Magdalene's Story
Tender Mercies: Elizabeth's Story
Woman of Redemption: Bathsheba's Story
Jewel of Persia: Esther's Story
A Heart Restored: Michal's Story

Beauty's Surrender: Sarah's Story
The Woman Warrior: Deborah's Story
The God Who Sees: Hagar's Story
The First Daughter: Eve's Story
The Ones Jesus Loved: Mary and Martha's Story
The Beginning of Wisdom: Bilqis's Story
The Shadow's Song: Mahlah and No'ah's Story
Days of Awe: Euodia and Syntyche's Story
Beloved Bride: Rachel's Story
A Promise Fulfilled: Hannah's Story

ORDINARY WOMEN OF THE BIBLE

From generation to generation and every walk of life, God seeks out women to do His will. Scripture offers us but fleeting, tantalizing glimpses into the lives of a number of everyday women in Bible times—many of whom are not even named in its pages. In each volume of Guideposts' Ordinary Women of the Bible series, you'll meet one of these unsung, ordinary women face to face, and see how God used her to change the course of history.

A Mother's Sacrifice: Jochebed's Story
The Healer's Touch: Tikva's Story
The Ark Builder's Wife: Zarah's Story
An Unlikely Witness: Joanna's Story
The Last Drop of Oil: Adaliah's Story
A Perilous Journey: Phoebe's Story
Pursued by a King: Abigail's Story
An Eternal Love: Tabitha's Story
Rich Beyond Measure: Zlata's Story
The Life Giver: Shiphrah's Story
No Stone Cast: Eliyanah's Story
Her Source of Strength: Raya's Story
Missionary of Hope: Priscilla's Story

Befitting Royalty: Lydia's Story
The Prophet's Songbird: Atarah's Story
Daughter of Light: Charilene's Story
The Reluctant Rival: Leah's Story
The Elder Sister: Miriam's Story
Where He Leads Me: Zipporah's Story
The Dream Weaver's Bride: Asenath's Story
Alone at the Well: Photine's Story
Raised for a Purpose: Talia's Story
Mother of Kings: Zemirah's Story
The Dearly Beloved: Apphia's Story

SECRETS FROM GRANDMA'S ATTIC

Life is recorded not only in decades or years, but in events and memories that form the fabric of our being. Follow Tracy Doyle, Amy Allen, and Robin Davisson, the granddaughters of the recently deceased centenarian, Pearl Allen, as they explore the treasures found in the attic of Grandma Pearl's Victorian home, nestled near the banks of the Mississippi in Canton, Missouri. Not only do Pearl's descendants uncover a long-buried mystery at every attic exploration, they also discover their grandmother's legacy of deep, abiding faith, which has shaped and guided their family through the years. These uncovered Secrets from Grandma's Attic reveal stories of faith, redemption, and second chances that capture your heart long after you turn the last page.

History Lost and Found
The Art of Deception
Testament to a Patriot
Buttoned Up

Pearl of Great Price
Hidden Riches
Movers and Shakers
The Eye of the Cat
Refined by Fire
The Prince and the Popper
Something Shady
Duel Threat
A Royal Tea
The Heart of a Hero
Fractured Beauty
A Shadowy Past
In Its Time
Nothing Gold Can Stay
The Cameo Clue
Veiled Intentions
Turn Back the Dial
A Marathon of Kindness
A Thief in the Night
Coming Home

SAVANNAH SECRETS

Welcome to Savannah, Georgia, a picture-perfect Southern city known for its manicured parks, moss-covered oaks, and antebellum architecture. Walk down one of the cobblestone streets, and you'll come upon Magnolia Investigations. It is here where two friends have joined forces to unravel some of Savannah's deepest secrets. Tag along as clues are exposed, red herrings discarded, and thrilling surprises revealed. Find inspiration in the special bond between Meredith Bellefontaine and Julia Foley. Cheer the friends on as they listen to their hearts and rely on their faith to solve each new case that comes their way.

The Hidden Gate
A Fallen Petal
Double Trouble
Whispering Bells
Where Time Stood Still
The Weight of Years
Willful Transgressions
Season's Meetings
Southern Fried Secrets
The Greatest of These

MYSTERIES OF MARTHA'S VINEYARD

Priscilla Latham Grant has inherited a lighthouse! So with not much more than a strong will and a sore heart, the recent widow says goodbye to her lifelong Kansas home and heads to the quaint and historic island of Martha's Vineyard, Massachusetts. There, she comes face-to-face with adventures, which include her trusty canine friend, Jake, three delightful cousins she didn't know she had, and Gerald O'Bannon, a handsome Coast Guard captain—plus head-scratching mysteries that crop up with surprising regularity.

A Light in the Darkness
Like a Fish Out of Water
Adrift
Maiden of the Mist
Making Waves
Don't Rock the Boat
A Port in the Storm
Thicker Than Water
Swept Away
Bridge Over Troubled Waters
Smoke on the Water

Shifting Sands
Shark Bait
Seascape in Shadows
Storm Tide
Water Flows Uphill
Catch of the Day
Beyond the Sea
Wider Than an Ocean
Sheeps Passing in the Night
Sail Away Home
Waves of Doubt
Lifeline
Flotsam & Jetsam
Just Over the Horizon

Find more inspiring stories in these best-loved Guideposts fiction series!

Mysteries of Lancaster County

Follow the Classen sisters as they unravel clues and uncover hidden secrets in Mysteries of Lancaster County. As you get to know these women and their friends, you'll see how God brings each of them together for a fresh start in life.

Secrets of Wayfarers Inn

Retired schoolteachers find themselves owners of an old warehouse-turned-inn that is filled with hidden passages, buried secrets, and stunning surprises that will set them on a course to puzzling mysteries from the Underground Railroad.

Tearoom Mysteries Series

Mix one stately Victorian home, a charming lakeside town in Maine, and two adventurous cousins with a passion for tea and hospitality. Add a large scoop of intriguing mystery, and sprinkle generously with faith, family, and friends, and you have the recipe for *Tearoom Mysteries*.

Ordinary Women of the Bible

Richly imagined stories—based on facts from the Bible—have all the plot twists and suspense of a great mystery, while bringing you fascinating insights on what it was like to be a woman living in the ancient world.

To learn more about these books, visit Guideposts.org/Shop

Printed in the United States
by Baker & Taylor Publisher Services